Finding June

Shae,
I hope you enjoy reading this as much as I enjoyed writing it! It was so great to meet you!

S.C.C.

Shannen Crane Camp

Published by Sugar Coated Press

ISBN: 1480260827
ISBN-13: 978-1480260825

Cover design by Jackie Hicken
Edited and typeset by Jackie Hicken

For Sharon, Ben, Darl, and Dean, who—against my will—taught me to love silent films, and for The Husband, who puts up with my odd taste in movies.

ALSO BY SHANNEN CRANE CAMP

The Breakup Artist

ACKNOWLEDGMENTS

Nathan Lee and Aaron White: Thank you for being my on-call film consultants.
Lizzi Relins: Thank you for being the one who made sure I knew English and British are not always synonymous.
Jackie: Thank you for . . . everything. Editing, making me a clay sculpture of my characters to keep me motivated, helping me with the titles, coming up with possible titles for a baseball book we've never read, and looking at 10,000,000 pictures of people in sunglasses to find a cover I ultimately didn't use.
Jolene Perry: Thank you for answering my endless stream of questions on everything in the world and knowing how to do . . . well . . . everything.
Cindy Bennett: Thank you for your endless help with navigating the world of publishing. You've been so awesome and our book signings are always full of candy and happiness, just like a book signing should be.
My amazing family: Thank you for being so supportive and listening to my endless brainstorming.
Janet Swenson and Haleh Risdana: Thank you for teaching me the beauty of well-executed injury makeup.
Every film teacher and film student I've ever worked with: Thank you for giving me random terms like C47 to throw out there so I look like I know what I'm talking about.

Shannen Crane Camp

CHAPTER 1

The thick green liquid in the glass in front of me bubbled ominously. I sniffed at it, hoping that it was like the green Jell-O we seemed to have at every church party—pretty disgusting looking, but overall quite harmless and kind of tasty.

"Why am I drinking this, again?" I asked my grandma, who sat next to me nodding her silent encouragement.

"Because, June, it will make your skin glow like a sunrise," she replied with a grand wave of her hand. I started to relax slightly.

"Okay, so then I'm putting this on my face?" I asked hopefully, praying silently that she would answer in the affirmative. She simply stared at me with one raised eyebrow, wordlessly asking why I was being so naïve. After all, this wasn't my first encounter with the dreaded health food monster.

"June, do you know what this really is?" she asked, though I was pretty sure it was a rhetorical question. She gave a dramatic pause for effect. "This is the difference between getting cast as the leading lady and being cast as frightened citizen number three."

"Does frightened citizen number three have any speaking parts?" I asked with a sly grin.

"Drink," she commanded, getting up from the table to answer her buzzing cell phone.

I sighed deeply and stared the glass down once more, trying to frighten it into tasting like something other than sour, gritty oatmeal. "All right I can do this . . . I think. It can't be any worse than the time I played a crash victim lying in the rain for eight straight hours."

The goop bubbled at me again, letting me know that it could, in fact, be worse than that. "You don't scare me," I said boldly as I picked up the full glass. I took a few deep breaths through my mouth to prepare myself for the horrid event before gulping the liquid down. Well . . . gulping as well as you could gulp something that was the consistency of applesauce.

My gag reflex instantly voiced its opinion of the health drink but I quickly regained control of my body, making sure I finished the entire glass. I was pretty sure that even if I did throw up, I wouldn't get out of somehow drinking this monstrosity. Gran would see to it.

My gran and I had a very complicated relationship. As much as I liked to pretend she's a slave driver, I had to admit I'd be lost without her. After my mom died she moved in right away and took up the role of "woman of the house," which turned out to be a good thing since my Dad constantly traveled for work. He was some sort of math genius, but we didn't actually know what he did. All we knew was that the government paid for his schooling and most of the time he wasn't at home. It was like being the daughter of James Bond . . . except with math instead of guns, I guess.

Most of the time it was just Gran and me. In fact, Gran was so much a part of the family that the house had been completely transformed into her own personal "acting Zen zone." I kind of liked it, and Dad wasn't really home enough to notice the very non-masculine vibe of the house.

"Did you drink it all, Bliss?" Gran asked as she re-entered the room. When she wasn't being stern or going all "acting coach" on me, she liked to call me "Bliss" because—

according to her—June was the marriage month, which made it the month full of bliss. Personally I thought that would make it the month full of chaos and fake tans, but maybe that was just me.

"Down to the last blob of green stuff," I said, smiling sweetly.

"Throw your sarcasm around all you want, but when Hollywood comes calling, you just remember who helped you get there."

"Duly noted," I replied, grabbing a non-fat bran muffin from the counter and taking a sizeable bite. "So, who was on the phone?"

Gran shot me a look for talking with my mouth full, but didn't scold me. It must have been an important call. "That, my dear little starlet, was a casting director I've been talking to. I have an audition for you tomorrow. He saw your headshot and asked to meet with you specifically," she said with a grin.

I waited to react, knowing that there had to be more since she looked like *not* spilling the news was physically painful for her.

"It's for a television show and . . . wait for it . . . it's a recurring role," she practically shouted.

My eyes widened slightly at this news. I had been on TV shows before, but never anything big. I mostly played an extra with a speaking part or just did commercials. Actually, my first role ever was for a diaper commercial when I wasn't even old enough to walk. That first commercial was the thing that firmly cemented the idea that I was destined to become famous. At least, that's how Gran felt.

"How many episodes do they want me to do? What's the show?" I asked, excited by the prospect of this new role.

"I can't quite remember the name of the show but it's one of those crime dramas."

"*Forensic Faculty*?" I offered, naming the most popular crime drama on TV. If I was going to dream, I might as well dream big, right?

I was, of course, completely shocked when Gran said, "That's the one."

"Wait, are you serious? The audition is actually for *Forensic Faculty*?"

"It sure is Bliss," she replied, tapping her nose knowledgably.

I sat back in my chair happily, wiping a few muffin crumbs off of my yoga pants as I did so. This was really big news. If they wanted me on the show in a recurring role, that probably meant I wasn't a dead body or a character that they suspected to be the murderer for ten minutes before catching the real killer. This could be a really big deal.

"So, what time is the audition?" I asked, having to pull myself back to reality for a moment, even though my daydreams were a far more pleasant place to be.

Gran looked down at her little black planner where she had quickly scribbled the details. "Twelve o'clock on the dot," she said, snapping her planner closed in a crisp, precise manner.

"Wait, twelve?" I asked, though I had heard her the first time.

"Is there something wrong with twelve?"

"I've got a test at twelve thirty. There's no way I'll make it back to school in time," I said woefully.

"What class is it for?" she asked over her shoulder while she put my now-empty glass in the sink.

"English," I replied, still trying to work out some way I'd be able to do both.

"Oh Bliss, that's an easy one. You had half of Shakespeare memorized before you were four. I think your teacher will understand why you can't make it for her little 'test' when you have much bigger fish to fry. Does she think Hamlet would come to school and take a test when the Danes are out there waiting for him to conquer them?"

"Gran, Hamlet was Danish," I reminded her.

"Regardless, she of all people should understand that sacrifices must be made for art," she said grandly. Gran always had a way of making everything she said seem grand and important. I wasn't quite sure if it was her larger-than-life gesticulating or just her grandiose tone. There was just something about her that seemed important. If she were still acting, I bet she'd always get cast as the queen in period pieces. She tucked a bright red strand of her short, curly hair behind her ear.

"I guess you're right," I conceded. "I'll just have to send her an e-mail tonight to see if I can make up the test."

"That's my girl," Gran said with a smile.

"So what else do you know about the role? Besides the fact that it's recurring."

"Not much. But Andy did mention something about the whole 1920s thing, which I thought was a bit odd. Isn't the show modern?"

"It is, but maybe they want to put a different spin on it," I replied, though I was equally as puzzled as to why a modern crime drama would want me to audition because I look old-fashioned.

It was no secret that I had a very distinct look, which made me kind of a novelty in the acting world. This did prove to be a little troublesome when trying to land more mainstream roles but so far it had actually helped me get a few artsy commercial parts.

When most casting directors met me, they'd say I looked like Lillian Gish reincarnated. Between my pale skin, long, curly, dark brown hair, bee-stung lips, and big brown eyes, I was like a walking silent film. Gran loved it. She said it was yet another sign that I was meant to be a great actor.

"Well, we don't question our good fortune, Bliss, so get lots of sleep tonight and be ready for me to pick you up from school at eleven. We don't want to hit traffic coming into L.A.," she said seriously.

"Aye-aye, captain." I said with a mock salute. Gran just rolled her eyes with a smile.

"Goodnight Bliss. I love you," she said.

"Love you too, Gran."

....

The second I went upstairs into my room, I pulled my cell phone out to tell my best friend about this unexpected opportunity. Joseph Cleveland had been in my life for as long as I could remember. Our moms had been best friends growing up, and for the short time my mom was with me before she died, she made sure Joseph and I had a play date just about every day. His mom, Claire, had always been like a second mother to me (Gran being the first) so it was only natural that Joseph and I were destined to be best friends.

I fell back onto my black wrought iron bed, which had a bronze and black 1920s art nouveau bedspread, as I dialed his number. I definitely played up my inner silent film star at every opportunity.

"Hey June," he said by way of greeting, never bothering to do the questioning "hello?" that we all seem to do, even when the caller ID tells us who's calling.

"Well, Joseph . . . I just thought you would like to know that your best friend might not be able to go out in public without being ambushed pretty soon," I said, in what I hoped was a cool and matter-of-fact way.

"Oh my gosh, June, how many times do I have to tell you it's really not that bad? Yes, it kills the first day and your face will swell up like a balloon, but that's when I'll come over with about twenty awesome movies and a shake with no straw to make it bearable," he replied with some exasperation.

"What the heck are you talking about?" I asked, so thrown off by his reply that I couldn't even begin to understand where it had come from.

"Wait, what are you talking about?"

"I have an audition for a pretty big part tomorrow," I replied, happy to finally be getting to the big news.

"Oh, okay. That probably makes more sense than my thing anyway," he said, embarrassed.

"And what thing was that?" I asked with a laugh.

"It's nothing. I just assumed . . . because you've been

stressing over it and everything. I thought maybe you were finally getting your wisdom teeth out," he said.

"Gross, no. I'm putting that day off for as long as possible," I said with a shudder. I've never been very good with dentists. Or doctors. Or even dermatologists, for that matter. There was just something about people poking you and the potential for intense amounts of pain that I couldn't get over. So unless my Gran was going to heavily sedate me and drag me to the dentist, I was never going to get my wisdom teeth out, which I told Joseph on a regular basis. Thus, any time I called him in a panic (or in this case, in extreme excitement) he assumed the day had finally come. I sometimes got the sneaking suspicion that he wished someone really would pin me down and pull them out so he wouldn't have to hear me stressing over it anymore. Luckily for him, he had already gotten his out. He called it mission prep.

"We'll see. One day when you least expect it, you'll get them out and then you'll figure out that I was always right and you were always wrong."

"And then we'll go to the park to watch the sunset with all of the pigs flying by," I said with mock sweetness. Joseph just laughed.

"All right, fine, you win for now. So what's this life-changing audition you have?"

"Tomorrow at noon I've got an audition in L.A. for a certain crime drama on TV . . . you might say it's the best crime drama . . . actually . . . I'm pretty sure everyone would say it's the best one. But maybe that's just me jumping on the bandwagon," I said with a grin, hardly able to contain my excitement.

"Maybe you should just tell me, because I'm afraid I'll shoot for the moon here, and then you'll get mad when it's something not nearly as cool as I'm thinking," he replied. I could hear the playful tone in his voice, but he was probably right. If he guessed something better than what I was thinking, I'd probably get upset. Luckily, he knew me well enough to figure out how to make me feel better if that happened.

"Smart thinking. All right so the show is . . . are you ready?"

"Yes, just tell me already!" he practically shouted.

"*Forensic Faculty*," I said proudly. His end of the phone was silent for a minute, making me wonder if he had heard. "Joseph?"

"Are you kidding me? You're not joking right now, right? Because I'll be so mad if you're making that up."

"No, I swear I'm not! The casting director saw my headshot and asked for me specifically!" I squealed, happy to be telling someone I knew would be excited for me.

"So basically what you're telling me is that when you walk down the red carpet, you want me to be your escort, right?"

"Naturally," I answered with a laugh. "But seriously, this could be a really big deal for me. You'd better be praying all day tomorrow that I get this part," I threatened.

"Like I wouldn't already June," Joseph answered. I smiled up at my ceiling.

"All right, well, I just wanted to let you know so you can send some good thoughts my way."

"Will do, kid," he said softly. "Does this mean you won't be auditioning for *Romeo and Juliet* with me?"

"Yeah, unfortunately I think my schedule will be pretty full. But hey, maybe Xani will play your Juliet. I'm sure that would make her life complete."

"Don't even joke about stuff like that," he said. I could almost hear his uncomfortable shudder at that unpleasant suggestion.

"You still picking me up for seminary tomorrow?" I asked as an afterthought.

"Dark and early."

CHAPTER 2

My alarm went off at four o'clock in the morning, making me seriously question why I had decided to take zero period theatre. I had even talked Joseph into taking it with me at six a.m., bumping seminary back to an unhealthy five a.m. As I lay in bed with a pillow over my face to drown out the sounds of Edith Piaf singing, "Non, je ne regretted rien," on my alarm clock, I contemplated "accidentally" turning the alarm off. I knew, of course, that Joseph would kill me, since he would soon be waiting outside in his car in the pitch-black night. Besides that, Gran was adamant about my going to school and seminary every day, even though she wasn't active in church anymore and most days she pulled me out of school for auditions.

"Thank you Edith," I mumbled in agitation at my alarm as I shut it off and rolled out of bed. You'd think that being an actress I'd be all high maintenance and take two hours to get ready for the day. But when I heard Joseph pull up outside the house forty minutes later, I had already showered, dressed, and done my hair and make-up. Not bad.

Before dashing down the stairs to meet Joseph, I gave myself a once-over in the mirror. For my audition, I had chosen a mauve and beige polka-dotted top with a big floppy bow attached to the neck, a high-waist beige A-line skirt, and some short close-toed heels. My makeup made my eyes look smoky and mysterious in contrast to my porcelain skin. I let my hair stay exactly how it was when I didn't touch it: long, dark, and curly. If 1920s was what they wanted, that's exactly what they were getting.

Gran was still asleep, so the house was dark and quiet as I grabbed a pear and headed out the front door into the cool, dark world. Joseph was standing in front of his old green Volkswagen Beetle, wearing a grin on his face and looking every bit as old-fashioned as me. Pretty much everyone said we'd get married one day because we fit together perfectly. In my opinion, though, it would be really weird to marry Joseph because we just didn't think of each other like that.

Joseph was a bit taller than me, with chocolate brown eyes and wavy brown hair that always fell right above his eyebrows. Today he wore fitted khaki pants, a white collared shirt with a brown skinny tie, and a gray button-up sweater. Honestly, he was a pretty gorgeous guy and if it weren't Joseph—who I'd known all my life—I'd probably be madly in love with him. But as it was, he was just Joseph, and that was just the way I liked him.

As I approached the car Joseph spread his arms wide to give me a congratulations hug, which I gratefully accepted, burying my head in his neck. "This could be big," I said, though my words were muffled on his shoulder.

"I know! This is honestly so exciting," he replied, pulling away to get a good look at me. "Nice choice for the audition," he said with a smile, indicating to my outfit.

"Yeah, I thought it would keep the look they're going for, but also look modern just in case I'm completely wrong and they aren't going in the old-fashioned direction at all," I said nervously.

"I think it's perfect," he reassured me.

The LDS Church building where we held seminary wasn't far away from where I lived, sitting right behind the high school. It only took us about ten minutes to get there, but Joseph and I liked to get hot chocolate at the gas station on the way, so he always showed up to my house early.

We drove in silence for a few minutes, blowing on the too hot and much too rich hot chocolate. It wasn't really all that great and it kind of hurt my stomach most mornings, but it was warm and it was tradition, so we got it every morning without fail.

"So, you might actually meet Will Trofeos," Joseph said suddenly. "I mean . . . meet him meet him. Not just say, 'Oh I saw Will Trofeos one day on Rodeo Drive,' but actually hang out with him." He sounded very surprised by this sudden revelation, which made me laugh.

"Forget Will Trofeos, I might meet Lukas Leighton if I get on the show," I replied, my voice sounding much higher and giddier than I had intended. Joseph just rolled his eyes.

It was a well-known fact that Will Trofeos was a huge star. Everyone loved him on *Forensic Faculty*. But it was an even better known fact that Lukas Leighton was completely and utterly breath taking . . . and probably the only reason every girl at my high school watched the show. Will Trofeos was way too old for anyone at school. Lukas, on the other hand, was only twenty, making him a perfect candidate for the "teen heartthrob" status he had so gracefully obtained.

"I don't like that guy," Joseph said simply, using his "I know more than you because I'm a month older" tone and annoying me to no end.

"Everybody likes him, Joseph," I replied matter-of-factly.

"Like that's a good reason for me to like him."

I just shook my head and smiled. Joseph said he didn't like Lukas Leighton now, but if he ever met him he'd be just as big of a dork as anyone else who watched the show. Taking great satisfaction in this fact, I simply said, "Good point Joseph," and continued to sip at my hot chocolate until we got to church. There were already a handful of cars parked outside of the building as we made our way inside through the dark chill.

A lot of our friends at school weren't members of our religion and couldn't understand why on earth we'd get up every morning at four a.m. to talk about "church stuff" for an hour. When they asked, I'd ask them why they'd get up at five to go to school and do "theatre stuff" for an hour. Their answer was: because they loved it. That helped them understand a bit where we were coming from, but secretly I think they still thought we were crazy.

I always loved going to seminary right before school. It was just so nice to get that uplift in your spirit before heading into the battleground that was Simi Valley High School. Walking out of the building after seminary, Joseph and I were much happier and had almost completely forgotten about our little disagreement from that morning. The sun was just starting to peek over the mountains, though pretty much everything was still shrouded in the darkness of the fading night. By the time we got out of our zero period theatre class it would be light out and the rest of the students would be getting to school. When we got to school in the mornings it was just the band kids, the unnaturally smart AP science kids, and us. It did, after all, take a special brand of student to take a zero period class. You either had to be really, really smart, or creative and a little crazy.

Sitting on the stage next to Joseph and listening to Mr. Carroll, our theatre teacher, felt like the most natural thing in the world. Joseph and I were lucky enough to have almost all of our classes together . . . although luck didn't really play a part in it, since we'd purposely arranged our schedules to match. History and math were the only two subjects we couldn't take together because Joseph was in AP calculus while I was stuck back in Algebra 2. Math was definitely not my strong suit.

While Mr. Carroll talked about the importance of stage presence, I daydreamed about my audition that day. I always hated having to do a cold read. Most of the time they'd send the script over the night before so you could get familiar with your lines, but it looked like I'd be going in blind today. My stomach turned at the thought, emitting a low, loud grumble. Joseph looked over at me with his eyebrows raised, a smile playing across his lips.

"Hot chocolate and nerves do not mix," I informed him under my breath. He just shrugged his shoulders and gave me a mock sympathetic pat on the shoulder.

As nervous as I was and as much as I tried not to get my hopes up, I couldn't help but wonder what my life would be like if I got the part. I'd get to be on a really popular TV show that pretty much everyone watched. People would actually see me and say "Hey aren't you that girl from *Forensic Faculty*?" How cool would that be? Not to mention the fact that I'd be working with Lukas Leighton, who was probably the hottest guy on TV.

"Do you think I'll get to do any scenes with Lukas?" I asked Joseph quietly. I could see the same annoyance return to his eyes. He really didn't like that guy.

"Maybe," he said simply, not bothering to elaborate. I shrugged off his odd behavior and continued to daydream about a scenario where Lukas fell madly in love with me and I became the famous girlfriend of Lukas Leighton . . . until the bell rang, bursting my perfect fantasy.

After theatre, Joseph and I had some time before we actually had to be to our first class, so we headed to the northeast side of the school where a little grassy area and some planters served as our usual hangout spot with a few other people from theatre.

"Joseph, I really enjoyed the scene you did on Friday," said Xani Tucker, tossing her short blonde hair and emphasizing her cute southern accent. While I liked Xani well enough, she was always throwing herself at Joseph, which I think made him pretty uncomfortable. I could tell she wasn't his type, but he was way too nice to ever say that to her, and so he just endured her endless praise and constant attempts to win his heart.

"Thanks. It really wasn't that great . . . I actually forgot my lines about halfway through and had to make the rest of the monologue up," he said modestly. Xani wasn't having it.

"No, you were fantastic! I think that just shows what a

great actor you really are," she cooed, leaning closer to him with a lovesick smile plastered to her face. Joseph simply stared straight ahead, his mouth pursed into a line, and looking more uncomfortable than I'd ever seen him.

"So, June has an audition today," he finally managed, his voice sounding a bit squeaky. I tried to hide my smile at his obvious discomfort, knowing it would only embarrass him more.

At the mention of my name Xani seemed to remember that she was, in fact, in public and not in one of her fantasies where she and Joseph were married with fifteen children.

"Oh," she said with a polite smile in my direction. Xani didn't really like me much. I'm pretty sure she thought I was trying to steal Joseph away from her, which couldn't be farther from the truth. But for whatever reason, she'd cemented this idea firmly in place and always made it known to me that she was after him.

"Tell her what it's for, June," he said in a pained voice, still staring straight ahead and trying not to look like his personal space bubble was being infiltrated.

"It's an audition for *Forensic Faculty*," I said, trying to sound like it was no big deal even though I was bursting with excitement. This actually pulled Xani's attention away from Joseph for a second.

"Seriously?" she said, staring at me suspiciously, as if I were trying to distract her so that I could lunge at Joseph and shower him with kisses.

"Yeah, she's got an audition at noon," Joseph answered for me, sounding much more like himself now that he didn't have Xani practically chewing on his ear.

"Do you think Lukas Leighton will be at the audition?" she asked, her voice suddenly rising a few decibels.

"I don't think he'll be at the audition, but I'm sure if I got the part I'd meet him," I said, now matching her tone and making Joseph look like he wanted to throw up. I think he would actually prefer fending off a thousand Xani clones rather than talking about Lukas Leighton anymore today.

"Oh. My. Gosh. June, if you meet him, I'm going to be so jealous. What if you guys date or something?" she asked, sounding as serious as she was about her Joseph obsession.

"I'm pretty sure June has enough common sense not to date someone whose greatest accomplishment is being seen at a different bar every night with his latest bimbo," Joseph said defensively.

"Maybe he's not drinking in the bars," I said dreamily, getting a faraway look in my eyes. "He just likes the atmosphere."

"And those girls could be related to him," Xani added, matching my dreamy tone.

"I give up," Joseph sighed. "You guys are hopeless and blinded by his 'good looks'," he said, putting air quotes around the last two words.

"Well, if I get the part we'll just see who's right," I said challengingly to Joseph as the bell rang for us to go to English.

....

English seemed to creep by the whole time we were in class. We were talking about persuasive essays and I knew I should be paying attention, but all I could think about was my audition. After English we'd have a fifteen minute break and then I'd only have to sit through half of math before Gran picked me up from school to drive to LA. Today was kind of a bad day to be picked up early since it was a "testing day" and I would only have half a math class before meeting in the cafeteria to take an AP English prep test. But like Gran said, I had to make sacrifices for my art, right?

All through English my foot kept bouncing up and down frantically, shaking my desk and making a rattling noise I was sure annoyed everyone. Joseph kept shooting me glances to remind me to calm down and breathe, but it was proving to be a very difficult task. After about two hours of foot bobbing and irritated looks from everyone in the room, the bell finally rang for break.

"You're lucky the class didn't stage a coup," Joseph said with a smirk as we walked back to our little grassy area. Xani was already there, waiting for us anxiously . . . well, waiting for Joseph, anyway.

"I can't help it," I exclaimed, "I'm so nervous about the audition . . . and excited . . . but mostly nervous."

"June, you're a really good actress and they handpicked you to audition. I'm pretty sure they already know they want to cast you; they just have to go through the process. Don't worry, you're definitely going to get it," he replied warmly, his chocolate brown eyes crinkling at the edges as he smiled at me.

"Thanks Joseph," I said seriously. I loved him for always knowing exactly how to clam me down. That's what best friends were for.

For the rest of break I went over audition tactics in my head while Joseph stared at the ground uncomfortably and Xani leaned over him. She was talking about the homecoming dance that was coming up in just two weeks and dropping hints like her life depended on it. Joseph nodded every once in a while, trying to look interested without encouraging any more physical closeness. This only made Xani scoot closer to him and rest her hand on his knee, turning Joseph's face a bright red for the remainder of our break.

When the bell rang Xani scuttled off to class, leaving Joseph and me alone. He turned to me seriously and put his hands on my shoulders so that our brown eyes were locked on each other.

"June, you're going to kill this audition, all right? Don't worry about anything. Just be yourself and they'll love you," he said evenly. "And remember not to agree to anything sleazy just so you can meet Lukas Leighton," he added as a humorous afterthought, though I wasn't sure how much of his warning was a joke and how much of it he really meant.

"Joseph, I wouldn't," I said, slightly offended. He just smiled and pulled me into a tight hug.

"Knock 'em dead, June."

CHAPTER 3

The car ride to the audition only seemed to take ten minutes, though in reality about forty minutes had passed since Gran picked me up from school. We both stood outside of the office building for a moment, staring up at the looming structure in silent awe.

"This is it, Bliss," she said with a slow nod. "Take it in, because this is the moment your life changes forever."

"Only if I get the part, Gran," I reminded her.

"Details," she muttered as we walked into the office.

After filling out some paperwork and reading old magazines for a good ten minutes, the receptionist came out from a back room and said, "Mr. Hill will see you now." It made me feel like I was at the dentist office and brought my anxiety up a few notches. Gran gave me an encouraging nod as I made my way shakily back into a large office with a long desk in it. Four people and a fifth man with a small video camera on a tripod sat behind the desk, staring at me. The man in the center was slightly overweight, the buttons on his white shirt straining with the effort of staying closed. Nevertheless, he looked well put together. The other two men at the table were dressed in a similar fashion, button-up collared shirts and slacks. A woman sat to the left of the man in the center. She wore her blonde hair pulled back into a

French twist, her deep purple silk top bringing out the green in her eyes. It was obvious she was trying to look professional and sexless so that she could compete in this industry. The man with the video camera looked like a film student. He had an artsy appearance that tried to look unintentional even though you knew every article of clothing he was wearing was carefully planned out to give him an indie air.

I walked up to the desk and placed my headshot and resume in front of them before walking back to the neon pink tape mark that had been placed on the floor for me. The people behind the desk all silently scanned my resume while I stood there awkwardly. Normally I would slate for the camera, which means I would say my name and what agency I was with, but they weren't looking at me, so I figured I'd wait until they gave me the go-ahead.

I stood there for what seemed like hours, trying to look like I was calm and collected even though my legs felt like Jell-O and my palms were sweating like a fourteen-year-old boy at a stake dance during a slow song. Finally the group looked up from my resume and gave me a once-over.

"All right June, can you please slate to the camera?" said the man sitting in the center of the table, clueing me in to the fact that he was the casting director I should be trying to impress.

I turned to the camera, plastered a bright smile to my face and said with all the enthusiasm I could muster, "Hi! My name is June Laurie, I'm sixteen years old and I'm represented by the Annette Adams Agency."

Slating was always kind of an awkward thing to do because you look at the camera and talk to it like it's your best friend while a group of people sit there and watch you. Then you have to turn back to face those people and act like you just did a completely normal thing by talking to a camera. The world of acting was a very strange place. At least it wasn't as weird as modeling—I didn't have to wear a paper bag over my head while people looked at my feet to see if I'd be a good shoe model.

After slating I'd normally start reading for the casting director while they filmed me, but again, this audition was proving to be a bit different since I didn't have a script yet.

"So, June, have you seen the show before?" asked the man who had told me to slate. I assumed this was Mr. Hill.

"Of course," I replied, still smiling but trying to act more relaxed than I had for my very stiff slate. "I think most people have seen it." They all smiled at each other, silently congratulating themselves, I guessed.

"So you're familiar with the characters and have a rough handle on their background stories and such?" he went on. This was by far the strangest audition I had ever been to. It felt more like sitting around and talking about the show rather than actually trying to be a part of it. When was I going to read lines for them?

"Yeah, I watch the show every week so I know all about the characters," I replied, this time a bit hesitantly. I wasn't quite sure where this was going.

"Well, we aren't really trying to bring a new main character onto the show, but it has been a bit stagnant lately and we felt that a fresh face could liven things up for a few episodes—throw a wrench into the normal operation of the team," he said. I simply smiled and nodded, wondering if they wanted my opinion or if they were simply letting me know what was going on.

"That's always a good idea," I answered neutrally.

"Wonderful," he said with a grin, though I was pretty sure he didn't need me to tell him it was a good idea. That's what the other people at the desk were paid to do. "What your character would add to the show is some conflict. You'll be playing Imogen Gentry. She's a vaudeville actress whose co-star Edward winds up dead. Of course you'll be a suspect, but Cutter is going to let his feelings for you cloud his judgment on the case, causing some contention between him and Charles."

My head was spinning as Mr. Hill described the part to me. Not only was I going to play a pretty big part in the show, but I was also going to be a love interest for Lukas Leighton's character Cutter. I didn't trust myself to speak, so I just nodded my approval of the part.

"Well, then, if you'll just take this script here and look over it for a moment, we'll bring someone in to read with you."

As they handed me the paper I began to feel more comfortable. This was more like a normal audition. Having scripted words in front of me was somehow easier than standing in front of this group of people and answering questions as myself.

One of the men left the room as I scanned the page and tried to get comfortable with the lines in the few short seconds I had to look at them. I knew I could just read from the paper, but it was so much better to have it memorized. It looked more natural. I made sure I memorized the key words in my lines that I knew would trigger the response from the other character in the scenes. That way if I forgot the exact line and had to improvise a little bit, the other actor would still pick up their cue from me.

As I took it all in, trying not to think of the camera fixed on me or the line of people staring at me, I heard the door open and close as the man re-entered the room with someone following behind him.

I kept my eyes trained on the page in front of me, but the first thing I noticed about Lukas Leighton was how amazing he smelled. This could have been due to the fact that I wasn't looking at him, so my other senses had to alert me that someone incredible had just walked into the room. The second his heavenly scent hit my nose I looked up from my script and into his perfect blue eyes.

"Lukas Leighton," I said dumbly. Honestly. That was the wittiest thing I could think of to say: his name. I was pretty sure he'd heard his name enough times that he didn't need me reminding him of what it was.

"June Laurie," he replied with a winning smile.

I let out a little laugh. It was all I could muster. Lukas

Leighton had just said my name. And he was standing two feet away from me. His ocean blue eyes. His perfect, full mouth. The gorgeous dirty blonde styled hair. His ever-present five o'clock shadow. That chiseled jaw. All right. I had to get a grip or I was going to make a fool out of myself on camera. And in front of the casting director. And most importantly, in front of Lukas Leighton.

"June, we'd like to have you read the lines with Lukas so we can make sure everything . . . fits," Mr. Hill said thoughtfully. "So whenever you're ready, you can start."

I was pretty sure I'd never be ready for this moment, but I tried to calm myself. Gran had been right after all. This really was the moment my whole life changed. I took a steadying breath and tried to quickly get in the mindset of the scene. From what I had gathered from the script, I was supposed to be emotional because Charles had been accusing me of killing my co-star for money. In this scene I was supposed to ask Cutter if he really thought I was capable of killing Edward. Luckily, I wouldn't have to act much to get myself feeling worked up and emotional—I was there the second Lukas Leighton walked into the room.

Turning and facing Lukas while still cheating out to the camera, I began with my lines, my voice full of emotion. "Cutter, I know all the evidence points to me and you really have no reason to believe me, but . . . you can't think I'm capable of something so . . . so horrible," I said, looking up at him hopelessly. My heart was beating out of my chest and I tried to harness that emotion into the character of Imogen Gentry.

Lukas took a step closer to me, closing the gap between us in just one movement. He stared down at me with his blue eyes and looked as if a thousand thoughts were passing through his head. It was incredible. This is what it felt like to act with someone who really knew what they were doing. I actually believed that he was thoughtfully considering how to answer my question, even though I already knew his answer, since it was written right under my lines.

"Listen, I know Charles can be kind of intense, but he means well," Lukas said softly, bringing his hand to my cheek. I had to bite my lip to keep from grinning like an idiot, which proved useful since it just made me look like I was fighting back tears. "He has to follow through with every possible lead. If he got distracted by every pretty suspect we had, he wouldn't be a very good detective, now would he?" His thumb lightly traced my cheekbone and I frantically tried to remember my next line. The fact that Lukas Leighton was touching my cheek really wasn't helping my concentration at all, but I didn't want to look down at the script and ruin the chemistry we were building. I remembered generally what I was supposed to say, so I took a shot in the dark.

"But do *you* think I did it?" I asked, this time with my voice barely above a whisper. I stared up at him in silent awe, waiting for his next line.

His big blue eyes were so easy to get lost in, and I forgot that there was a whole desk of people watching us until Mr. Hill said, "That's all that matters to me." It instantly tore my attention away from Lukas.

"What?" I asked, looking over at Mr. Hill.

"That's your next line," he said with a raised eyebrow.

"Oh, right! Sorry," I said quickly, turning back to Lukas and trying to get back into the moment. I thought I saw frustration pass over his face, but the emotion disappeared so fast that I couldn't be sure. I took another breath and moved my expression back to one of distress. Lukas instantly brought his hand to my cheek and resumed caressing my cheekbone with his thumb once more. I could feel blood rising to my face and I hoped I wasn't turning red. That was the last thing I needed right now.

"That's all that matters to me," I went on, saying my line with a voice full of emotion. I took advantage of what assets I had, knowing that in the presence of this perfect man, I didn't have many. I widened my dark, soulful eyes, looking up at him with a gaze full of intensity. I thought I saw a flicker of a smile pass over his full lips, though I didn't know why that would have made him smile.

"Maybe this will answer your question," he said so quietly that I wondered if the camera had caught his line. I tried desperately to remember what came next, hoping I hadn't forgotten a line again. But as Lukas moved his hand from my cheek to the back of my head I instantly knew what was coming. He moved his face closer to mine, making my breath catch in my chest.

This couldn't actually be happening.

I held my breath, waiting for him to close the now-minuscule gap between us, when Mr. Hill loudly announced, "Thank you Lukas, that's perfect."

I couldn't believe it.

I had been so close to actually kissing Lukas Leighton. I mean, I could actually feel the warmth from his lips right before he pulled away. If I had gotten a small shiver, we would have been kissing. That's how close we were. And the magical moment was stolen away from me by "Mr. Casting Director." Wasn't he the one who wanted to see if we "fit"? What better way to tell? I thought of bringing this up in a moment of sheer desperation, but luckily someone else spoke before I could make the suggestion.

"We'll see you on Thursday, Lukas," the woman in the purple top said.

"Thanks guys," he said quickly, dropping his hand from my head and walking out the door without so much as a glance in my direction. The whole thing happened so fast that I couldn't really tell if he was being rude or if he genuinely looked like he was in a hurry. Maybe I was just so worked up that everything seemed to move in fast forward. That was probably it. Lukas was a gentleman and I knew he wouldn't just leave like that if he didn't really need to.

"Well, June, that was marvelous. Now let's talk business."

CHAPTER 4

The rest of the meeting was a bit of a blur. I tried to take in all of the instructions the casting directors were giving me, but it was so hard to get that image of Lukas out of my head. The look on his face right before he was supposed to kiss me could have melted butter in the dead of winter.

From what I could recall (between daydreams of Lukas Leighton), I had gotten the part and they were very happy with my performance. The team gave me a packet full of filming times, paperwork to sign, and some general information. They also gave me a script, background information on my character, and pretty much everything else I needed to know to be ready for our read on Thursday. In exchange, I gave them my measurements for the costume department and some other schooling information they'd need to get me a studio teacher.

When Gran pulled onto Pullman Avenue where we lived, I saw Joseph's forest green car parked outside of the house.

"That boy has been calling every five seconds to ask if you're out of the audition yet," Gran said with slight exasperation, even though I knew she loved Joseph. I smiled at Joseph's interest and couldn't wait to tell him I got the part . . . and all of the other exciting things that had happened that day. "I think he likes you," Gran said mischievously.

"Gran, I only met him today," I said with a grin, but I secretly hoped she was right. Lukas did look very passionate when he was about to kiss me. Never mind that he had been duped by Mr. Hill.

"I meant Joseph, Bliss," she said with a roll of her eyes. "Don't you get all wrapped up in Lukas Leighton. It's never a good idea to date someone you work with. Besides, you just can't trust actors," she said knowingly.

"But you're an actor . . . and I'm an actor . . . and Joseph's an actor," I said, ticking each of us off on my fingers. Gran simply shot me a silencing look.

"You know what I mean, Bliss."

I smiled at her and jumped out of the car the second we pulled into the garage. Joseph scrambled out of his own car, holding a miniature cooler and searching my face tentatively.

"I brought you ice cream," he said carefully.

"What kind?" I asked.

"Both."

We were silent for a moment while I let the suspense build. Joseph knew me so well that it was scary. Whenever I was sad, I ate my weight in Praline Pecan ice cream. Whenever I was happy, I ate my weight in Huckleberry ice cream. Either way, I probably shouldn't be eating my weight in ice cream no matter what my mood was, but that wasn't the point. The point was that Joseph thought of everything.

He continued to look at me with his dark brown eyes, practically pleading with me to tell him what had happened.

"Break out the Huckleberry," I said with a grin.

"No way," he exclaimed, dropping the cooler onto the ground and picking me up in a tight embrace. "No way," he just kept saying over and over again while I laughed like a maniac. I was sure anyone driving by would think we had completely lost our minds. When he finally released me from the hug he just held me at arms length and smiled. "I can't believe this," he finally said.

"How do you think I felt when they told me?" I said breathlessly. "I'm actually going to be on *Forensic Faculty*! And from the scripts they gave me, I'll be on at least four episodes. Maybe more if they decide they really like me."

"June, this is a really big deal," he told me, as if I needed reminding. "I say we go inside, you eat the Huckleberry and I'll eat the sad ice cream and we go over your lines."

"I think that's a perfect idea," I said, linking my arm through his. As we walked inside, Joseph said hello to Gran for a moment while I grabbed two spoons from the drawer and raced him up to my room. We didn't bother with bowls on special occasions; we just ate the whole pint right out of the carton.

"All right, where do you want to start?" Joseph asked, skimming the pages of the script and scooping a huge amount of ice cream up with his spoon.

"Honestly, I don't really say much until my scene with Lukas that I auditioned with today. Most of my scenes before that are just a few angry lines that I yell at Charles, but I'd rather practice those on my own. Angry lines are always kind of embarrassing to practice in front of someone," I said with a shrug.

"Agreed," he replied. "All right, so you start here, right?" he asked, pointing halfway down a page in the script.

"Yep." I took a deep breath, trying to get myself back to the heightened emotional state I was in this afternoon. Joseph and I sat side by side on the ground, our backs against my bed and our shoulders touching lightly. I cleared my throat and began the lines I had already gone over today in the audition and about a thousand times in my head on the drive home.

"Cutter, I know all the evidence points to me and you really have no reason to believe me, but . . . you can't think I'm capable of something so . . . so horrible," I began, the dialogue sending a chill up my spine as I remembered the look in Lukas's eyes.

"Listen, I know Charles can be kind of intense, but he means well," Joseph said, smiling as he read the lines. "I just can't get over the fact that you'll be saying these lines on the show," he said with a grin.

"So unprofessional, breaking character like that," I said in mock seriousness, shaking my head and closing my eyes. Joseph pulled a face at me and went on reading his lines. Joseph and Lukas definitely approached acting differently. Lukas seemed like he stayed in character and didn't really like to break it when reading his lines. Joseph, on the other hand, was all fun and games until the second he had to be in character, when he somehow magically turned into someone else completely.

"He just has to follow through with every possible lead. If he got distracted by every pretty suspect we had, he wouldn't be a very good detective, now would he?" At this line Joseph tried to suppress a laugh but ended up snorting.

"What?" I demanded, wondering what he could possibly find so funny.

"You didn't tell me Cutter was going to be all smooth toward you on the show. It's a little disturbing," he said with a shudder.

"What's wrong with it?" I asked, now a little defensive.

"Well, for one thing, his character is named Cutter. I don't really need to expand on that. And for another thing, aren't you supposed to be a murderer? Isn't he the good guy?"

"I am not the murderer!" I exclaimed, trying to defend myself as if Joseph were actually accusing me of being a killer. "They just suspect me. A suspect and a murderer are not the same thing."

"My mistake," Joseph replied, though I could still see the smile in his eyes. He was teasing me. "Sorry. Back into character now," he said, his face instantly melting into an expression of the utmost seriousness. I followed suit.

"But do *you* think I did it?" I asked Joseph, now turning to him and gazing into his eyes. The moment didn't hold the passion of my audition, but that probably had something to do with the fact that Lukas wasn't in the room, sending chills up my spine every time he breathed. "That's all that matters to me."

Joseph held my gaze for a moment before looking back down at the paper to read his line. "Maybe this will answer your question," he said before pausing abruptly. A look of great concern passed over his face and he looked up at me questioningly. For some reason the look made me very uncomfortable.

"Don't worry, Joseph, you don't actually have to kiss me. We're just reading through the lines," I said, trying to play off how heavy the room had suddenly gotten.

"This is the scene you did today?" he asked. I nodded silently, not sure why that mattered. "With Lukas Leighton?" I nodded again, this time with a grin spreading across my face. "You kissed him?"

"No, I didn't kiss him," I said, as if that were the most obvious thing in the world. Joseph visibly relaxed at that news. "I was so close though," I said sighing and laying back against the foot of my bed, closing my eyes. "I know you're a guy so you don't care, but it was honestly the most exciting experience ever. We were this close," I said, turning and showing him an almost nonexistent space between my finger and thumb.

"Great," he said with at least some enthusiasm. I should have known not to bring it up to Joseph—he was such a guy about things sometimes. But he was my best friend also, so it felt like he should be the one I told about this kind of stuff. Maybe I'd just have to suck up my pride and tell Xani tomorrow morning. Letting out a deep breath, I closed my eyes once more and laid my head on Joseph's shoulder.

"This part is going to be so great," I breathed. Joseph tilted his head down against mine, but didn't say anything.

CHAPTER 5

The next morning Joseph and I were late to theatre because we were held up by dozens of questions from kids in our seminary class. Somehow word had gotten out about my audition going well. I had no doubt Gran had something to do with the news leak, but at that moment, I wasn't exactly angry. Instead, I was reveling in all of the questions and the fact that I suddenly seemed very important.

As Joseph and I ran into the auditorium for zero period theatre, Mr. Carroll gave a slow applaud, causing the other people in the class to join in. I blushed a deep shade of scarlet and tried to look modest while Joseph just beamed over at me like a proud parent.

"As I'm sure some of you know, our very own June Laurie just got a part on the TV show *Forensic Faculty*," Mr. Carroll announced happily. I imagined this was every theatre teacher's dream come true—to feel like they'd contributed to helping someone reach their goal with acting. I simply continued to smile as Joseph and I took a seat in the audience of the auditorium with the rest of the students. Xani soon appeared next to Joseph, flashing him her perfectly bleached teeth.

"Now, getting on to business. I've decided that I'm going to break the class into groups for our next acting assignment," Mr. Carroll began. "I'm going to have each group perform a skit for the rest of the class that will require a great range of emotion. I'm talking tears, laughter, panic . . . the whole shebang," he said with a wide gesture of his hands. "I've assigned the groups and the skits, so I'll pass these out right now while you turn in your play analysis from last week."

As I scrambled through my backpack to find my play analysis, Xani leaned in to Joseph and whispered something that made him go white. It instantly brought a smile to my face. It really wasn't that I liked to see my friend constantly embarrassed by Xani's attention—I just liked that he was so surprised to be getting attention from a girl. Joseph didn't realize his potential no matter how many times I reminded him of it.

"I think the groups are already assigned . . . so we don't know who will be in what group," Joseph said stiffly to Xani, making her pout.

"June and Joseph, of course," Mr. Carroll said absentmindedly as he shuffled through the pile of scripts in his hands, not responding to what Joseph had said, but simply thinking out loud as he often did.

I gave Joseph a thumbs up and a cheesy smile, knowing Xani was about to try to pout her way into our group. I'd let Joseph deal with that. Luckily for him, Xani was soon put into her own group and couldn't keep trying to bribe Mr. Carroll into putting her in ours.

"All right, let's do this," Joseph said, rubbing his hands together as I handed him his script. We made our way into the green room behind the stage to rehearse, as per Mr. Carroll's instructions. We only had a few days to perfect our skit, and if we wanted to win this self-proclaimed competition, we were going to have to start practicing now. Joseph kept subtly dropping hints about how I'd better not let my newfound stardom affect my commitment to winning our class competition, and I kept playfully deflecting his accusations with a coy smile and a few well-placed winks.

"All I'm saying," Joseph began, as we settled into the green room to practice before the bell rang for our next class, "is that I'd better not see an amazing performance on *Forensic Faculty* and then a crap one in class the next day."

I could tell he was joking, so I tried my best to annoy him. "But what I was thinking is that we could try a different approach from everyone else in the class. You know everyone is going to try to do well, right? So let's just be awful! Then we'll really stand out," I said, as if he should have thought of this ages ago.

"Very funny, June," Joseph replied, shaking his head at my suggestion and quickly reading over the script we had been given. "Hey, I get to be funny," he said, suddenly excited. "Well . . . for about two seconds."

Joseph *loved* funny parts. I figured it was because he'd always loved Harold Lloyd. He repeatedly insisted that Harold was one of the few people who truly sacrificed for his art (which wasn't true at all). Of course, he didn't sacrifice in the typical sense of the word. He was a silent film star who had a few fingers blown off during a photo shoot when the prop bomb he was holding exploded unexpectedly. Macabre story? Yes. But for some reason Joseph loved it.

"Oh . . . " he said out of nowhere. "Awkward."

"What?" I asked, skimming the script quickly to find what could possibly be labeled as "awkward." It wasn't too hard to locate.

"Huh," was all I could say, once I saw the four-letter word printed on the page I held. "Kiss?" I read the word in puzzlement, as if it were foreign to me, (although the word definitely was well known, since it was the only word I'd been thinking of since I found out I'd be kissing Lukas Leighton on the show). Instead of saying, "Let's see if Mr. Carroll will give us a different script, because this is way too weird," I simply shrugged my shoulders at Joseph, pretending it was no big deal. He seemed to take his cue from me and nodded in agreement, though his face looked like he had just been called to serve a mission in the Bermuda Triangle.

"No big deal," he said slowly under his breath, almost as if he were giving himself a pep talk.

"Maybe for today we'll just rehearse the rest of the skit. No need to practice that . . . other part . . . for a while," I said with a sense of authority, as if I knew what I was talking about.

"Good point," he agreed a bit too quickly.

The instant we began rehearsing the non-kissing part of the script, I could see why Mr. Carroll had given it to us. The scene was supposed to be acted out as a black-and-white movie. The couple, played by Joseph and me, were unorthodox bank robbers who'd narrowly escaped being caught by the police. We were supposed to be hiding out in an abandon store near the bank while the search for us continued, and while inside, we would get into an argument. Mr. Carroll's only direction was that he wanted it to be big and a little overacted, which suited us just fine. It was always nice to be able to do something different.

Joseph started our scene off by pacing back and forth in the green room, tripping over his shoes on one jaunt across the room and stumbling to regain his balance. I sat in a chair, my head following his movements. As he regained his balance, he rounded on me, waving his imaginary gun in my direction.

"What could you possibly be thinking?" he spat, his hand gestures very big and dramatic. "Robbery is an *art*, not an excuse to throw a brick through a window!"

I stood up indignantly, pulling my own imaginary gun out of my imaginary pocket and stepping close enough to him that my pointer finger gun barrel stuck into his chest.

"What's more artful than smashing a window, taking the cash, and still not getting caught?" I inquired, my eyes narrowing at him dangerously. He waited a beat before answering, letting the intensity hang in the air like a thick fog.

"If you don't point that thing somewhere else, I'll have to reconsider my idea of working as a team," he whispered darkly, his face forming an expression I'd never seen my sweet Joseph wear. It was actually a bit terrifying and it caught me off guard for a moment. I had to collect myself before going on.

I dropped my hand from his chest and turned as if I were about to walk away from him.

"Where do you think you're going?" he asked.

"To find a new partner," I shot back at him, putting as much ice into my voice as I could.

"Perfect. How about while you do that, I'll stay here and count all that money you just made me," he said condescendingly, causing me to stop in my tracks and turn slowly toward him again. He kicked his backpack on the ground, indicating that it would act as our bag of money for this rehearsal. I tried to make it look as if I were thinking hard about a way to turn this situation in my favor and had suddenly discovered the perfect ploy. I walked over to him slowly, looking up at him from under my eyelashes, my lips turned up into a half smile.

"I see your point," I said finally, sounding as if I had just realized how foolish I was being. I injected as much sweetness into my tone as I could muster while trying to look seductive. "Really there's no reason to fight, right?" I asked as I finally closed the distance between us. I rested my arm on his shoulder and let my fingers play with the back of his hair. "We're on the same team aren't we?" I said sweetly, moving my face close enough to him that I could feel his shallow breathing on my cheek. While doing this, I moved the "bag of money" behind me with my foot, trying to be graceful as I did so—which proved to be difficult, since he had so many books in his backpack.

Joseph's face was bright red and he looked a bit like a deer in the headlights, but he still managed to say his line, however broken it sounded. "Um . . . yes . . . Yes, we are on the same team," he said shakily, sliding his hand around to the small of my back while using *his* foot to slide the "bag of money" back behind him again. I could feel his hand shaking on my back, but I tried to ignore it. I assumed he was probably just nervous about performing this very intimate scene in front of our class. No one in the class ever let you live down a kissing scene.

He was looking at me intently now, his brow furrowed slightly and a look in his eye that I couldn't quite put my finger on. He pulled me closer to him, causing my heart to race for some reason and making the blood rush up to my cheeks. I swallowed loudly, almost comically, as I tried to keep my focus on the scene. Joseph and I had been in dozens of plays together, but we'd never had a scene like this. I had always wondered what it would be like to have to act something like this out, but now that it was here, I was actually in a state of mild panic.

By this point, Joseph's eyes were closed and his hand had tightened its grip on my back. As his lips were only inches from mine, our noses touching lightly, I pulled back abruptly, startling him. Apparently he had gotten a bit lost in the scene as well. I cleared my throat in an attempt to gain my composure and get my cheeks to stop flushing.

"All right, and so this is where we would kiss and both reach for the bag at the same time, catching each other in the act, right?" I asked, looking down at the floor rather than at Joseph. I wasn't sure why I wouldn't look at him. Maybe I was worried about what I might see in his face, or maybe I was a little worried about what I might feel if I looked at him. Joseph and I did not see each other in a romantic way—at all. It was probably just my constant fantasizing over Lukas that had gotten me so off balance. I was confusing my feelings; confusing *who* I was having the feelings about.

Joseph cleared his throat as well, apparently trying to pull himself back to reality. His cheeks were still red and he was still breathing hard, though I pretended not to notice. "Yeah," he said finally, sounding distant. "Yeah, we'll need to make sure when we both reach for the bag we . . . um . . . we really play up the look we give each other in the end… that's where the comedy will be, if we can do it right."

"Perfect," I said, trying to sound bright and cheerful,

though my words just sounded odd, like yelling in an insulated room with no echo. Finally, I looked up at Joseph and was startled to see him staring at me intently with a confused look in his eyes. We didn't say anything for a moment, and the silence in the room was deafening. Joseph eventually opened his mouth to say something, but was cut off by Xani bursting into the room. Her unexpected entrance caused us both to jump in alarm, as if we'd been caught doing something wrong.

"I've been looking *everywhere* for you guys!" she exclaimed in her southern accent. "The bell's just about to ring and—," she let her words trail off, looking from me, to Joseph, and back again. "You guys just have a séance or something?" she asked with a small laugh. "Looks like ya'll have seen a ghost."

I was the first one to stop acting like a complete idiot. "The auditorium *is* supposed to be haunted," I said cheerfully, figuring I should do some actual acting today.

"Wait, you didn't really, did you?" she asked, a little slow about catching on to my joke. "Never mind. Not important. What *is* important is that you tell me absolutely everything about Lukas Leighton right now!"

Xani pulled me violently by the arm, barely giving me the chance to grab my backpack off the floor before she'd forcibly led me out of the green room. Joseph seemed to finally regain his composure and hurriedly picked up his backpack to run after us.

"So, what did he smell like?" Xani asked seriously.

"Heaven," I replied, finding that this conversation was clearing my mind of its recently confused contents. "I don't even really know how to describe it." Xani just beamed at me as if this were the best news she'd ever heard.

"Was he nice? I'd hate to think he was one of those celebrities who're big jerks to everyone who isn't famous," she said with a shake of her head.

"He was so nice! Well . . . I mean, I didn't get to talk to him much out of character," I admitted. "We only said a few words to each other before rehearsing the scene . . . but he seemed really nice for those few sentences," I said, trying to sound as reassuring as I could. Joseph was walking a few steps behind us, muttering something under his breath. I ignored him.

"But didn't y'all have a chance to talk after the audition?" Xani asked, sounding a bit disappointed that I didn't have more to tell her.

"Well, he had to leave right after we finished our scene. I'm sure he's really busy."

Xani nodded slowly at this revelation. "Makes sense," she agreed as the bell rang.

After Xani left us, I turned to Joseph, determined not to let things be weird at all. "Well, I'm off to learn about all sorts of interesting, non-math related subjects," I teased.

He just rolled his eyes and adjusted the way his backpack sat on his shoulders. "Yeah, thanks June," he deadpanned, before winking at me and making his way to his next class.

Maybe things wouldn't get weird after all.

CHAPTER 6

The rest of the school day was uneventful. Joseph and I went to Spanish and Art History together, and then said our goodbyes after he dropped me off at home, never once mentioning the weirdness of that morning. Gran was already waiting for me in the kitchen with some new, bizarre concoction that would make me a better actress somehow. She wore a deep emerald tracksuit that made her flaming red hair stand out from miles away. I took this apparel to indicate that today was going to be a workday. I sighed deeply, but wasn't let off the hook. Surrendering, I changed into my black yoga pants and oversized purple v-neck T-shirt to prepare for what would undoubtedly be a grueling workout. I pulled my curly hair back into a high bun and secured an elastic headband in place to hold any stray hairs back.

"What have you got for me this time?" I asked Gran when I returned to the kitchen. I rubbed my hands together, ready to take on any weird tasks she would throw at me. After all, I was now on a hit TV show. I could handle anything, right? Gran didn't say a word, but pushed over a glass of blue-ish, purple-ish sludge. At least this time it wasn't green.

"Drink," she said with a knowledgeable smile, as she always did when making me try some strange new concoction. I raised an eyebrow at her skeptically. "Oh relax,

Bliss, it's just a berry smoothie." That put me at ease exponentially and I happily accepted the drink.

"No green goop today?" I asked.

"Not today. Besides, berries have antioxidants, which are good for your skin. We don't want you to show up to your first table read looking like your skin is made of rice paper, now do we?" she asked. I instantly brought my hand up to my cheek in horror and she realized her mistake. "You don't have rice paper skin Bliss. I'm just making sure it stays that way," she clarified.

"Thanks Gran," I said with a grin. "Bottom's up!"

This drink pleasantly surprised me. Even though Gran had called it a berry smoothie, I still expected it to have some hidden green or brown thing in it. However, it was actually pretty good, which made the drinking process much easier than it had been with the green goop. I polished the drink off with gusto and jumped out of my seat to show I was ready for the day. It was hard to tell where my newfound energy had come from, but the fact that I had a table read with Lukas Leighton in only two short days may have had something to do with it.

Gran seemed ecstatic about my enthusiasm and beckoned me into the living room, where she had lined the floor with the silk Indian pillows that seemed to be coming out of every corner of the house. "I thought we'd start off our workout today with a little yoga," she said, as she lit some incense in a stone holder.

I feel that before I go on, I should point out that my grandma is a bit of a hippie. She's completely dedicated to the art of acting, of course, but her methods are a bit . . . well . . . hippie-ish. Dad always called her a high-tech hippie because she was all earthy and organic, but couldn't go anywhere without her smart phone. So, as I prepared myself for a round of yoga that I was sure would kick my butt, I tried to ignore the heavy perfume coming from the incense holder.

After a few minutes of "clearing my mind," (or at least clearing it of everything except a certain someone I would be seeing again on Thursday) I arranged myself into my least favorite pose: Garudasana, or the "Eagle Pose." It wasn't that this pose was terribly difficult—for most people. Unfortunately, I lacked a basic sense of balance, so to stand on one leg with my other foot tucked behind my knee and my arms twisted like a pretzel with no chance of catching myself if I fell . . . well, needless to say, it was a pretty deadly combination. I stared intently at a spot on the floor, trying to maintain my balance and actually managing to clear my head—until Gran spoke.

"Now, June, I want to talk to you about your shining new opportunity on *Forensic Faculty*," she began, instantly making me wary. "You're going to be on set a lot—more than a month, if you only do four episodes. You'll have a studio teacher on set for those days you're filming for eight hours. But just because you aren't technically in school doesn't mean you can slack on your school work," she said with a note of finality.

I tried to respond and reassure her, but even thinking about speaking made me wobble in my current yoga stance. Instead, I settled for a reassuring (though pained) smile in her direction while I tried to ignore the bead of sweat running down the side of my face. She took it as her cue to keep talking.

"I know I've never put much stock in school . . . or at least I've never told you how important it is. I just want to make sure you haven't gotten the idea that I think school isn't important, Bliss," she said from her position next to me. Gran was simply amazing. She was obviously much older than me, (she was my grandmother, after all) but she could hold a yoga pose better than me. Probably better than anyone, really.

I finally managed to speak, feeling that this one-sided conversation wasn't going to reassure her. "Gran, I promise I'm still going to get good grades. I'm not going to get into BYU by batting my eyelashes at the admissions office," I said, causing me to lose my balance and fall into a heap on the floor. Now I could see why the pillows were scattered everywhere. Gran had taken precautions against my notorious clumsiness.

"Well, good. I just wanted to make sure we were on the same page . . . And on that note, I wanted to mention something else," she started, though she quickly interrupted herself by saying, "Natarajasana, Bliss," indicating that I should get into the "Lord of the Dance" pose. I did as I was told, bringing my leg up behind my back and reaching back over my shoulder to grab my foot. Needless to say, it was painful and very unstable.

"I know you know this, but when you're actually in the thick of things it becomes easy to forget . . . well . . . to forget what's important," she said seriously, easily holding a "Tree Pose" as she spoke. "Just remember that being around the same people in such a unique situation every day can skew reality a bit. You grow close to people faster than you normally would, and sometimes you think you have feelings that aren't really there."

I dropped the foot I was holding behind my head to turn to her. "Are you talking about Lukas Leighton?" I asked, coming off a bit more defensively than I meant to.

"I know you've only met him once, but I can see those stars in your eyes, Bliss. I just want you to be careful and keep your real friends close," she said, bring her hands up in surrender, preventing any fight that could have started. "Whenever you need a break from the limelight or a reality check, you should give Joseph a call. He's a very grounded young man."

I sighed deeply and wiped my wet forehead with the back of my hand. It was amazing that standing still could be a workout. "I know, Gran. I'll make sure I stay grounded," I told her. "It's only a small part anyway; I don't think you have much to worry about."

"You'd be surprised how much popularity can come to a pretty girl like you from just a small part," she warned, making me wonder if I'd been a little naïve about what I was getting into. "But I'm not trying to spoil this for you. I just want to make sure you're going into this whole thing with your eyes opened."

"Thanks Gran," I said honestly, feeling that if I had someone with her experience on my side, I'd be all right.

"Well, that's enough serious talk, Bliss. While you do your aerobic workout, I'll make you some grilled salmon . . . it's good for you hair," she said with a smile, even though she knew I hated fish.

"You know dark chocolate is loaded with antioxidants," I countered at her retreating form. "It was worth a try," I mumbled to the empty room.

CHAPTER 7

Wednesday came and went with lots of stomachaches throughout my classes and Joseph constantly reassuring me that I had this whole thing in the bag. By the time I woke up at four o'clock a.m. on Thursday morning, I was ready to call it quits. My stomach had been in knots all night, making it impossible to sleep, and I already had four panic attacks and one minor nervous breakdown in the time it took me to get ready. I didn't really know if I could handle this.

For the table read today, I chose my powder blue knee-length sundress. It had ruffled cap sleeves and a V-neck with a sash that tied around the back. I wore this dress whenever I could because I loved the pattern. The entire dress was printed with white flowers and red and yellow birds, making it look very 50s. I only wore mascara on my eyes today, to offset the red lipstick I was wearing (I didn't want to look like I had used a spatula to put my makeup on). And my wild curls were pinned strategically so that they piled up on the back of my head in a mass of curly chaos.

I slipped on some powder blue ballet flats as I ran out the door to meet Joseph outside. My table read wasn't until one, so I'd make it to most of my classes before Gran picked me up at noon. That gave me approximately seven more hours worth of nervous breakdowns and worst-case scenarios playing out in great detail in my head.

Joseph stood outside of his car, looking as comforting as ever, though his eyes were a bit red and tired. I smiled guiltily at him. I'd texted him about a hundred times throughout the night, unable to be left alone with my thoughts of everything that could possibly go wrong today.

I walked up to him and gave him a tight hug, scrunching my eyes closed in an attempt to make the outside world disappear for a second. Now, don't get me wrong. I was absolutely thrilled to be going to my first table read for *Forensic Faculty*, but the idea of being the newcomer in a room full of seasoned veterans was completely and utterly terrifying.

"I'm sorry," I finally said after Joseph and I got into his car.

"Don't worry about it, June," he answered warmly. "I'm your best friend. It's my job to stay up until three in the morning comforting you," he remarked with a yawn.

"There are just so many ways I could screw this up today," I admitted. I knew this because I'd already made a mental list of the various ways I'd make a fool out of myself.

"There are a lot more ways you could blow the entire cast out of the water," he countered matter-of-factly.

"Like what?" I asked skeptically. As a general rule, it wasn't nice to put someone on the spot when they're trying to cheer you up, but I was scared out of my wits and needed some reassurance.

"How about the fact that you look like a perfect little silent film star?" he began, holding up his pointer finger as he drove. "Or the fact that you're by far the best actress Mr. Carroll has ever seen," he said, still counting. "Or your very hip and awesome entourage." I looked at him, puzzled for a moment. "Me, June," he said, as if I'd just blanked on what 1+1 equals.

"Oh, right!" I exclaimed, embarrassed by my complete lack of comprehension this morning. "And what a supportive entourage you are," I commented with a grin. Joseph just glanced over at me and scrunched up his nose like he always did when I made a sarcastic remark.

"So, I know this is the last thing on your mind right now, but I was just thinking about homecoming," Joseph said as we pulled into the gas station to get our hot chocolate.

"That's coming up soon, isn't it?" I asked, having forgotten all about it in the excitement lately. Homecoming wasn't really a big deal to me, mostly because it wasn't like I had some crush that I wanted to ask me. More than likely, Joseph and I would go to homecoming together, stay for about five minutes before realizing all of the music was horrible and it was just an excuse for people to be . . . well . . . very close to each other (to put it nicely), and then we would go back to my house and watch a movie.

"We're still going, right?" he asked, glancing at me sideways a bit uneasily.

"Yeah, definitely . . . unless you wanted to ask Xani to be your date," I teased, poking him in the shoulder.

"You got me," he said sarcastically, getting out of the car while I followed suit.

"She's a cute girl—that's all I'm saying," I told him in a singsong voice as the bell above the gas station door announced our entrance.

Hazel, a beautiful girl with skin the color of cherry wood, stood behind the front counter, flipping through a magazine. She smiled by way of a greeting as we walked in. She always worked the early morning shift, so she'd quickly grown used to Joseph and me stopping in every weekday at the crack of dawn.

"I think I may pass on the hot chocolate today," I admitted to Joseph, watching while he filled up his cardboard cup with steaming, too-rich hot chocolate.

"Knowing your stomach, that may be the best idea," he agreed with a nod. "I'll just pay really fast and then we'll get this show on the road."

I stood back by the hot chocolate machine while Joseph paid for his drink. He talked avidly with Hazel about whatever she was reading in her magazine. She said something that made him laugh, and I couldn't help but notice how his smile made his eyes crinkle up in the corners. It was his squinty smile; my favorite one. Joseph was just one of those people who was nice to everyone he met—even crazy Xani, who always threw herself at him.

Joseph began to walk toward the door, waving for me to join him. As he stepped outside, he pulled his grey button-up sweater tighter around him.

"Skinny tie not keeping you warm?" I asked teasingly.

"For your information, all the best people wear skinny ties," he countered. "Harold Lloyd wore one."

"Did Buster Keaton? Because if he did, then I'd be convinced," I said with a wink.

"Didn't he wear bow ties? Maybe not . . . I think I'm confusing my actors." Joseph scratched his head in a contemplative way, and we spent the rest of the drive to seminary arguing over who was better between Buster Keaton and Harold Lloyd. What can I say? We were nerds.

After seminary, we actually managed to make it out the door and in to zero period theatre on time. Mr. Carroll wasn't standing on the stage in his normal "lecturing" position because he was giving us today to work on our skits. This revelation gave me a small jolt as I realized we'd be performing those skits tomorrow. I wasn't quite sure how I was supposed to handle having so much going on at once. We hadn't even started filming the show, but I already felt overwhelmed by school and my new part.

Joseph and I resumed our practice in the green room where we'd been rehearsing for the past two days—without the kiss in the scene. Today, however, Joseph had brought our actual bag of money and we were ready to pull out all the stops. Of course when I say "actual bag of money," I mean, "actual pillowcase stuffed with board game money." He plopped the sack down next to him and began his pacing back and forth to start the scene off. I tried my best to forget about all of the stress I'd been feeling this past week and focus on the task at hand. After all, I had promised Joseph I wouldn't have some great performance on the show and hang him out to dry on our skit.

"What could you possibly be thinking?" Joseph asked me harshly, letting me know the scene had started. "Robbery is an *art*, not an excuse to throw a brick through a window!"

I let him pace back and forth a few more times, just to get the point across that he was fuming. Once he'd taken a few trips across the floor, I stood up to begin my lines. I walked behind him silently so that when he turned around to continue pacing, he ran into me, with my water gun sticking into his chest. The water gun was neon green, which wasn't very convincing, but Mr. Carroll thought it might not be a good idea to bring black water guns to school. I have to say, I didn't blame him for thinking this.

"What's more artful than smashing a window, taking the cash, and still not getting caught?" I asked, pushing my water gun into his chest hard enough that it made him stumble back a few paces. Joseph looked down at me through narrowed eyes for a moment and then leaned in close.

"If you don't point that thing somewhere else, I'll have to reconsider my idea of working as a team," he said icily, still giving me chills with the way he could instantly become so dark and threatening. I balked for a moment at his sudden change of tone and let my mouth drop open a fraction to show my surprise before turning and beginning to walk away.

"And just where do you think you're going?"

"To find a new partner," I threw over my shoulder.

"Perfect. How about while you do that, I'll stay here and count all that money you just made me," he said with a sneer, patting the bag next to him loudly. Just as we had rehearsed, I stopped dead in my tracks and turned my head so the audience would be able to tell I was considering this without turning enough to be looking at Joseph. Taking a deep breath, I spun around to face Joseph, who looked a bit comical. It looked like he was trying to keep his sneer in place and look tough, but I could see just a hint of nerves somewhere around his eyes. I dropped my water gun on the floor and put my hands up in mock surrender before walking slowly toward him.

"I see your point," I began, letting my lips form an alluring smile, walking closer to Joseph until I was right in front of him. I let my arm rest lightly on his shoulder as I had done every time we rehearsed this scene the past two days. My fingers spun his wavy dark brown hair into little curls behind his head while I continued to look at him.

"Really, there's no reason to fight, right?" I asked innocently, looking up at him through my eyelashes while I moved our pillowcase full of money behind me with my foot. Joseph looked at me intently, his brown eyes dark and intense. He was a good actor—I had to give him that. I let my face move incrementally closer to his as I said my last line. "We are on the same team right?" Joseph continued to stare at me, and I couldn't tell if he had forgotten his lines or was pausing for dramatic effect.

"Yes, we are," he finally said slowly, the words coming out just above a whisper. For a moment I hesitated. This was going to be weird. I was going to kiss my best friend. But then again, it was just for a skit, so it wasn't *really* like I was about to kiss my best friend, right? Just before I urged myself those last few inches, I thought of all of the stress and stomachaches I had put myself through these last few days by over-thinking things, and I made a resolution: this scene would be one less thing for me to over think.

I looked up into Joseph's brown eyes one last time. He seemed to be holding his breath as he stared back down at me. This was it. I closed my eyes and pressed my lips against his. At first it was just like holding hands—it didn't feel intimate at all. But as the kiss deepened and Joseph wrapped his arms around my waist, I could tell this wasn't really a stage kiss. I ran my fingers through his hair, pushing his face against mine as he pulled me tighter against him, and for a second, I felt all of my stress melt away in his warmth. It was a perfect moment where the only thing I was concentrating on was letting my breath come out in a slow, even pattern, and how soft Joseph's lips were. I guess I hadn't ever given him much thought in that way. As much as I was letting myself enjoy the kiss, Joseph must have enjoyed it more, because he didn't seem to want to let go of me.

By the time we pulled apart, we were both breathing hard and red in the face. Most of that, I soon realized (much to my horror), was because of the red lipstick I had decided to wear that day. I kept my fingers tightly entwined in his hair and his arms were still firmly around my waist as we stared at each other, dumbstruck.

"Sorry," I said sheepishly, although I wasn't quite sure what I was sorry about.

"Wow," was all he said. His eyebrows were raised as if he was surprised and his lips were pursed together.

"I've just been so stressed and I really, honestly, didn't mean to . . . attack you," I finally said. This made him laugh as he let go of me, somewhat reluctantly, I thought.

"Attack me?" he repeated with just a hint of mischief in his smile. "Yeah, I'd say that's a good way to describe what just happened here."

"You have lipstick all over your face, by the way," I said in embarrassment, bringing my hand up to my mouth, partially to remove the lipstick from my own face, but mostly to hide the blush that was rising in my cheeks. Joseph wiped at his face, rubbing most of the red away except for a small trace right around his lips. I quickly wiped it away with my thumb. He placed his hand over mine for just a moment before letting it go.

I stood in front of him, looking at the ground and feeling slightly ashamed that I had pounced on Joseph just because I'd been so stressed. It wasn't his fault he happened to be the innocent bystander of "June's mental meltdown."

"I really am sorry," I said again. Joseph opened his mouth to talk, but I quickly cut him off, wanting to make sure he understood me entirely. "It's just everything's been so crazy lately and I've been stressed about the show and even about the skit. And I guess I was thinking if I just let go for a minute I could maybe . . . get rid of some of the stress. But I didn't mean to attack you and I definitely don't want you to think I'm some crazy hormone-filled girl like Xani," I said all in one breath. Though I expected Joseph to look relieved by my revelation, he just looked a bit disappointed to me.

"Don't worry about it," he said somberly. I couldn't figure out exactly when we'd gone from being happy and full of jokes right after our kiss, to being suddenly all somber and depressed. "We did forget the last part of the skit though," he said with a halfhearted smile.

"Well, tomorrow we'll be much better," I said resolutely. "I promise. I won't attack you again, all right?" Joseph nodded, his pursed-lipped smile still in place.

We didn't talk about the kiss at break. Or in Spanish. Or during lunch . . . well, the whole fifteen minutes I was at lunch before Gran came to get me. As I left our spot, I gave Joseph a little wave over my shoulder and smiled at him. He returned the wave but his smile just looked sad. I hadn't upset him *that* much by kissing him, had I? I asked Gran on the way to the table read what she thought of the whole situation, needing some input from someone I trusted.

"Bliss, you're a smart girl. How can you not see this?" she asked in exasperation.

"See what?" I replied, confusion and stress clouding my mind.

"Joseph likes you. He's probably wanted you to kiss him since you were five and now that it's happened he's probably hurt that you tried to downplay it so much," she explained, sounding wise and sure . . . even though I knew she was completely wrong.

"First off, Joseph's not a girl. He doesn't get his feelings hurt over things like that," I told her matter-of-factly. "And second, I know that because we're such good friends it seems like we like each other in that way, but we really don't. We've just always been really close."

"So you're telling me you don't feel anything other than

friendship toward that boy?" Gran asked skeptically. I thought about it for a moment. I had definitely always treated our relationship as a friendship. Did that really mean I didn't have feelings for Joseph? Or was I just constantly telling myself we were just friends to make sure I didn't spoil something I *knew* we had for something we *might* have? I decided to go with the former.

"That's what I'm telling you," I said at last, making Gran shake her head in an "I give up" kind of way.

We spent the rest of the drive to the production office discussing what I should expect from this table read today. The more we talked about it, the more nervous I became, and soon all thoughts of my kiss with Joseph that morning were gone, replaced by the hypothetically traumatizing situations I could possibly experience today.

By the time I walked into the designated room for that day's table read, I was about as stable as a bowl of Jell-O. None of the other actors were in the room when I took my seat and began to read over the script for the millionth time. Three long tables were set up in a U shape in the small room. There were a few crewmembers there, and Mr. Hill gave me a quick briefing of what we'd do today. Once he finished talking, I sat awkwardly by myself, waiting for the other actors to trickle in.

The first two to show up were Ryan Hex and Benjamin Hampton, who played Rich and John on the show. They were the notorious comic-relief detectives who got all the clever one-liners and catchphrases that people printed on T-shirts. They were both in their 20s and couldn't have looked more different from each other if they tried. Ryan had fair skin, short blonde hair, and deep blue eyes. Benjamin, on the other hand, had dark brown skin, brown hair, and brown eyes. Even though they looked so different, I could tell instantly that they had great chemistry as they bounced jokes off of each other while walking into the room. The second they spotted me, they flanked me—Ryan with a wide, inviting smile, and Benjamin with a sideways smirk.

"New Girl," Benjamin said, pointing to me. I wasn't really sure if this was a question or simply a statement. I worried they were trying to put me in my place right away, but quickly found that wasn't the case.

Ryan put his arm around me and gave me a tight squeeze. "So, New Girl, I hear you'll be joining us for a few weeks," he said. He shifted, putting his elbows on the table in front of him and resting his jaw on his fist. From the way Ryan and Benjamin stared at me, I could tell they were sizing me up.

"Yeah, I hope so," was all I could think of to say. How did you reply to that? Especially when you'd never met the people before in your life? On top of just being a socially awkward person, I was feeling a bit star-struck at meeting the cast of *Forensic Faculty*. I smiled at them sweetly, trying to look friendly even though I was scared out of my wits.

"You're adorable, New Girl," Benjamin said, also resting his elbow on the table and looking at me from the other side. The whole situation was pretty awkward, to say the least.

"She's like a reincarnated . . . oh, what's that girl's name? Greta Garbo?" Ryan asked Benjamin. I knew exactly who they were thinking of, but thought it best to just keep it to myself and let them hash it out.

"Greta Garbo was blonde," Benjamin said, looking at his friend as if he were a complete idiot. "It's the brunette you're thinking of. With the big eyes."

"Mae West?" Ryan said.

"Well, Mae West didn't have big eyes she just had . . . well . . . never mind," Benjamin trailed off, giving me an apprehensive look.

"Lillian Gish?" I finally chimed in helpfully.

"Yes!" they exclaimed together, making me grin at how much they were like their characters in real life.

"So you're our new big star in 'Vaudeville Vice'," Benjamin stated in an overdramatic way, referring to the name of the first episode I'd be in.

"Oh yeah," I said jokingly. "I'm the biggest star you'll ever see."

"I like the New Girl," Benjamin said over my head to Ryan, on my other side.

"She's funny," he agreed with a grin.

As they continued to talk over my head, the next star to walk in caught my attention. Anna Farthing, who played Captain Juliana Ryder, was the hard-nosed woman in power on the show. She was in charge of everything and often hindered the actual process of getting things done because she wanted her team to follow the rules. Of all of the characters on the show, she was the one I was most intimidated to meet. If she was anything like the character she played, then she was a pretty terrifying person.

The boys must have seen my eyes watching Anna like a hawk, because Ryan quickly said, "She's not a man-eater in real life."

I started, surprised by his sudden exclamation right next to me. I turned to him with big eyes. "Was I that obvious?" I asked sheepishly.

"Not really," he said, shooting a sideways glance at Benjamin, who snorted to cover up a laugh. "You may have looked like your puppy got run over when she walked in—"

"But other than that, you were very collected," Benjamin finished with mock seriousness. I sighed deeply at the two of them. This was going to take some getting used to.

As soon as Anna set her large leather purse down, she walked over to me and extended her hand. "You must be June," she said in a thick British accent. The fact that she had an accent caught me off-guard, but I tried to recover quickly as I shook her outstretched hand.

"Yes, I'm June," I said, sounding brilliant, I'm sure.

"I'm Anna," she explained, though I knew exactly who she was . . . and I'm sure she knew that too.

"It's very nice to meet you," I replied, hoping I didn't sound too star-struck, even though I was doing flips inside.

"Very nice to meet you too," she answered as the phone in her hand buzzed. "Sorry, I've got to take this," she said, looking down at the screen in concern before leaving the room with one hand over her ear and the other holding her phone.

"She's British?" I asked the two boys the second she was out of earshot.

"Happens every time," Benjamin said with a sad shake of his head.

"Why is it that no one ever knows when a British person puts on an American accent, but the second I do my English accent, people are all over me about how awful it sounds?" Ryan asked Benjamin and me.

"Probably because your English accent *is* awful," Benjamin replied with a laugh. Ryan reached behind my back and shoved him playfully, but Benjamin had gotten his phone out and barely noticed as his thumbs flew across the keyboard.

"Hey, Candice is picking up coffee. What do you want?" he asked without missing a beat in his text.

"Iced café mocha," Ryan said, now looking down at his phone as well.

"New Girl, what do you want?" he asked, still not looking up.

"I don't drink coffee," I said simply. Both boys stopped texting and looked over at me as if I were from an alien planet.

"That's weird," Ryan finally said, as if he had made a study of me and had come to this conclusion after much deliberation.

"You don't drink it ever?" Benjamin asked, unable to comprehend this.

"Never," I said, feeling very out of my element. The uncomfortable moment was gratefully interrupted when an angel walked into the room. The angel, of course, was Lukas Leighton. Today he was wearing tight jeans, a plaid button-up collared shirt and aviator sunglasses, making him look like a walking piece of art. He had his trademark five o'clock shadow covering his cheeks, and his dirty blonde hair stuck up stylishly in every direction.

He was staring down at his phone when he walked in and didn't look over as he took his seat at the table opposite us. I didn't take this as rude, however, since he was obviously very preoccupied with his phone. It was probably someone important. He kept his head down, engrossed in his phone and occasionally touching the screen.

"Here we go," Ryan said in hushed tones.

"Another one bites the dust," Benjamin agreed in an equally reverent voice.

I turned a playful glare on them. "Do you guys have to have a running commentary on everything?" I asked. They nodded in unison, their faces completely serious.

"Listen, New Girl. I don't care if you like the boy . . . just please don't sleep with him until after we do your episodes," Benjamin said, making me blush a deep crimson.

"It'll really make your on-screen chemistry awful," Ryan agreed.

"I can absolutely promise you that won't be an issue," I reassured them as I shifted uncomfortably in my seat. Benjamin shrugged his shoulders and turned his attention back to his phone, but Ryan apparently wasn't giving up that easily.

"You're kind of conservative, aren't you?" he asked, the joking tone gone from his voice.

"Yeah, something like that," I replied, trying not to bring up the fact that I was Mormon. It wasn't that I was ashamed of my religion—not by any means. Mostly I just didn't want to get into a religious or political argument during my very first table read. I was used to getting weird questions from people at school, and it had kind of trained me to know when the mention of my religion would be a teaching opportunity or when it would turn into an argument or an excuse to make fun of it.

"Good for you," he said unexpectedly, smiling and making me feel like I had already made a friend in the cast.

"Thank you," I replied, in an equally as good-natured tone.

Anna eventually returned to the room and took her seat

near Lukas. He looked over at her and the two began to talk about something. I strained my ears to try to catch snippets of the conversation but couldn't really hear anything. I normally wasn't a nosey person, but when Lukas Leighton was sitting a few feet away from me, you could bet I was going to try to hear what he said.

Right before one o'clock, the last two stars on the show walked into the room together, talking in low, playful tones. Joann Hoozer, who played Jackie the medical examiner, was in her mid-twenties and absolutely gorgeous. She had long blonde hair, honey brown eyes, and a smile bright enough to land airplanes on. She was tall, skinny, and graceful, just like a movie star should be.

With Joann was Will Trofeos, the actual star of the show. Everybody loved him as the hotshot detective Charles Bagely, who had taken Lukas Leighton's character Cutter under his wing to teach him the art of deciphering a crime scene. He was probably in his mid-to-late forties, though I wasn't exactly sure of his age. That was the thing with Hollywood—everyone looked a lot younger than they really were. He had a thick Spanish accent, dark skin, black hair, and chestnut eyes. For an older guy, he was definitely good-looking.

Joann and Will sat in the two seats right next to Lukas, and the rest of the crew soon joined us at the table. I was glad that Benjamin and Ryan were sitting on either side of me. They had been so friendly already that it felt like they were my own private moral support. Looking around the room, I couldn't help but notice how glamorous everyone looked. Joann was leaning on her elbow and talking to Will, her diamond encrusted watch catching the light perfectly as her blonde hair cascaded down her bare shoulder in loose curls. Even Lukas, who you could tell was trying to go for the artsy "I don't care about wearing trendy clothes" look, had probably spent more on his plaid shirt than I had on my entire wardrobe.

Something about these people just said they were important, and I suddenly felt inadequate in the sundress I had bought at the thrift store because I thought it made it more "vintage." I tugged at one of the cap sleeves on my dress uncomfortably, wishing it looked more expensive in this room jam-packed with designer labels. Ryan and Benjamin somehow sensed my discomfort, because they exchanged a quick glance before leaning in to me again.

"Just relax," Benjamin said quietly.

"Yeah, table reads are honestly no big deal, all right? Half of the time we don't even act . . . we just read through the script like robots so that the department heads can stop us every five seconds and tell us what kind of clothespins they'll need to keep the lighting right . . . or something," Ryan said in exasperation.

"Most of the time we have no idea what the crew is talking about. They have weird names for things," Benjamin said, looking confused at the mere mention of these supposedly odd nicknames.

"Like what?" I asked. I was actually pretty interested in what new vocabulary I'd pick up on set. That, and I really wanted something to distract me from my nerves.

"Well, like clothespins. They call them . . . what is it, Benjamin?" Ryan asked, snapping his fingers as if that might help him remember.

"C47s . . . or C42s . . . I'm not sure. I know it has the letter C in it though."

"Right! Why not just call them clothespins? Is it really that much easier to say C47?" Ryan asked, to which I just shrugged. Benjamin looked like he had thought of a clever response for Ryan, but he was silenced when Mr. Hill stood up at the table to indicate we'd be starting the table read.

"Okay, so today we'll read the script for episode ten in season six, titled 'Vaudeville Vice'," he said stiffly, looking like he'd done this so many times that it now bored him to have to be here. "We've got a new face with us today," he said, instantly making my stomach churn. "Give a little wave, June."

I waved nervously at the room full of faces I'd seen every

Thursday night for years. Joseph and I watched the show every week, never missing an episode. And now we'd be watching me. This was all so weird. As I looked at the people surrounding me, I started to feel like maybe I could do this. Everyone seemed to be smiling, except for Joann—she just wore an expression of pained boredom. I couldn't tell if she had spaced and didn't hear Mr. Hill ask me to say hello, or if she just didn't care and therefore didn't acknowledge my existence. Whatever the answer was, I was glad that everyone else seemed happy to see me. This might not be too bad after all.

After my brief introduction, we began the table read. I didn't have a single line until halfway through the script, so I let myself get lost in everyone else saying their lines. It was so bizarre to see all of the characters around me, acting like they were in character, but not actually moving around and doing the things they were talking about. It took me a few pages to get used to the actors saying lines like their characters would, but then breaking character to look at one another, laugh at a line they had said wrong, or ask a question about how a scene should be played. It didn't feel like watching actors playing a character; it felt more like the people I had seen on TV all these years suddenly stepping out of their typical personalities.

The first half of the script seemed like a normal episode of *Forensic Faculty*. I was actually in the very first scene, but all I did was scream. I was supposed to be onstage during a performance; the "lovely assistant" to my magician co-star. In the scene, he steps into our disappearing man trick (a large painted box on the stage) and instructs me to close the box. I wait and make a few grand gestures before reopening the box, only to have my co-star's body fall out—dead as a doornail. Then I scream and the opening credit sequence rolls.

There was someone sitting near Mr. Hill saying all of the non-speaking parts of the script. He was a mousy little man with thinning hair and thick-rimmed glasses, but he spoke his part with gusto. He read the descriptions, actions, and settings between dialogue to give the cast some exposition for the scenes.

After my mostly silent opening scene, the cast fell comfortably into reading their lines. The case of Edward, my dead co-star, made its way to the detectives, where Rich and John (played by Ryan and Benjamin) made a few cracks about vaudeville being dead. I had to stifle a laugh at the easy way they said their quick back-and-forth remarks across my seat between them, but was quickly silenced by Anna's terrifyingly powerful voice as she read in character as Captain Juliana Ryder. Her British accent had vanished completely. The captain was, of course, telling off Rich and John for the cavalier way in which they discussed the crime scene, as per usual. While the captain was scolding the boys, Charles Bagely and Cutter came into the scene, ready to be assigned to the case. That's when the real action of the script began.

Lukas and Will read their parts, which seemed to make up a good chunk of the script. At one point their characters visited Jackie, the medical examiner, and it was the first time I'd really heard Joann speak since she'd come into the room. Her voice was deep and smooth, instantly making me think of a smoky-voiced lounge singer. She twirled her blonde hair as she read, and I couldn't help but stare at how elegant she was. There was something about her that just made me feel like I was a little girl in a room full of grown-ups: tolerated, but not really expected to participate.

After Charles and Cutter talked to Jackie to discover the means of the murder (arsenic), they decided to head over to the theatre, where they'd meet me. Up until this point I'd been relatively relaxed about the read through. Honestly, it felt like I was watching another episode of *Forensic Faculty*. But now I was actually going to have to participate. I cleared my throat nervously and scanned my lines to make sure I wasn't about to sound like a five-year-old trying to read Shakespeare.

"Interior. Day. Charles and Cutter walk into an empty dimly-lit theatre," the mousey man next to Mr. Hill read.

"This place is a dump," Will Trofeos read, pulling a face as if he were actually looking at a dingy theatre. I tried to pay close attention to exactly what Will was doing. I wanted to make sure I didn't sound like I was reading the script and have the whole cast think I couldn't act, but at the same time, I wanted to make sure I didn't over-act and seem like I didn't know what to do at a table read.

"Yeah, and they hire killers," Lukas said with a smirk at Will. I couldn't tell if Lukas was smirking at him because that's what Cutter would do, or if he just thought the line was funny. Was I supposed to be making my character's facial expressions? Should I gesture too, if the script called for it, or should I hold the script and not move my hands at all? I was definitely over-thinking this whole thing. I really needed to take a step back and relax. It wasn't that big of a deal—I just had to do what I've been doing my whole life.

"We don't know that, Cutter," Will said, his tone suddenly serious. "Remember what I told you about coming onto a crime scene? You have to go in with a blank slate or you let your judgment get clouded by preconceived notions," he chided in his thick Spanish accent.

"Got it," Lukas mumbled moodily.

"All right, so the body was found in that box over there," Will said, pointing across the room at me and making my heart skip a beat.

"Who found him?" Lukas asked, glancing at his phone under the table. I peeked around the room to see if anyone else had noticed, but they all had their eyes trained on the script, so I quickly dropped my eyes back to the page.

"His assistant found him during the performance. Sent him into the box to disappear—guy comes out thirty seconds later ready for the freezer."

"It was her," Lukas said matter-of-factly.

"Cutter," Will answered in an exasperated tone, like a father rebuking his son.

"What? Who else would know exactly when he'd go into that box?"

"I don't know," Will answered with strained patience. "That's what we're here to find out."

"Fine, but I say we talk to her first," Cutter stated in the cocky tone I'd heard so many times on the show before. That was usually the first giveaway that he was wrong.

No matter how innovative a crime show tried to be, there always seemed to be a pattern. On *Forensic Faculty*, for example, the detectives would question a series of suspects in the first fifteen minutes. They would strongly suspect someone who would ultimately be innocent, and then they'd find another person to blame who would also prove innocent. About ten minutes before the end of the show, they'd catch the real killer, who would almost always be someone they questioned but assumed wasn't the killer because they had an alibi or gave the team seemingly helpful information to send them in a different direction. Sometimes it would be a person they only mention in passing so the viewer would think they didn't have a big role to play in the story.

I listened to our action reader inform the room that Cutter and Charles had walked over to where I sat stone-faced backstage. This was it. Time to prove what I was made of . . . And hopefully what I was made of wasn't bad acting.

"Imogen Gentry?" Will asked me. I didn't actually have a line yet; I was just supposed to nod. I inclined my head incrementally at Will across the room, unsure if I should actually perform the action or just wait for him to continue with his lines. "We have some questions for you regarding the death of your co-star Edward King," he went on, his brow furrowed.

"Of course," I said, my voice cracking a bit as I talked. This made me flush slightly, but it actually sounded like I was a bit choked up, so my nerves were working in my favor. Maybe they'd think I was a better actress than I really was.

"Where were you at the time of the victim's death?" Lukas asked, causing Will to look over at him in exasperation. "Right," Lukas said quickly, realizing why his question had sparked such a reaction. "Sorry . . . habit," he amended.

"Imogen, do you know of any problems in Mr. King's personal life? Anyone who may have wanted to harm him?" Will asked, his tone smooth and professional.

"No one that I can think of," I said softly. "Our profession is a dying art. There's not much competition amongst the practitioners, just a mutual respect for a shared interest," I confessed, allowing my voice to sound fragile and helpless.

"I see," Will began, "And you can't think of anyone who would benefit from his passing?"

I paused for a moment, letting them know I was thinking about this query. "Honestly, I think I'd be the one to benefit most from his death. I was his apprentice—his assistant. With him gone, I would be the one to take over the show," I said hesitantly. Lukas looked over at Will with a bemused expression. I was hoping that look was given to Charles from Cutter to tell him that he had been right about me; not from Lukas to Will asking him why they'd hired me for this part.

"Well then, you'll excuse me if this next question is a bit bold, Miss Gentry, but did you have anything to do with the death of Mr. King?" Will asked, his voice candid.

"N-no," I said quickly, "No, I was just as shocked as anyone when he fell out of that box. Edward has always been so kind to me. I couldn't ever hurt him."

"You couldn't even hurt him to become the star of the show?" Lukas asked coldly, causing Will to jump in.

"Cutter, that's enough," he said quietly, before turning his attention back to me. "Miss Gentry, can you remember anything out of the ordinary on the night of Edward's last show? Did he seem worried or paranoid at all?"

I paused again, still unsure if I was supposed to be putting pauses into the scene or if I should simply read the lines to get through the script. "I don't think so," I said with a shake of my head. "And the only people who would have had access to the box were the stage manager and the prop masters. I mean, the theatre isn't exactly Fort Knox, but

Edward was always very particular about keeping his magic tricks under lock and key," I told Will, glancing up at him and feeling quite shocked when I saw that he was staring at me intently, his chin resting on his hand as if he were actually trying to determine my innocence. It was the same look I'd seen him give suspects on the shows millions of times. He winked at me before looking back down at his script for his next line, and I tried to hide an embarrassed smile.

"Very well Miss Gentry. Thank you for your time," he said. And that was it. My first scene was over and I had managed to do a pretty good job. I let myself relax down into my seat and gave myself a mental pat on the back, which was followed by an actual pat on the back from Benjamin, accompanied by a thumbs-up from Ryan. I smiled at them, glad that they had approved of my first scene, and beginning to feel much more confident in my ability.

CHAPTER 8

After the whole script had been read through and all of the notes had been taken by the department heads, Mr. Hill dismissed us, stating that he'd see us on Monday morning to begin shooting the episode.

Ryan and Benjamin turned to me in unison, both sporting big cheesy grins.

"New Girl, you are awesome," Benjamin said, accepting a coffee from a cute, short girl who had just walked in the room. With her long black hair, brown, slightly slanted eyes, and grand height of 4-foot something in heels, I guessed she was at least partly Asian. She didn't look a day over sixteen, but I assumed she had to be in her early twenties to be working on the show.

"New Girl, Candice. Candice, New Girl," Ryan said by way of introduction.

"Nice to meet you," I replied, smiling at her sheepishly. I didn't recognize her, so I was guessing she wasn't an actor on *Forensic Faculty*, but I couldn't figure out any other reason why she'd be here if she wasn't somehow affiliated with the show.

"Candice is the head of the makeup department," Benjamin explained, as if he had read my mind. "But we like to keep her around because she's funny," he added thoughtfully as he sipped his coffee.

"And to bring them their drinks, apparently," she said in a deep dry monotone that didn't really fit her "cute" look. I'd expected a high, pitchy voice to come from her small frame.

"She's a chipper one," Ryan remarked very seriously, throwing Candice a quick, playful smirk. She just rolled her eyes at him and walked away, though I did see her smile as she turned her back on the boys, giving me the impression that she might not mind Ryan and Benjamin's teasing as much as she let on.

"So, how did your first table read feel?" Benjamin asked me.

"It felt really good," I answered with a smile. "I wasn't nearly as bad as I thought I'd be."

"Yeah, you weren't as bad as we thought you'd be either," Ryan agreed. I shot him a playful glare.

"I'm serious," I went on. "Reading through the script actually has me excited about Monday. An hour ago I worried that I'd come to the studio on Monday, pass out from sheer terror, and that would be the end of my *Forensic Faculty* adventure."

"That could still happen," Benjamin said, looking at his coffee cup as if he was worried it was about to come to life and attack him. "This tastes a little off."

"Maybe Candice is trying to poison you," Ryan said in a hushed tone.

"I wouldn't put it past her," Benjamin agreed in a comically loud voice so that Candice, who was standing a few feet away talking to someone, could hear. "Sneaky little vanity department."

"We are *not* the vanities," Candice said in an annoyed voice, walking over to Benjamin and plucking the cardboard coffee cup from his hands. "No coffee for you."

Benjamin just watched her walk away with his mouth hanging open in shock. "What was that about?" he asked us.

"Department envy," Ryan informed me. "Costume and makeup are called the vanities. It never did sit well with Candice. She says it's a derogatory term and if it weren't for her, we'd all look as much like corpses as our victims on the show."

"Well, then, I guess you'd better start being nice to her," I advised with a grin.

"June?" a heavenly voice said from behind me, causing me to whip around in my seat. There stood Lukas Leighton in all his glory. He was smiling down at me, and my heart rate instantly picked up the pace. "I didn't really get to introduce myself properly a few days ago and I wanted to get the chance to talk to you. Do you have a second?" he asked.

"Of course," I answered, trying not to sound too anxious.

"Yeah June, you should go and see what a proper Lukas Leighton introduction is like," Ryan said in a quiet, sarcastic tone. I think Lukas heard him, because he shot him an annoyed look. I ignored Ryan and got up to leave with Lukas, though I made sure to bump Ryan with my purse as I left, making him roll his eyes at me.

Lukas and I walked through the halls of the production office toward the parking lot. I knew Gran wasn't there yet because I hadn't called to tell her when the read through was over. I figured I should probably do that, since it would look a little weird to walk with him to his car and then turn around and go right back into the building. Then again, I was with Lukas Leighton—I wasn't about to interrupt this moment to call Gran to come pick me up. That would just make me look like a five-year-old. I really needed a car.

"You did a good job in there," he said finally. I had to try pretty hard to keep myself from proclaiming my love for him.

"Thanks. I was really nervous," I replied, looking up at his perfect face.

"Well, I couldn't tell, if that makes you feel any better," he said with a dazzling smile. "I'm glad you'll be on the show for a while. It's been getting kind of dull always doing the same thing in each episode. We needed to spice things up a little." We left the production office and walked through the bright parking lot where Lukas's motorcycle sat waiting for him.

"This might be a weird question, but is it hard for you to

watch the show? Since you're in it, I mean. I know I've always watched the show, but I feel like watching the episodes I'm in will be so bizarre," I said.

"I guess I'm used to it," he replied with a shrug. "I've been watching myself on the show since it started years ago, so I've never seen it without seeing myself. I can understand how it would be weird for you, though." He looked down at his bike then back up at me. "You want to go for a ride?" he asked, his smile instantly convincing me that he was the most beautiful person on the planet.

For a moment, I seriously considered going for a ride with him, even though I knew Gran would kill me, Joseph would be all weird about it, and I was in a sundress, which wasn't really conducive to riding a motorcycle. But I let my better judgment take over, much to my own dismay.

"My ride is going to be here soon," I said with a regretful sigh. "I'm really, really sorry," I added, hoping he could see just how sorry I really was. I couldn't believe I was actually turning him down. An incredibly good-looking famous actor had just asked me to go for a ride on a motorcycle with him. How could I be dumb enough to turn him down?

"Don't worry about it," he said. "I'll see you Monday?"

"Yeah, definitely," I replied, suddenly at a loss for words in the presence of this perfect man.

"Bye June," he said with a nod before leaning in and giving me a quick kiss on the cheek.

I stood in stunned silence as I watched him drive away. I had no idea why he had kissed my cheek, but I did know that I'd never wash that cheek again. I exhaled deeply, wishing I was a little more like glamorous Joanne Hoozer at that point and a little less like boring, responsible June Laurie.

....

By the time Gran pulled into the parking lot of the production office, I was mentally kicking myself for being so responsible. I was a teenager after all, wasn't I? Didn't that mean I was supposed to do irresponsible things like go for rides on dangerous motorcycles with beautiful boys I'd just met? Okay, maybe it was a bad excuse to do anything like that, but my less rational mind was doing a really good job at convincing me that it would have made perfect sense to take off with Lukas.

When I hopped into Gran's old-fashioned red car, I was met with a pile of shopping bags.

"Oh no," I said with an accusatory look in her direction. "What happened here?"

"Oh honestly, Bliss," she said with a wave of her hand, though I could see the guilty look in her eyes. "I've lived on this planet for . . . well . . . the exact number of years isn't important. My point is, I think I have the right to do a little shopping every now and then."

"Yeah, but Gran, you don't have to buy the whole store," I said with a laugh, looking at the array of brightly colored bags. "I mean, can we really afford all of this?" I motioned to the mountain of bags between us. Gran wasn't really a huge spender, but when she went on a spree, she made sure she did it thoroughly.

"Some of it is for you," she said matter-of-factly, instantly piquing my interest. "So, how was the table read?" she asked as I rifled through bags for anything that could possibly be for me. I pulled out a headband with a few peacock feathers on it hopefully. Gran looked at the headband warily before nodding that it was for me. Obviously she hadn't bought it with that intention, but I was glad she had surrendered it over to my possession.

"It was actually really good," I answered with a smile. "I even made a few friends in the cast already. I think I'm fitting in pretty well so far."

"I didn't doubt for a second that you would," she replied warmly. "Do they have your measurements for the costume department?" She asked the question as though she'd just remembered how important this detail was.

"Yeah, they do," I reassured her. "I wonder what kind of costume I'll wear."

"Probably something very pedestrian, I'd imagine. I haven't seen the show much, but don't they all dress pretty normally?"

"They do, but my first scene is as an assistant in a vaudeville magic show," I said with a grin, imagining the great costumes they could put together. "So hopefully I'll get to wear something really different."

I relayed the table read to Gran on the way home, making sure I mentioned every detail so that she could interpret every look the actors had given me and what it might mean. After we ate dinner I retreated into my room to call Dad with all the details of the day and to do my homework.

It was hard for me to imagine how school would be on the set. I was the only one on the show who was young enough to require a studio teacher, so it would pretty much be like having my own private tutor. I guessed that they would follow the same curriculum as my high school so that my transition from the studio teacher and my high school teachers would be a smooth one. It would be odd to go to school on set for a week and a half at a time, and then going to my normal school between episode shoots. I was going to have to make sure I really focused to keep everything straight.

After I finished my homework at about seven o'clock and changed into my tight black yoga pants and a fitted emerald green T-shirt, I quickly pulled out my phone to text Joseph.

I bought some Huckleberry, so you should come over.

In all honesty, I couldn't really blame Gran for forcing me eat super healthy at the house, since I ate ice cream every chance I got—probably not the healthiest thing for me. As I sat in my room painting my short nails a dark crimson that almost looked black, a sudden thought struck me. Maybe Joseph wouldn't text me back. Maybe he didn't want to come and hang out with me after our last awkward encounter.

I put the nail polish brush back in the bottle and turned to my phone suspiciously. I pressed the button once to illuminate the screen and saw that I had no new messages, which made me frown. I kept my gaze trained on the phone as my imagination did what it did best: created worst-case scenarios.

It was possible that, because of our little incident this morning, Joseph didn't want to come and be alone with me. Maybe he was scared that I'd attack him again, or maybe he was trying to think of a nice way to let me know we shouldn't be friends anymore. Both of those situations would be utterly devastating, since we'd been best friends since we were in diapers. I tried to push these thoughts from my mind, but it was difficult with my dark, silent phone sitting beside me.

"June, pull your hair back and meet me in the kitchen," Gran said, suddenly popping her head in my room to relay her cryptic instructions. I didn't argue or even question why in the world I'd need to pull my hair back. Instead, I checked to make sure my nails were dry and then arranged my hair in a high curly bun with an elastic headband holding flyaway hairs back.

I met Gran in the kitchen, while Joseph's silence left a nervous feeling building in my stomach. He almost always had his phone with him—mostly to answer my texts, since no one else really texted either of us. I placed my phone on the counter next to a bowl full of yellow, pulpy goop. Gran pointed to a bar stool, indicating that I should sit, although she still failed to offer an explanation of what I was doing with this bowl of . . . whatever it was.

"Lean your head back and close your eyes," she said mysteriously.

"Gran, what are we doing?" I asked, though I did as I was told.

"I'm helping, as usual," she replied matter-of-factly. "Bliss, I said keep them closed," she threw in as an afterthought, since I kept opening one eye to glance at my phone.

I jumped slightly as Gran plopped the yellow mixture onto my face and couldn't help but notice the refreshing tingle that was spreading all over my cheeks. I sniffed a few times, recognizing a citrus-y smell.

"Is this pineapple?" I asked, puzzled.

"It's supposed to make your skin whiter," she said, a hint of skepticism in her voice. "I assumed it couldn't hurt, and if it works, even better."

"At least it smells good," I said, smiling and taking in another deep breath of the sweet, tangy fruit. A knock at the front door caused me to jump slightly. Not being able to see apparently made me a very paranoid person.

"Stay here and don't open your eyes. The vapor might sting them," Gran instructed artfully, as if she had been putting pineapple on people's faces her whole life. I heard her footsteps retreating from the room and strained to hear who was at the door. All I could make out was a muffled voice and the sound of two sets of footsteps coming back into the kitchen.

At that moment, I wasn't sure where my logic went, but my first panicked thought was, "get this stuff off of your face—Lukas Leighton is about to walk into the room." A mild panic began to rise within me at this far-fetched idea. I cupped my hands and tried desperately to scrape the yellow goop from my face, managing to spill most of it in my lap and down the front of my shirt.

When Gran and Joseph appeared in the kitchen, I realized how foolish my thought process had really been. Joseph instantly burst into a fit of laughter at the sight of me. Honestly, I couldn't blame him.

"Did you and Annette get into a food fight?" he finally managed to ask. It was always a little odd when I heard people call Gran by her first name, though I used it every time I slated for the camera and I named her as my agent.

"For your information, this will make my skin more porcelain than Clara Bow," I said sarcastically, standing up and smearing a handful of pineapple pulp onto Joseph's cheek, much to Gran's horror.

"Honestly, Bliss, I don't know what to do with you sometimes," she said in an overly dramatic tone. "You just make sure you clean this up," she threatened, nodding toward the mound of pineapple now on the wooden floor as she left, muttering about high-maintenance actresses.

I looked back to Joseph, grinning wickedly and relieved that he didn't seem to harbor any animosity for my attack on him that morning. He simply swiped a finger full of the fruit on his face and licked it.

"Is this pineapple?" he asked surprised.

"Apparently it makes your skin whiter," I said knowledgably.

"So, does that mean I'm going to have one white cheek and one normal cheek?" he asked jokingly, though I could detect a hint of worry in his voice. I squinted my eyes at him, leaning in closer.

"Wow, you know what? I think it's already working," I said, my tone full of amazement. Joseph's eyes grew wide as he quickly wiped the pineapple from his face. I laughed at his obvious distress and shook my head. "I'm joking," I reassured him.

"Funny, June. Very funny," he deadpanned. "How about you wash the produce off your face while I get the stuff on the floor? That way we can get to our night full of eating too much ice cream and watching *Forensic Faculty*." I nodded my agreement and we soon were sitting comfortably on the couch in the living room with big bowls full of huckleberry ice cream. Joseph tossed a few Indian pillows onto the ground, since there were always so many on the couch that you could barely find a place to sit.

"Do you think it'll be different to watch the show now that you've met everyone?" he asked, spooning ice cream into his mouth and making me smile.

"I think it'll be a little different, but it probably won't really be weird until I'm on the show. Then I think it may be difficult just to watch," I admitted.

"How was Anna Farthing? Is she really as scary as her character on the show?" Joseph asked, suddenly very intrigued by the fact that I could give him the inside scoop. I wished beyond anything that I could bring him to set with me. I knew I'd be so much more comfortable with him by my side, and he'd love to meet everyone in the cast. But sadly, that wasn't a possibility, so he'd just have to settle for my stories.

"She was actually really nice! And she's British, which caught me off guard."

"Wait, she's British?" he asked, just as shocked as I was when she had first spoken to me. I nodded with a grin. It was kind of fun knowing all of these little facts about the show.

"Everyone was pretty nice to me. Will Trofeos actually winked at me while we were reading our lines," I said, crinkling my nose. "Is that weird?"

"A little," Joseph answered with the same unsure look on his face. "Was he being funny?"

"I'm not sure," I said with a laugh. "But I'm pretty sure I'm not his type . . . since I'm like, thirty years younger than him."

"Well, let's hope not," he said emphatically.

"The only person who wasn't all that nice to me was Joann Hoozer," I confessed, remembering the icy looks and indifferent stares she had given me throughout the table read.

"I can see that," Joseph said with a nod of his head. "She seems like a bit of a diva."

I thought about his statement for a moment, realizing how little I knew of the people we had watched every week for years. "I guess I never really thought about it," I said with a shrug. "I always assumed they were all like their characters . . . although Benjamin and Ryan are exact replicas of their characters." Rich and John were Joseph's favorite characters on the show, so I knew he'd be excited to hear that they weren't huge jerks in real life.

"I want to meet them," he whined, giving me a pouty look.

"Who knows, maybe we'll become great friends and they'll hang out with us so you can meet them too," I said enticingly. Joseph laughed, giving me a nudge with his shoulder and then not moving back to his side of the couch after. We stayed shoulder-to-shoulder while we watched the show, and I couldn't help but notice how much I liked how comfortable we were around each other. After a day of tension and nerves, it was nice to just sit with Joseph and forget about all of the scary things coming up.

CHAPTER 9

Just as she did every morning, Edith Piaf interrupted my blissful dreams with her low, resonating voice. I rolled over, my eyes still closed, and hit the snooze button. I was always pretty good about getting up in the morning, but that didn't mean I had to enjoy it. I rubbed my eyes wearily and wondered how my bed managed to become so warm and inviting the second I had to leave it. I pulled my fluffy comforter up around my face and tried to hold on to the last fleeting memories of my dream.

Five minutes later, I was staring blearily into the mirror in my bathroom, trying to tame my wild mass of curls. I had fallen asleep on Joseph's shoulder the night before. When he finally left, I was too tired to shower, and now my mane of hair was very vocally lodging a complaint, with ringlets sticking up in all directions. Most of the time my hair had a medium wave that curled naturally. Today, however, the lack of washing had turned it into a giant mass of curling chaos.

I gathered my dark hair up at the back of my head and began randomly shoving bobby pins into it, hoping that it would form some semblance of a proper hairdo. In the end it actually looked quite nice, although some of the ringlets were escaping wildly around my face. I did my makeup light today, sticking with a peaches-and-cream color pallet.

As I re-entered my room to get dressed, I heard Joseph pull up outside. I looked around in confusion, wondering why he was so early, only to find that I was actually the one falling behind on our normal schedule.

"Shoot," I muttered under my breath, tripping over my backpack in my attempt to hastily get dressed. My phone buzzed by my bed as I threw on a pastel pink tunic top and some faded gray skinny jeans.

Running late are we? my phone read, much to my annoyance. Joseph knew that if my bedroom light was still on when he pulled up, we were in trouble.

Two seconds, I texted back, realizing that if I had not texted him, I might already be out the door. I quickly put on some cream-colored peep-toe heels, grabbed my backpack, and ran out the front door, sticking light pink feather earrings through my ears as I rushed down the driveway. I could see Joseph smirking from the driver seat of his Beetle.

"I have no idea how that happened," I said, referring to my late arrival.

"Maybe we'll skip the hot chocolate for today?" he asked, with a questioning glance in my direction.

"Well, it is Friday, so someone's going to bring food to seminary, right?" I asked. Fridays were the best. It was almost the weekend, everything went by faster, and someone was assigned to bring treats to seminary for everyone.

"I think Grace is bringing them," Joseph said as he pulled away from my house.

"Oh, do you think she'll bring that fruit Danish thing? It's amazing," I said closing my eyes at the mere memory of the delicious dessert.

"We can only hope," Joseph answered with a laugh. "You know, I think this show is already starting to wear you out," he said, suddenly changing the subject. "The second they revealed who the killer was last night, you were out like a light."

I blushed slightly at the memory, knowing I had fallen asleep on his shoulder. I couldn't help it that his shoulder was right there next to me, just begging to be slept on.

"I thought for a minute I was going to have to carry you up to your room," he said with a grin.

"Lucky for you, you didn't," I reassured him. "I'd like to see you try to carry my dead weight up those stairs."

"I've had to carry your dead weight a lot of places over the years. I don't think the stairs would've put up much of a fight," he countered playfully. I rolled my eyes at him while I secured a long strand of brown pearls around my neck.

Walking into the classroom that we used for seminary in our church building, Joseph pointed to the pizza-shaped dessert sitting on a table and gave me a quick thumbs-up. I smiled at him but refrained from laughing. Our seminary room was always so quiet in the morning before our lesson started. I liked to think it was because everyone was being so reverent, but I knew it was most likely due to the early five o'clock hour. There were only about ten people in our seminary class, since most of the kids our age went to the later one at six. Only we zero period kids got up to learn about the gospel that early, when a lot of people were just getting into bed.

Joseph and I took our seats in desks toward the side of the room and pulled out our notebook and scriptures. Seminary was nice because it was a lot like auditing a class in college—you can go to class to actually learn, not because you know you'll be tested on the material or will have to turn in assignments, but rather because you want to be there. We didn't even need to take notes on the material; I just liked to write down little thoughts that would come to my mind while Sister Pond taught.

Slowly, people trickled in and took their seats, some in pajamas, others fully dressed, but everyone looking like it was a struggle just to keep their eyes open. Joseph looked around the room, a bemuse expression on his face.

"Maybe we should move to Utah so we can have seminary in the middle of the day," he whispered. I nudged him playfully but didn't respond, finding that I was too tired to think of a clever comeback. Maybe Joseph was right—the stress of the show was already taking its toll on me, and we hadn't even started filming yet.

Since it was Friday, our lesson in seminary wasn't straight out of the scriptures like it normally was. Instead, we would break into groups, read a story or talk given to us, then get up in front of the class and tell them about it, making us the teachers. I always liked this idea because it shook things up a bit. Plus it was really easy to let your eyelids droop so early in the morning with just one person talking for an hour.

Sister Pond passed out papers to each group and gave us ten minutes to figure out how we were going to present it. Joseph and I had been given a talk from General Conference on charity. Some people would stick to the standard method of standing there and talking, while others would try to be more creative by acting their lesson out or playing a game.

Joseph and I would normally try to be pretty creative with our lesson, but today I was just too exhausted to think of a clever tactic. Instead, we opted for playing a game of hangman with the class to get them to guess what the topic of our lesson was before we taught what we had learned from reading the talk.

After seminary was over, we grabbed a slice of the fruit Danish, thanked Grace, and hopped back into Joseph's car to go to theatre. Joseph had eaten his Danish in about two bites, but I savored mine, trying not to eat it too fast. It was some sort of pastry crust with cream cheese frosting, cherry pie filling, and sugar glaze. I was pretty sure if heaven had a taste, this dessert would be it.

"Are you going to eat it or marry it?" Joseph asked me jokingly.

"I'm still not sure yet," I replied happily, making every bite count.

"I don't think I've ever seen someone who loves dessert as much as you," Joseph said with a shake of his head.

"And if I play my cards right, you never will," I answered. We drove for a moment in silence as I finished my Danish. I felt as if Joseph was gearing up to saying something important. His mood had quickly gone from lighthearted and joking to tense and quiet.

"You remember that we're supposed to perform our skit in class today, right?" he asked finally, revealing what the cause of his tension was. He was afraid I would attack him again.

"Yeah, I do," I answered carefully, not sure exactly where he wanted this conversation to go.

"Are you ready for it?" he asked, equally as carefully.

"I am," I replied. This was ridiculous. Joseph and I were never weird around each other. It was blatantly clear to me that I'd have to be the one to make this situation less awkward. "We don't have to actually kiss in the skit if that's what you're worried about." I said, proud of myself for being so bold.

"What?" he asked. I couldn't tell if he sounded puzzled or a little upset.

"Well, that's what you're worried about, isn't it? Me attacking you again?"

"No, June. You can attack me any time you want," he said with a laugh, though he went quiet right after the laugh had escaped him. "I mean . . . that came out wrong," he muttered. "I think the kiss is fine . . . I just want to make sure it's okay with you if we do that."

I thought about this quietly, puzzled by what he had said. Why would I mind? I wasn't the one who had gotten all weird after we had rehearsed the kiss, was I? I tried to think back to yesterday, which seemed like years ago already. Maybe I had acted a little weird.

"I'll be fine," I said. "Now that I know you're fine with it, I won't be concerned at all. I just thought maybe the whole thing made you uncomfortable or bothered you or something," I said with a shrug.

"It definitely doesn't bother me," he said with a smirk, though just as before he let his face melt instantly into a mask of neutrality. "That came out wrong again," he amended. I giggled at his odd behavior but wondered inwardly what it meant. He was definitely not acting like his usual self.

When we pulled into the school parking lot, we were already running late for class. Joseph quickly grabbed his backpack and our fake sack of money while I shoved the neon green water guns into my bag. We ran to the theatre, which proved to be very difficult in my heels, and made it just as the first group was getting up to perform their skit. Joseph and I slumped into some seats in the audience, trying to keep our panting to a minimum. Almost instantly Xani was sitting next to Joseph. I couldn't help but wonder how she would react when she saw our kissing scene. I half thought she might think I had planned this all along—that I had somehow bribed Mr. Carroll into pairing us together and giving us this script. But maybe it was just my exhaustion talking.

The first group to perform consisted of four people. They acted out a scene where two of them were on a date with each other while the other two stood behind their respective person and voiced their thoughts. It was actually amusing to watch the difference between what the sitting people on the date were saying and what they were thinking. The skit ended with the girl's thoughts walking over and slapping the boy's thoughts, while the sitting girl simply said, "Check please." Joseph glanced over at me and shook his head sadly.

"They got to be funny," he said.

"You get to be funny too," I said helpfully, though the way we had put our script together meant it ended up being less funny and more intense.

As soon as the first group sat down, Xani popped out of her seat to walk up on stage. She threw Joseph a wink over her should and mouthed, "Wish me luck," as she went.

"You little heartbreaker," I whispered to him.

"None of that is my fault! I've done nothing! I just come to class to learn. Is that such a crime?" he whispered back dramatically.

"Save the acting for our skit," I shot back with a wicked grin.

Xani's skit consisted of her and a girl named Laura. They were supposed to be new roommates who were meeting for the first time, only to find that they were complete opposites. They walked around the stage, arranging their imaginary rooms and talking about their likes and dislikes. While Laura's back was turned, Xani would rearrange her things so that they weren't on "her side," only to have Laura do the same thing to Xani as her back was turned. This all occurred as the girls continued to talk about how well they were going to get along despite their differences.

"Even Xani got to be funny," Joseph said in a singsong voice under his breath.

"Well, then, why don't we show them why we're good even without a funny script?" I challenged.

"Fair enough," he replied happily.

Right as Xani sat down next to Joseph and leaned over to talk to him, he bolted out of his seat and hustled to the stage, obviously happy to avoid any close contact Xani would force upon him. I followed suit and sat down on a black wooden block, right next to where Joseph had dropped our pillowcase full of board game money.

Glancing at the audience, I felt a wave of nerves go through my body as my palms began to sweat. I loved acting, but being in front of a crowd always made me nervous. On top of that, Joseph and I had to perform a pretty intimate scene in front of our classmates, which was never something you wanted to do. It didn't help knowing that all of the skits thus far had been funny—it just made our skit seem out of place. Also, as paranoid as I'm sure it made me, I couldn't help but feel my classmates would be more critical of my acting ability now that they knew I was on *Forensic Faculty*.

I cleared my throat and gave Joseph the smallest of nods, letting him know I was ready to begin. I saw him pause for a moment before completely altering his expression to one of pained frustration. I was always amazed at his ability to do that. He began pacing back and forth across the stage, making sure to throw an exaggerated trip in there for at least a little bit of humor. The class laughed and I saw the smallest flicker of a smile cross his lips.

"What could you possibly be thinking?" he finally spat at me while he continued to pace. He kept his head down with his eyes trained intently on the ground in front of him, as though it took all of his concentration not to shoot me right then and there. I wondered for a moment if anyone else in the class thought it was a bit terrifying to see Joseph so worked up, even if it was fake. "Robbery is an *art,* not an excuse to throw a brick through a window." His voice was full of venom, as if I were a complete imbecile whose only goal was to drive him crazy.

I stood up from the black wooden box on stage, making sure Joseph was pacing away from me so he couldn't see me pull out my neon green water gun. I silently padded up behind him, so when he spun around he was met with a very angry June holding a gun hard against his chest. He stared at me intently, his eyes burning a hole through my head. Even when we had rehearsed, Joseph hadn't looked that angry. It left me speechless for a moment.

"What's more artful than smashing a window, taking the cash, and still not getting caught?" I countered, pushing my water gun against his chest even harder so that he stumbled backward a few paces. This only intensified his look of utter disgust and hatred. I didn't like this angry Joseph. Without warning, he grabbed me by the wrist of the hand that was holding the gun and pulled me in close to him. I didn't have to fake my look of shock on this one, since this wasn't how we had rehearsed the scene.

"If you don't point that thing somewhere else, I'll have to reconsider my idea of working as a team," he threatened in an icy tone before angrily releasing my wrist. I stood for a moment, staring at him in shock that was half acted and half real. When I finally came to my senses, I turned around on my heel and began to walk away from him, my shoes clicking loudly on the stage.

"Where do you think you're going?" he asked.

"To find a new partner," I yelled over my shoulder, keeping my gaze straight ahead as I walked across the stage.

"Perfect. How about while you do that, I'll stay here and count all that money you just made me?" he replied, walking over to our bag of money and kicking it with his foot.

I stopped dead in my tracks. The effect was much better than I had hoped because just as he finished speaking and I stopped walking, my heels stopped clicking on the stage, casting the entire auditorium into a tense silence. I reveled in the unexpected dramatic effect for a moment before saying my next line.

"I see your point," I confessed, turning slowly to face him. I placed my gun on the ground to indicate a truce before I began walking slowly toward him, trying to muster any feminine wiles I possessed. I tilted my chin toward the ground so that I could look up at him from under my eyelashes and let a small sideways smile play on my lips.

"Really, there's no reason to fight, right?" I asked innocently, stopping in front of Joseph. Just as we had rehearsed, I rested my arm on his shoulder, letting my fingers play with his hair. I could see the color begin to rise in Joseph's cheeks and tried to ignore the fact that our whole class was staring at us in silent suspense.

"We're on the same team, aren't we?" I asked, now close enough that our noses were touching. As smoothly as I could (in heels) I used my foot to push our pillowcase full of money behind me, getting a few scattered laughs from the audience. This must have boosted Joseph's confidence, because his entire look suddenly changed. Rather than looking timid and afraid, he suddenly looked purposeful and sure of himself.

"Yes, we are," he said, using his foot to move the bag of money so that it was between us, the top of the pillowcase sticking up high enough that we could grab it while standing. Joseph looked at me for a moment in the silent theatre, his dark eyes full of determination.

And then he kissed me.

It was difficult to get lost in the moment right away with

so many people watching, and the handful of whistles from our classmates didn't help at all. But as Joseph wrapped his arms around my waist and kissed me hungrily, I couldn't help but enjoy it, tangling my fingers in his hair.

I wasn't sure how long the kiss should last and it really didn't seem like Joseph was going to end it anytime soon, I gave him a quick squeeze with my hand that was resting on his back to indicate that I'd be reaching for the bag of money. It was almost comical how obvious the difference between a real kiss and a staged one was. Practically the instant Joseph realized we still weren't done with the skit, the kiss lost its passion. His lips were still pressed against mine, but it felt like kissing a wall. There was just nothing there.

I kept my eyes closed as I reached blindly for the top of our bag of money, and I began silently cursing myself for not rehearsing this part with Joseph. We had always gotten so distracted by the kiss that we never actually went over this part—we just talked about how we would do it.

When my hand finally made contact with the top of the pillowcase, I was glad to feel Joseph's hand there as well. We opened our eyes, pulled apart, and looked down at the bag of money before bringing our gaze back up. I gave Joseph a little smile to show that I was on to him, and then the scene was over. We had managed to make it through without a single mishap or forgotten line.

The reaction from the class was a combination of applause and catcalls. I rolled my eyes with a grin as we walked offstage to a chorus of whistles and jokes about our kiss. Joseph squeezed my hand as we made our way back to our seats and I held it tightly until we were safely seated and the next group had started their scene. I could feel the blood in my cheeks and was glad that the auditorium was dark so Joseph wouldn't notice.

"That wasn't so bad, was it?" I asked, glad that we had decided beforehand that we weren't going to let things be weird between us after the kiss.

"It was perfect," he whispered, turning and smiling

warmly. I beckoned him closer with my finger so I could whisper in his ear.

"I don't think your girlfriend is too happy with you right now," I joked. Joseph glanced to his side where Xani sat fuming. Her eyes were trained straight ahead and her arms were folded across her chest. I was pretty sure if I stumbled into her line of sight, she'd burn a hole through my head with her gaze. Joseph turned back to me with his eyebrows raised.

"Don't leave me alone with her after class," he murmured. "I think she might kill me."

CHAPTER 10

I made sure I did all of my homework for the weekend the second I got home from school. That way, Joseph could begin his long process of distracting me from my own thoughts for two days while I pondered how many ways I could ruin the show. He picked me up in the early evening and I got in the car with absolutely no idea of what we were doing.

"Phase one complete," he said slyly as he drove down East Los Angeles Avenue, which, despite the confusing name, is actually in Simi Valley.

"Phase one of what, may I ask?" I replied, hoping I'd get some sort of information out of him.

"June, you have to respect the articles of secret agent lingo. I can't tell you or else the whole cover will be blown."

"That sounds promising," I said sarcastically, looking out the window at the trees flying by. We drove for about ten minutes, with Joseph telling me all about the benefits of sucking up my cowardice and getting my wisdom teeth out. I, of course, nodded and smiled as I tuned him out, not wanting to hear anything about that horrible process.

Joseph turned right onto Hidden Ranch Drive and into the parking lot for the Rancho Santa Susana Community Park. I turned to him with a grin.

"I'm on to you," I said, tapping my nose for effect. "But if I get a tan from being in this sun, it'll be you who has to explain it to the makeup department on Monday. And trust me, she's a scary one."

"Oh, don't be dramatic. Just put some pineapple on your face. You'll be grand," he said with a fake Irish accent and a dismissive wave of his hand.

We got out of the car and began walking through the grass, going nowhere in particular. I was glad I had changed out of my heels after school, opting instead for beige ballet flats. Joseph was carrying a tan messenger bag, which he flatly refused to tell me the contents of. As we approached the swing set, Joseph stopped and looked over at me as if he were sizing me up.

"June, it's time for you to get used to making a fool out of yourself," he said seriously, pulling a Polaroid camera out of his bag.

I looked at him quizzically. "All right, first, where did you get that thing? And second, what are you talking about?"

"This," he said, patting his camera affectionately, "I got at a thrift store. She's beautiful, right?"

"Does it work?" I asked skeptically. The camera looked like it would turn into a pile of dust at any minute.

"Of course *she* does," he said, emphasizing that the camera's feelings may have been hurt by the fact that I referred to it as an "it."

"Well then, what are you and *she* going to do?" I asked, humoring him.

"Who? Me and Lola?" he asked, giving me a wicked grin, which I rolled my eyes at. "We're going to get you ready for Monday."

"Of course. What else would my crazy best friend and his sidekick Lola be doing on a Friday after school?" I asked no one in particular.

"Make fun all you want June—"

"Okay."

"—But this is going to make Monday much easier for you.

What is acting, if not an excuse for people with a camera to make other people in front of the camera act like fools?"

"That's about what it is," I agreed.

"So go over to those monkey bars," he instructed. I looked around the small playground, taking in my surroundings to see just how embarrassing this was going to be.

"There are kids on the swings," I stated with so much obviousness that it caused Joseph to shake his head.

"And some on the slide," he pointed out as well, making me feel a little foolish.

"And parents watching those kids," I added helpfully.

"All the more reason to do this. When you start filming, you're going to be sitting in a completely silent studio with dozens of people staring at you while you scream at a tennis ball on a stick as if it were a huge monster."

"Well, I doubt there'll be any monsters on the show," I said.

"You get my point," he replied. "Acting is embarrassing. It's even more embarrassing when the stakes are as high as this show. So, why don't we just get you used to doing embarrassing things now, so that when Monday rolls around, it won't be such a shocker?"

I looked at him for a moment and then looked back around at all of the parents and children in the park. Sighing deeply, I nodded, knowing that as much as I didn't want to do this, it would be good for me. I was never very good with the embarrassing part of acting.

"What should I do, Coach?" I asked. Joseph gave me an impish grin, obviously happy I was going along with this.

"Well, I'm trying to think of what would be the most embarrassing thing for you to do."

"Which I will obviously lend you no assistance with," I stated playfully.

"Fair enough," he answered deviously. "Why don't you climb on top of the monkey bars . . . so that you're sitting on top of them rather than hanging off," he instructed.

I walked over to the monkey bars and regarded them dubiously before doing as I was told. I must say—if you were ever considering buying monkey bar chairs for your living room, you should reconsider. Sitting there was incredibly uncomfortable.

"Okay, now for the fun," he said, walking underneath the bars. "I want you to crawl across them, but look down through the bars at me so I can snap pictures. Oh, and I'll tell you what emotion I want on your face every few seconds."

"How do you even think of this stuff?" I asked, very painfully getting on all fours on top of the monkey bars. The metal dug into my knees with ruthless vigor.

"Crawl," was his only response. I began to carefully pick my way across the bars, trying desperately not to fall and feeling completely ridiculous as one of the kids pointed me out to their mom. "Okay, now look down at me and give me anger," he said, sounding very much like a parody of a high-fashion photographer.

"That won't be too hard," I countered, trying to look angry while my knees were screaming out in pain.

"You just look uncomfortable," he said, disappointment filling his voice. "Look angry, June!"

I knitted my eyebrows together, formed my mouth into a thin line and looked down at him. I didn't have to work too hard to "pretend" I was unhappy.

"Much better. Now be really happy—like those models advertising nail polish or whatever they're supposed to be promoting."

"I really hate you right now," I said with a laugh.

"As long as you look really happy while you do it," he said in a singsong voice.

"How's this?" I made my eyes big and round while putting on a bright smile and repeating, "I really hate you right now," through gritted teeth.

"Perfect!" he exclaimed. By now, most of the kids in the park had stopped swinging and were watching our antics, hiding little giggles behind their hands. Joseph seemed like he didn't even notice them and continued to snap away with his camera, catching each picture as it came out.

"Now growl," he said with a snort, trying to keep himself from laughing.

"Fat chance," I said simply, twirling back around so that I could jump down. I landed in the sand with a soft thud and punched Joseph playfully on the shoulder. "You're the devil," I said as we began to walk away.

"We'll be here all week," Joseph said jokingly to the now-disappointed children who were watching us go.

"Are we done making me look like a fool yet?" I asked Joseph over my shoulder. He snapped a quick photo of me as I did this. "Apparently not."

"That was the last one," he promised, catching up to me so that we were now walking toward his green Beetle. He waved the picture around in the air, trying to make it develop faster. "Are you hungry?" he asked, keeping his eyes trained on the ground.

"Starving," I admitted, realizing I hadn't eaten after school. I was too anxious for my "de-stressing session" . . . which mostly had turned into a "stressing session."

"I brought a blanket and some sandwiches . . . you know . . . just in case you were hungry . . . at all," he stammered. I couldn't understand why he suddenly seemed so nervous, but I had to admit, nervous Joseph was adorable to watch.

"That sounds wonderful," I said warmly. I set up the blue and brown quilt under some large trees and Joseph brought a cooler over to our picnic spot.

"A basket would have been much better," he said regretfully, "but a cooler is more practical."

"The cooler works just fine," I reassured him. "So, what's on the menu?"

"Well, as you know, I am a gourmet chef," he said, shaking his head "no" even as he spoke so confidently. "So I made us peanut butter and banana sandwiches, some barbeque chips, and orange soda."

"You made us orange soda?" I asked skeptically.

"From scratch," he answered as he popped open the tab of a very obviously store-bought soda.

"Well, you certainly know how to woo a girl," I said with a giggle. He handed me the can of orange soda before opening his own and bringing it up in a toasting gesture.

"To looking stupid in front of large groups of people," he said, smiling.

"I will definitely toast to that," I answered, raising my can so that it hit against his.

The sun was beginning to set and a comfortable orange glow enshrouded the park as we ate. It warmed my skin in the chill October air, and I closed my eyes against the sun for a moment, taking in the smell of the park and the fact that Joseph was with me.

"This is perfect," I said, finishing off my sandwich and laying down on the blanket. A soft breeze blew my stray curls across my face, tickling my nose. Joseph lay down next to me and looked up at the hot pink clouds scuttling across the darkening sky.

"I agree," he said quietly. He moved his arm behind my neck so that I could rest my head on his shoulder. He settled his cheek against the top of my head and I smiled.

"I'm glad I have you," I admitted, breathing in the combination of Joseph's scent and the freshly cut grass surrounding us. "It's going to make the craziness of filming so much more bearable."

"As long as you don't completely forget about me," he joked. "I mean, you'll be surrounded by famous people all day. Do you really think you'll be able to reduce yourself to hanging out with non-famous me?"

"As if you even need to worry," I laughed.

"I know I don't really need to worry too much about you, but make sure you don't let anyone on set make you think you've got to be bad to be cool," he said out of nowhere. "Your innocence is a huge part of your charm. You don't need to change anything to fit in."

"Joseph, are you talking about Lukas Leighton?" I said

accusingly. He shrugged but didn't answer my question, which actually did answer my question. "I don't think you need to worry. He wouldn't be interested in me anyway. Especially when he can have any beautiful actress he wants."

"June, you know you're ten times prettier than any of them," Joseph said matter-of-factly, making me blush. I was immensely glad I was lying on his shoulder so he couldn't see it.

"I don't know about that, but thank you," I answered modestly. Joseph gave me a tight one-armed squeeze and I nestled my head against his chest, still staring up at the now-purple sky. I could hear his heart beat speed up a bit but pretended not to notice.

"We should probably get going," Joseph said a bit regretfully.

"Yeah, you're probably right. It's getting cold," I agreed. As we stood up, Joseph took off his grey cardigan and handed it to me. I accepted it gratefully and helped him fold the large quilt.

"Thank you for today," I said sincerely as we walked back to his car in the fading twilight.

CHAPTER 11

On Saturday, Gran signed me up (without my knowledge) for her own personal acting lessons. We went over the script for the first episode about a million times, all the while eating disgustingly healthy food, forcing ten bottles of water into my system, and putting all manner of odd food beauty remedies on my face. By the end of the day, I was worn out and smelled faintly of pineapple—a smell I was quickly growing to hate.

I scrubbed my face until it was red and shiny before falling down onto my bed with a loud sigh. It was dark outside of my window and I couldn't help but feel that my weekend had just started and was already almost over. It was funny how time did that. If you're looking forward to something, it always takes ten years to arrive, but the second it comes, it's over before you have time to blink.

I hadn't bothered drying my hair after my shower that night. I figured that with church starting at ten, I'd have time to do it in the morning. My wet, springy curls fell across the back of my neck, making me shiver as I drew my comforter tighter around me. I closed my eyes and tried desperately to sleep, but no matter how persuasive I was at willing myself to fall asleep, it just wouldn't happen. Every time I tried to drift off, I'd think of Monday. I could see Lukas and all of the other cast members staring at me like I was an idiot for some little faux pas or other. I knew somewhere in the back of my mind that once I was there and actually filming, I'd be all right. It was the waiting that was killing me.

Emitting a low grumble, I turned off the lamp on my bedside table and picked up my phone, determined to get some comfort.

Angry face, I texted Joseph, wondering if he could pick up on what I was trying to say with such an obscure hint.

It was always fun seeing how well Joseph knew me. Most of the time I could say one phrase to him like "jasmine soap" and he'd reply, "You're right, green would be a nice color for your bedroom wall." That was just the kind of friendship we had. So I wasn't at all surprised when I received a reply from Joseph one minute later that said, *June, they have tons of people watching the monitors. They'll tell you if you look like you're thinking too much.*

It was a sad (but true) fact that whenever I was concentrating, I made a face that resembled a scowl. Joseph was the first one to point it out to me when we started acting together. Ever since then I'd been trying to reverse this cruel trick of nature. Unfortunately, every now and then there was just nothing I could do. The scowl would present itself.

It's scary how well you understand me, I answered, yawning quietly into the darkness of our house.

I speak June fluently. I've had 16 years of classes, was his instant response. I smiled to myself and nestled down into my fluffy art nouveau comforter, suddenly finding that sleep was within my reach. I held my phone to my chest, closed my eyes, and allowed my dreams to take me.

....

Sunday passed with lots of encouragement from Joseph all throughout church. This encouragement came in the form of little doodles scribbled on the back of the sacrament program, but as much as I appreciated it, nothing could prepare me for the sense of dread and sheer panic that I felt as Gran drove me to the studio on Monday morning.

Gran had picked me up right after seminary with Joseph shouting, "It's okay to look like a fool," as we drove away, causing Gran to look over at me quizzically. I waved away her unsaid questions and closed my eyes, trying to keep myself from throwing up from all of the excitement. My actual call time was seven o'clock, so leaving right after seminary at six was worrying me a bit.

"Do you think we'll hit a lot of traffic?" I asked anxiously as I stared at the glowing numbers on the car clock.

"It's L.A., Bliss. The only way we wouldn't hit traffic is if it was the end of the world . . . although even then I think we'd probably still have trouble," she replied evenly. I could tell she was attempting to hide any emotion in her voice, fully aware that the slightest misunderstood tone might send me into full breakdown mode.

Even with the normal L.A. rush hour traffic, we made it to the studio with enough time for me to stall in the car for five minutes until Gran forcibly pushed me out. I had already gotten off to a late start that morning, realizing much too late that I had to have my hair washed before I got to the studio. And so, terror bubbling up within me, I ran into the makeup and hair trailer, panting and clutching my purse.

"Are you all right?" Candice asked skeptically when I entered. I had totally forgotten that she was the head of the makeup department and it was nice to see a familiar, if not entirely friendly, face.

"Running late," I managed between deep, gasping breaths. She looked me up and down, assessing what she had to work with, I guessed.

"Well, I'll go tell them you're here and find out where they want to stash you," she said dryly. "Sit down and take off your coat."

I plopped down in the barber chair in front of the light bulb-lined mirror as she walked out of the trailer. I looked over the stacks of makeup, brushes, and odd things that I didn't recognize and suddenly realized how real this whole thing was. Looking over my shoulder to make sure Candice wasn't on her way back, I pulled my phone out and snapped a quick picture in true "fangirl" style. I quickly typed a message and sent the picture to Joseph, closing my phone just as Candice re-entered the room.

"They're running a little late," she remarked with a roll of her eyes, as if this was a usual annoyance to her. "After I finish your hair and makeup, you can eat some breakfast. Then come find me and I'll show you where your locker is."

"Thanks," I said with a nervous smile.

"You really need to relax," she said over her shoulder as she unfolded a black plastic cape. She draped it over the front of me and fastened it tightly around my neck. "This really isn't that big of a deal . . . I mean, it is, but you're going to be fine."

I looked at her reflection in the mirror as she stood behind me and ran her fingers through my hair, assessing what she would do with it.

"I'm sure I'll be fine, but I just worry, you know? Maybe I happened to read well the day I auditioned, but once I start acting they'll figure out it was a huge mistake," I said, confessing my fears.

"All right, do you want me to tell you something that will make you feel a lot better?" she asked, to which I nodded. "Don't tell anyone I said this, because I don't want to be out of a job for being a set gossip, but Joann Hoozer really isn't that great of an actress," she whispered conspiratorially.

I turned around to look at her skeptically, my hair falling out of her hands and across my shoulders. "What do you mean?" I asked. I couldn't really believe it was true since I'd watched the show since day one, and Joann was always very good at what she did. My only guess was that Candice was trying to make me feel better about myself, and really, who was I to complain about this kind gesture?

"I mean, she's a good actress eventually, but the director really has to work to get the talent out of her. She's mostly just a pretty face who can act if you're willing to spend the time it takes to help her," Candice said with a shrug. "It'll be good to have someone on set who's just raw talent. You won't have to worry about them getting frustrated with you—anything you could put them through, they've already gone through with her."

I pondered this silently for a moment, wondering if it really made me feel any better that they could handle my bad acting just because they'd seen it before. Oddly enough, at the end of my inner conflict, I discovered I was okay with this. Still, one additional thing was bothering me.

"At least she's got a pretty face to hide behind," I muttered, feeling very inadequate with my eyes that were red and puffy from lack of sleep, and my hair that had turned frizzy because I didn't have time to dry it that morning.

"That's what I'm here for," Candice stated matter-of-factly, though I did see a wisp of a smile form fleetingly on her face. I got the feeling that was the most smile I'd ever get out of her. "Now, down to business," she said. She instantly pulled me out of the little moment we had shared when I saw the shiny reflection off of her metal scissors. Instinctively I put my hands over my head and slouched down in the chair.

"What are you going to do with those?" I asked, suddenly frightened on behalf of my hair.

"Relax. I'm just getting rid of the split ends and cleaning it up a bit," she answered in her trademark monotone.

"But you won't chop it, will you?" I ventured, still not entirely sure I trusted Candice with the scissors.

"If you don't sit up straight I might," she threatened, causing me to instantly straighten my posture. "Better."

I tried to keep talking to Candice in order to distract myself from the small chunks of dark hair falling on the floor around me. Every snip I heard seemed to be taking off more hair than I wanted to lose, though somehow my hair wasn't really looking any shorter. Candice might have actually known what she was doing.

"If you're the head of the hair and makeup department, shouldn't you be working on Joann Hoozer and Will Trofeos first? Or are they not here yet?" I asked, slightly confused (but definitely not complaining) about my VIP treatment.

"Well, normally I'd be the one to work on The Tall Ones, but they're all too famous for me now. They bring in their 'crew' of hair and makeup people so I get to work on the extras," she said disdainfully.

"Thanks," I replied, matching her usual dry tone.

"You know what I mean. It's not as glamorous, but it does mean I get to do lots of injury makeup, which is right up my alley," she answered with a grin, giving off more enthusiasm than I had seen from her so far.

"Silver lining," I agreed. "So when you say 'The Tall Ones,' you mean Will and Lukas?"

"All of them, really. They're all too high and mighty for me. Except for Benjamin and Ryan. I still do their hair and makeup. Unfortunately," she said, puckering her lips in concentration as she continued to snip away at my hair.

"I think you secretly love them," I remarked, staring at my puffy, tired reflection in the mirror.

"Yeah, like a psychopath loves a murder," she answered with a scoff.

"Candice, you didn't murder another extra, did you?" I heard a familiar voice ask behind me.

"Get out of here Ryan. I'm not ready for you yet," Candice shot venomously at him.

"There's nothing like the melodic sound of Candice's voice in the morning," Benjamin said, walking into the small trailer behind Ryan. "And look, an extra pair of seats just for us," he sang sweetly, beaming all the while at the scowling Candice.

"And of course we have our favorite New Girl, looking dashing as per usual," Ryan noted, setting his coffee down on the makeup table.

"If you didn't bring me any coffee, you'd both better learn how to do your own makeup and get out," Candice threatened, putting the scissors away and pulling out armfuls of product and bobby pins for my hair. She began spraying things over my head and wildly pinning my dark curls up as if she were possessed by some demon hairdresser.

"Now that you mention it, we did bring you some sustenance," Benjamin said, taking one of the three remaining cardboard cups from the holder. "And we brought New Girl a hot chocolate since Ryan reminded me you don't drink coffee . . . which is weird . . . but I can get over it one of these days."

I smiled over at Ryan, pleasantly surprised that he had remembered the little detail he found so odd. "Thank you," I said to them both, gratefully accepting the hot chocolate and hoping it would help me wake up without making me sick.

"Put that down. It's makeup time," Candice said, just as I brought the cup to my lips to take a sip. I glanced in the mirror and was completely taken aback by my reflection. My hair was piled high on my head in a mass of curls with a few long dark ringlets falling down my back and numerous stray curls framing my face. The effect was breathtaking (without sounding too conceited) and I was amazed that she was able to make it look so nice so quickly.

"Wow," I said simply, summing up my feelings on her ability in those three letters. "Candice . . . you're amazing."

She simply shrugged this statement off, but I did see a faint ghost of a smile on her lips, as if she appreciated this rare appreciation of her gifts. Picking up a black binder, she looked it over quickly before snapping it shut again.

"We need you to be in full vaudeville costume and makeup for the first scene you're shooting, but the rest call for more . . . normal looks. After you finish your first scene, you'll come back here and I'll make you boring," she said as she tilted my head back, smoothing something as soft as heaven over my skin.

"What is that?" I asked in awe. It felt as if she were rubbing air over my cheeks.

"Silicone based primer. It feels like silk wrapped in satin and dipped in heaven," she said in what I would describe as a dreamy voice but was, in reality, probably just a less monotone voice. "It makes your skin look flawless and helps the foundation stay in place. Now close your eyes."

I did as I was told, allowing her to fix all of the damage I had done by stressing and staying awake all night while I listened to Ryan and Benjamin bicker about some app they had just downloaded.

"Because it doesn't actually work," Ryan was saying.

"But it's a strobe light. It's just . . . funny," Benjamin replied, his voice full of fervor.

"Do you really get yourself into that many situations where you think 'Hmmm, if only I had a strobe light app on my phone'?" Ryan asked.

"You'd be surprised," Benjamin said with a mischievous grin.

"Never mind. I'm sorry I asked."

"Don't open your eyes. I'm putting fake lashes on you," Candice said, interrupting my eavesdropping.

I kept my eyes firmly shut, not wanting to have her miss and glue my lids together. Even though it was early in the morning and I was scared out of my mind for the inevitable humiliation I'd have to face in front of the camera, I couldn't help but notice how at home I felt in the little trailer with Candice, Benjamin, and Ryan. It was pretty clear to me who my on-set friends were so far, though I could only hope that Lukas would soon become another on-set friend . . . or boyfriend . . . whichever I could manage, really.

"Uh-oh," Ryan said, sounding suddenly close to me. "Look at the grin New Girl has."

"Do you have any scenes with him today?" Benjamin asked knowingly. I felt myself blush under the freshly applied makeup and hoped Candice had put enough on me that the others couldn't see it.

"Wait, are you talking about that tool Lukas Leighton?" I heard her ask behind me.

"New Girl has a crush on him," Benjamin confirmed sadly.

"Oh please. The guy is dumb as a rock," Candice said.

"He seems sweet," I said timidly.

"Great," she replied sarcastically. "Just find out for yourself, then. Don't let us persuade you. You're done, by the way."

I opened my eyes to see if Candice had been able to fix all of my red puffiness and—much to my amazement—she had. I was assuming that my vaudeville makeup would be dramatic, but I didn't realize just how striking the effect would actually be. My lips were painted a deep red, my porcelain skin looked almost transparent, and my eyelids were smoky black with shadow smudged right under my lower lids. The most dramatic thing, however, were the fake lashes she had applied. They had to be almost an inch long.

"You look like a porcelain doll, New Girl," Benjamin said approvingly.

"But you might actually cause a wind storm every time you blink with those lashes, so you may want to be careful," Ryan added with a smirk.

"Candice, you're incredible," I said, almost not recognizing this dark and mysterious version of myself.

"I'm okay," she answered modestly.

"Humility isn't a good color on you, Candice," Benjamin said seriously while he texted. "You already know you're good. Don't put on a show for New Girl."

"You're right. I am pretty brilliant," she confessed happily. "Anyway, you can go get some breakfast now if you want."

"I'll show you where the cafeteria is," Ryan offered, picking up his coffee and leading me out of the trailer. "Do Benjamin first, I'll be back soon," he added to Candice.

"New Girl, you can mess up the lipstick, but if you ruin your eye shadow there'll be hell to pay," Candice yelled out the trailer door as I walked away with Ryan.

"That was a frightening mood swing," I said with a giggle as we entered the small cafeteria, which was really just a room in the production office filled with long picnic tables and a buffet table pushed against the wall.

"That's Candice," he stated, studying my face.

"What?" I asked, suddenly self-conscious.

"Nothing. You're just mixing a few time periods here," he said with a grin, his deep blue eyes sparkling with his own private joke. "You're dressed very fifties, but then you have this turn-of-the-century hair with twenties makeup. The effect is very . . . confused," he laughed.

"I'm sure it'll fit once I'm in costume—and how do you know so much about fashion?" I asked.

"I watch a lot of movies," he said.

"Period pieces, though?" I asked skeptically.

"Any movie. I don't have very discriminating taste," he answered with a shrug. "Speaking of which, do you see anything you want to eat?"

I looked at the buffet table, which was loaded with fruits, bagels, toast, and little cereal boxes. I plucked a red apple from a nearby bowl and turned my attention back to Ryan.

"Done," I said happily.

"Apparently you don't have very discriminating taste either," he joked as we walked back to the hair and makeup trailer.

"Exactly," I replied, taking a crunchy bite out of my apple and smearing my red lipstick all over it.

"So, you and I don't have a scene together until Thursday," Ryan said, stopping right outside of the trailer.

"We have a scene together?" I asked. I couldn't remember ever reading anything with Ryan in the script.

"Well, sort of. We don't speak or anything, but we are in the same scene . . . " he trailed off. "But it should be fun, anyway. At least you won't feel like you're outnumbered by The Tall Ones," he said, using Candice's phrase to refer to the show's stars.

Mentally going over the cast list, I could see why Ryan and Benjamin chose to isolate themselves from the rest of the cast a little . . . or maybe why the rest of the cast kept them at a distance. Will Trofeos, Lukas Leighton, Joann Hoozer, and Anna Farthing were all big names in Hollywood. They were constantly in movies and the paparazzi followed them obsessively. Ryan and Benjamin, on the other hand, were best known for *Forensic Faculty*. They had been in other movies before, and every once in a while I'd find a picture of them in a magazine, but they didn't cause the same feeding frenzy the rest of the cast caused. It was like they were part of the show, but not part of that elite group of acting royalty. Somehow, as crazy as it seemed, it made me like them more. It made them feel more approachable.

"Well, at least I know I'll have someone to talk to on Thursday if it turns out Lukas isn't as sweet as he seems," I said with a wan smile.

"I know we teased you about him, but I think he's a pretty good guy. I mean, I haven't spent much time with him outside of work, but he's a nice guy to work with so I don't have any complaints. We just know his reputation, which is why we feel the need to warn you. If what they say is true, then he'd love to snag some sweet, innocent, unsuspecting victim like you," Ryan said darkly.

"I appreciate your concern," I said honestly, "but I'll be fine."

CHAPTER 12

The chaotic atmosphere on set was far different from the laid-back feeling of the makeup trailer. I had already changed into my costume and was now sitting on a chair behind the camera while a stand-in took my spot under the glaring lights. They measured the distance from her nose to the camera, made little changes in lighting, and did all sorts of imperceptible alterations that required a warm body to be in my spot.

My studio teacher and I had met earlier that morning, so I used my free time to work on the assignments she had given me. It was definitely nice that my on-set curriculum corresponded with my actual classes, because it made the transition between the two seamless. I was able to complete assignments in fast motion without the distractions of school, though, and I soon ran out of work, leaving me to stare at the crew as they bustled about. I looked over my shoulder every five seconds to see if Lukas Leighton and Will Trofeos had come in yet, but they were running late.

I let out a deep sigh and closed my eyes, trying to steady my nerves for the moment when I actually had to do some acting. The studio was cold, since acting under all of the lights would be like sitting in an oven. Behind the camera, I was forced to wear a coat over my costume to I wouldn't become a human popsicle. There wasn't a whole lot to my costume, and I couldn't help but wonder if Gran would be a bit angry with me when she saw how immodest it was. Granted, it wasn't immodest for normal TV standards, but I can safely say it wasn't something I would ever wear to a church dance.

I was supposed to be dressed as my character, Imogen Gentry, after she had come home from a performance. I had on black fishnet tights, low black heels, and the most amazing dress I had ever seen. The bodice was tight black satin with a corset back that they had laced so tight I could hardly breathe. It had thick straps and a sweetheart neckline that, combined with the corseting, emphasized my . . . well . . . we'll say, womanly features. It was definitely not something I was used to flaunting, that's for sure, and I was feeling distinctly uncomfortable being so on display. I had even loosened the laces of the corset when the crew wasn't looking, just a bit to make me feel at least a little more modest.

The skirt of the dress was the really incredible part of the costume. The entire thing was made of long, iridescent, dark green feathers that ended a few inches above my knees and bustled out behind me, giving me a very particular Victorian Gothic look. The crowning jewel of the costume was a black lace choker with a single dangling ruby pendant that, I felt, looked like a target to draw attention to my bust. The more I thought about it and the more looks I got from the crew, the more I felt like I wasn't being paranoid. That was definitely what they were going for with this particular piece of jewelry.

The sound of a door opening behind me announced the entrance of Will and Lukas, and my stomach automatically tightened once more. I tried to keep the blood from rising up in my cheeks and took a steadying breath before standing up to greet them. Will got to me first, since Lukas had stopped to check his reflection in his phone screen.

"Miss Laurie, you look beautiful," Will Trofeos said in his thick Spanish accent. His eyes roamed over me appreciatively and I resisted the urge to shudder a bit at this blatant display of admiration. I was definitely going to have to talk to the costume department about my revealing outfit. "I'm sure it will be a pleasure working with you," he stated with a wink before walking over to the director. I watched him walk away, getting a distinctly creepy vibe that made me wonder how I had ever thought he was charming and attractive. There was a big difference between thinking an older man is attractive on TV and having him hit on you in real life. Maybe "big difference" isn't the right way to put it—there's a very creepy difference.

"You clean up nicely," said a decidedly more welcome voice, so close to my ear that I could feel his breath on my neck.

"Lukas," I replied breathlessly. It appeared that the only way I could ever greet him was by saying his name.

"Are you nervous for your first scene?" he asked, his eyes roaming in the same way Will's had, though I did notice I didn't mind this nearly as much.

"Very," I admitted.

"Well, don't worry too much. If you just do as well as you did in the audition, you'll be just fine," he said kindly, smiling down at me. I couldn't help but feel drawn to his smile—not because it was perfect and famous, but because it seemed so sincere.

I could hear the warnings of Joseph, Gran, Candice, and Benjamin in my head, but they didn't matter to me. They could have been wrong. Even Ryan had admitted that he didn't know enough about Lukas to make a fair judgment; he was just going off of the rumors. Everyone knew tabloids would stretch the truth to its breaking point to make a story sound better.

"Thanks," I replied, looking (I'm sure) very intelligent. I couldn't help it. I was helpless in the face of such beauty.

"All right, June, can you come and stand here please? We're ready for you," Charlie Bates, the director, said.

Suddenly feeling very naked despite my efforts to sabotage the revealing costume, I took my place under the glaring lights. I was positioned so that I was leaning over a table in Imogen's apartment a few days after the initial discovery of the body. The table was covered in my own "research" on the murder case, which would, of course, look very bad when Cutter and Charles burst in with their suspicions that I may have something to do with the murder. I was fully aware that my leaning position did nothing to make me feel more comfortable about my tight and too-low bodice, but I didn't know what to say. I couldn't just put the entire cast and crew on hold because I was feeling uncomfortable, could I? I knew what Gran would say to that question: *Isn't your personal integrity worth more than avoiding a socially awkward situation?* I closed my eyes against her imagined words and tried to put the thoughts out of my mind, convincing myself that this is what I had to do if I wanted to be a famous actress.

I tried to pull the bodice up when Bates had his back turned, but the thing wouldn't budge. It was just tied too tight. Giving up, I prepared to resign myself to discomfort for the sake of the craft, although one last tug proved effective enough to bring the neckline up a few centimeters.

Once Lukas and Will were on their marks and ready to start filming, something odd happened to my body. As the director settled into his chair behind the camera, preparing to start shooting, my tongue went numb and a slow, creeping sweat began to spring up all over my body. I tried to give myself a mental pep talk, but my whole body felt weird, as if it were shutting down pore by pore. The air around me seemed to pulse, and then one word brought me instantly back to reality.

"Action!"

Cutter and Charles burst through the door into my apartment and I looked up at them from my leaning position over the table. They crossed the small threshold of the set in a few long strides and came to a halt right in front of me. It was difficult to ignore the cameraman moving around us, but I summoned all of my acting experience and immersed myself in the emotion of the scene.

"What are you doing here? You can't just break into my apartment without a warrant," I exclaimed, drawing myself up to my full height to confront them.

"We do have a warrant," Charles said in a controlled-yet-sinister voice. "And judging by what we have here," he went on, gesturing to the table full of research, "we got one just in time."

"This isn't what it looks like," I pleaded, trying to look as desperate as I could in the face of such overwhelming evidence. "I wanted to try to help solve the murder myself."

Charles just scoffed at this, but Cutter shot him an icy look. "She could be telling the truth," he said defensively.

"Would you keep your hormones in check long enough to see the obvious?" Charles said with no measure of kindness in his voice. Charles made a grab for my wrist, but Cutter hit him away, ensuring that he didn't touch me. "Are you insane?" he asked Cutter, his eyes flashing dangerously.

"You don't have to manhandle her. If you ask her to come to the precinct with us, she will," he said in a low voice. Cutter looked over at me to confirm that I would, in fact, come quietly. I looked between the two men for a moment, assessed the situation, and nodded slowly, letting my big doe eyes proclaim my innocence.

"And cut," Bates said happily. "That was brilliant, guys." He said it with so much enthusiasm that I wondered if he'd even want us to run the scene again.

So naive.

We probably ran that same exact scene about fifty more times, from seven more angles, before they were satisfied with what we had done. After the second or third take, I became immensely at ease in front of the camera and *slightly* less uncomfortable in my revealing costume under the warm lights on set. If I had to be immodest, at least it was serving the purpose of keeping me from getting heat stroke. By the time we were finally finished, I walked back to my seat and drank my entire bottle of water, finding that I had somehow become dehydrated.

"June, we're going to have you stay in that costume and makeup for this next scene," Bates said, catching me off guard with this deviation from the original shooting schedule. "We're going to have you do the scene where you find that your files are gone and you run out of the apartment over to the precinct next. Then we'll do your sleeping scene, and then your last scene of the day with Lukas," he said, ticking off a list on his fingers.

"That sounds good to me," I said cheerfully, though I wasn't sure he was asking for my opinion. Will had already left the set—apparently he was needed for another scene somewhere else—but Lukas lingered behind for a moment, walking over to where I was watching the crew prep for the next shot.

"I really enjoyed acting with you," he said smoothly, moving a stray curl away from my face with his strong hands.

"It was a lot less stressful than I thought it would be," I offered, glad that I had managed to get a whole sentence out despite my heart pounding like a drum.

"You have to have fun with it, June," he said with a slight smile, taking a step toward me and dragging his heavenly scent with him. "Acting can be a lot of fun when you're not worried about what everyone else is thinking."

"I definitely believe that after today," I replied, shifting my weight so I was leaning toward him. I was trying not to be too obvious about my desire to wrap my arms around his neck and kiss him right then and there.

"Good. I look forward to our scene later today," he said softly.

I could suddenly feel his large hand on my corseted waist, sliding slowly to my hip. He brushed his lips over my cheek and then pulled away, giving me one last smile before leaving to join Will in their next scene. I watched him go mournfully, wishing he could stay a little longer. My legs still felt like Jell-O when the director called me back to the set to do my next two scene, and all I could think of during those scenes was the way Lukas's lips felt against my skin.

Oh yeah. I was in serious trouble.

....

"I am speechless New Girl. You look good," Benjamin said as I walked into the makeup trailer to ask Candice where I was supposed to go for my next scene.

"Do you ever actually act on the show?" I asked, trying not to blush too much from his compliment. "Or is your only job to hang around the makeup trailer all day?"

"His main job is annoying me, I think," Candice said drolly.

"Wow," I heard Ryan say behind me as he walked into the trailer. "They were definitely going for a . . . certain look . . . weren't they?" he said with a wry laugh, bringing whatever blush I had suppressed right back again. "You may want to wrap something around your neck to cover up your feminine wiles, or the rest of the crew won't be able to get on with their jobs."

"Ryan, stop. You're embarrassing her," Candice said in a rare show of loyalty.

"I'm sorry June. You look lovely."

"Thank you," I muttered, still feeling very uncomfortable walking around in this costume. All I could do was hope that my next costume would be a bit more dignified, or I might have to stand up for myself like I had failed to do earlier that day. "So, do I come to makeup first for my next scene, or costume?"

"How is it that they're getting so disorganized?" Candice asked no one in particular. "Go to the wardrobe department and they'll give you your next costume, then you can come back here and I'll do your makeup. Have you already had lunch?"

"Yeah, I ate after my second scene. I also had my schooling for the day, so I'm a little ahead of schedule," I said proudly.

"Good job," Candice replied, not sounding at all like she

cared. "Now go change into something that will distract the boys a bit less and get back here so I can do my job."

....

A little while later, standing outside of the makeup trailer and willing myself to walk in took all of the courage I could muster. I had to summon what dignity I could so that it wouldn't be obvious how disappointed I was in my new costume. It didn't help that the second I walked in, Candice burst into laughter and Ryan and Benjamin (I swear they didn't do any actual acting on set) let their mouths drop open.

"Oh no, New Girl," Ryan said apologetically.

"This is just ridiculous," Benjamin agreed with a nod.

"It's like they're doing it on purpose," Candice chimed in. There I stood in Imogen Gentry's pajamas, which consisted of nothing more than a pair of very short black silk boxers and a dark red lace spaghetti-strap top that revealed about an inch and a half of my stomach.

"I think they hate me," I wailed, trying to keep it together even as my eyes welled up. It wouldn't be so bad if the people on set were the only ones who would ever see this costume, but it was going to be broadcast all over America, not to mention everyone in the world who could see it online. I was absolutely trapped and had no idea what to do. It wasn't like they would have a spare costume just in case the little Mormon girl playing Imogen didn't like her pajamas.

"Actually, I think they really like you," Benjamin corrected.

"He does have a point," Ryan agreed. "They want to show you off."

"You're like the hidden gem they found to guest star on the show, and they want everyone to know how clever they were for taking a chance on a nobody," Benjamin explained.

"He doesn't mean 'nobody,'" Ryan quickly added, seeing my face fall even more.

"This is just humiliating," I said in distress. My tears were threatening to fall now.

"You are definitely a different breed, New Girl," Benjamin said with a shake of his head.

"I'd have to agree with that. I don't think I've ever had an actress on the show complain about looking too sexy. Most of the time I have to argue with the corpses over how much makeup they get to wear," Candice remarked.

"I just *really* don't feel comfortable being sexy," I admitted, taking a few calming breaths to ensure that I didn't burst into tears over the humiliation my costumes were causing.

Ryan looked sympathetically over the top of the magazine he was reading but said nothing, obviously knowing that there wasn't a whole lot either of us could do about the situation.

"The clothes really aren't that bad," Benjamin said suddenly. "I think you feel like they're a lot worse than they are because you aren't used to dressing like that."

"And you're not used to the way people respond to 'sexy June,' so it makes you uncomfortable," Ryan finished.

"I guess you're right," I acquiesced, trying to convince myself that this was something everyone my age would wear. (Although everyone my age wouldn't be seen by the nation in these clothes, but I'd just push that little detail to the back of my mind, along with the crushing guilt I was definitely feeling for not living up to the standards I was always so proud of.)

....

As I walked somberly to the set in the scraps of cloth they called pajamas, I decided to take a sporadic detour to the costume room. I stood outside of the door for a moment, taking a deep breath and saying a silent prayer that this would go over better than I expected it to. Giving a quick knock, I stepped into the small room that was stuffed with clothing, and was glad to see that none of the other actors were there.

The costume designer, Marc, sat sketching something in a notebook at his desk. He was an older guy with gray hair and thick black glasses, and he boasted a resume most people would kill for. Giving one last silent prayer, I cleared my throat, trying to get his attention.

"June Laurie, what are you doing back so soon?" he asked, his warm smile lighting up his kind face as he turned. Maybe this wouldn't be too difficult after all.

"Hi Marc," I started, my voice shaking a little.

"Is something wrong?" he asked, picking up on my obvious distress. "I didn't leave a pin in something, did I?"

I had to laugh at his guess, despite the fact that my tears were two seconds away from ruining my makeup. "No, you didn't leave a pin in my costume," I assured him.

"What's wrong, sweetie?" he asked again, using the kind, fatherly tone I noticed he never used around The Tall Ones.

"Your costumes are brilliant. You know that already, I'm sure."

"But?"

"There's not really a 'but'. I mean . . . not a real one. It's just that, I have certain—"

"Standards?" he offered, as though he had been expecting me to come and say something to him. I didn't say anything, but nodded in agreement, wondering how much of a diva I looked like right at that moment. Here I was, refusing to wear the costume someone had handmade for me. "Ryan and Benjamin told me about your hesitation with the vaudeville costume earlier," he elaborated, making me instantly want to go and hug both of them for standing up for me.

"I don't want you to think that I'm ungrateful for all of the work you've put into my costumes, it's just that, I can't feel good about myself in something like this, and if I'm feeling this uncomfortable, I think it'll come through in my acting," I explained all in one breath, knowing that if I didn't get the truth out right then, it would probably never come.

"Listen, I can make some compromises on your costumes from here on out now that I know you're uncomfortable being overly sexy," he began, hinting that there would be a stipulation. "But your main vaudeville costume is pretty much locked in. I don't think I could get approval for a change on that costume at this point even if I wanted to."

"I totally understand," I said, hoping that he could tell how grateful I was that he was being so wonderful about the situation. "Is it too late to change this costume?"

Marc looked me over for a moment, surveying the short shorts and tank top I wore. "They might kill me for making a last-minute change," he said, looking over his glasses as if to make sure I understood the gravity of what he was doing. "But I should have a fitted black T-shirt that's about your size and some red lace shorts that are *slightly* longer. That's the best I can do for you on such short notice."

Without a word, I ran over to the man I had just met that morning and threw my arms around his neck, giving him a tight hug. "Thank you so much," I said over and over as I released him. "I'm sorry I'm such a pain."

"You're not being a pain if you're being true to yourself," he said wisely. "I expect you won't judge my lifestyle, so I won't judge yours. Besides, now that I know what you're comfortable in, it won't be very difficult to adjust accordingly for the next few episodes."

"I really do appreciate it," I said, meaning every word. Relief swept over me as I began to feel like I wasn't a complete sellout.

"That's the only reason I'm helping," he answered kindly.

....

By the time six o'clock rolled around and I was ready to do my last scene, I was feeling exhausted. Candice sprayed some water on my face out of an aerosol can to "freshen me up," though I doubted it would do anything to hide my fatigue. The twelve-hour days on set were going to take some getting used to.

"This looks much better," Candice remarked, referring to my last costume of the day.

"I still wouldn't wear it, but it's better than a corset or those impossibly short shorts," I admitted, feeling much better after my little talk with Marc. My last costume was Imogen's everyday clothes, though they weren't exactly "everyday," since she was supposed to be so involved with vaudeville. I wore white socks that ended just above my knees, a pair of high-waisted black shorts, and a white, cotton, cap-sleeve button-up shirt tucked into the shorts. It looked very hipster while still managing to be old-fashioned. Actually, if anything, I thought it looked like some sort of Japanese street fashion.

"Wish me luck," I said to Candice as I left the makeup trailer for the last time that day. Benjamin and Ryan were surprisingly nowhere to be seen, and I assumed they must have actually had a scene to act in.

"No," was Candice's reply as she popped the tab on a can of soda and pulled out a magazine. Her abrasiveness was definitely something I'd have to get used to. It did help that I knew how she'd act if she actually didn't like me, though—she would just treat me like she did The Tall Ones. But that was the least of my worries at the moment. The thing that had been occupying the back of my mind the entire day (well, the entire week, if I'm being honest) was my next scene.

The anticipation that I felt for this last scene for today's shoot made me feel tingly and even a little giddy. I hardly noticed anything around me as I walked to the set and made my way back to Imogen's apartment with Lukas. We were the only two people in this scene, and I was almost a little sad that they saved it for the last shot of the day, since I was tired and might not be able to enjoy my first (but hopefully not last) kiss with Lukas Leighton properly.

In all honesty, I hardly paid any attention to the lines leading up to our kiss during the first take, and I probably stumbled over all of mine, but nobody called "cut," so it must not have been too bad. The only thing I cared about at that moment was getting to kiss the oh-so-coveted Lukas Leighton.

And here it was.

He was standing right in front of me, saying some line from the script that I had completely forgotten and looking exactly the way every boy in the world should look. I was vaguely aware that Lukas had given me my cue by saying, "Maybe this will answer your question," though I wasn't even sure if that's what he said. Instead, I did my best to look sultry and kept my eyes locked on him.

Lukas's hand cupped my face, his thumb running across my cheekbone, and he closed his eyes and leaned in to kiss me. I must admit that it took all of my strength not to collapse into a heap right at that moment. That particular response wouldn't have benefited me at all, since it would mean that I didn't get to kiss Lukas. Instead, I braced myself for what I was sure would be the best moment of my life. Lukas's free hand had gone to the small of my back, but was now lurking dangerously close to him getting slapped. Not that I would have considered slapping him . . . especially with the cameras and entire crew watching.

I followed his lead and closed my eyes until I felt the pressure of his lips against mine. It was definitely a very different kiss from the one I had shared with Joseph on stage. This kiss was more skillful and experienced, like kissing was an art that Lukas Leighton was very practiced in. Something about the way he kissed me was heavy and important, like a statement that goes over children's heads but adults nod somberly in response to, as if they could understand the weight of a single uttered phrase from their years of experience. This kiss definitely held significance that I couldn't understand with my years of stage kisses and lack of real kisses.

When Lukas pulled away and looked into my eyes, he wasn't red in the face or embarrassed like Joseph had been. Instead, he was sure of himself, and some dark joy played in his crystal blue eyes. All I could do was stare at him helplessly and feel like I had just had my legs taken out from under me. I completely forgot to act at all as I stared at him with unabashed adoration.

Apparently my candid reaction was exactly what Bates had wanted, because the second he yelled "Cut!" he poured praise over Lukas and me. I tried not to smile too much at how perfectly the director felt the scene had played out, but I did make a mental note at what good natural chemistry Lukas and I had. It made me wonder if maybe we could be together. I could imagine the headlines in the magazines without trying too hard. They'd call us LuJu, or Jukas, or—okay, the nickname needed work, but we could be Hollywood's perfect couple—the kind that people were jealous of because of how blissfully happy they were.

It's not really getting ahead of yourself if your fantasies are true, right?

CHAPTER 13

When Joseph and I got to school on Tuesday morning, I had already told him everything that had happened on set about a million times. He was amusingly excited to hear about Ryan and Benjamin and how nice and quirky they were, but he didn't really do much to hide his dislike of Lukas when I told him about our scenes. I ignored his less-than-enthusiastic response to my favorite part of the story and decided to just focus on the rest of my experience, knowing I could at least count on Xani to be excited about Lukas.

"Were your costumes really that bad, or were you just overreacting?" Joseph asked as we walked through the quiet, dark school to zero period theatre. "Because I could see how the fact that you're brought up to be modest might make a 'normal' outfit seem uncomfortably immodest."

"Well, my pajama shorts went up to here," I said, indicating a place on my leg I didn't even realize it was possible for shorts to end. "And my dress pushed me up so much that I practically had cleavage up to my neck," I said the second part a bit too loudly.

"Whoa, June. There are some things I really don't need to know," he said, bringing his hands up as if to wash them clean of my misfortune, smirking all the while.

"Yeah, you can go ahead and joke about it now, but when

you see just how terrible the costumes really were, you'll be on my side."

"Well, maybe by the time you go back for your scenes on Thursday they'll realize the error of their ways," Joseph suggested doubtfully.

"Actually, you'll be very proud to know that I spoke with the costume designer and he agreed to make me more modest costumes from now on," I informed him, beaming at my own personal triumph.

"Wait a minute, let me get this straight," Joseph said. "You—June Laurie—stood up for yourself?"

"Amazing, isn't it?" I asked. "He even changed my awful pajamas so they weren't all that bad."

"I'm impressed," Joseph said sincerely, giving me a quick squeeze as we walked.

The immodest costumes wouldn't have been such a big deal to me normally. I mean, I am an actor and I've worn tank tops or short-ish shorts in a lot of the school plays, and they never really bothered me. I think the reason this situation felt different was because they were obviously trying to make my character sexy, rather than someone who just happened to wear those kinds of clothes. I definitely didn't feel comfortable being portrayed as "sexy" June. On my most sexy day I was prettily awkward at best.

The second we sat down in the auditorium to wait for Mr. Carroll to start teaching, Xani was flanking me, asking endless questions about Lukas Leighton.

"June doesn't really enjoy talking about Lukas Leighton, so you may be hard-pressed to get any information out of her," Joseph said sarcastically. Xani and I responded by rolling our eyes in unison.

"Did you kiss him? Was it perfection? Oh, I bet he's just the most amazing kisser," Xani gushed in her thick southern drawl. Joseph looked like he might be sick, as per usual, when Lukas was involved.

"My kissing scene with him was at the end of the day, so I was really tired," I said regretfully. "But even then, it was the most perfect thing ever. He's just so good at it!"

"You're so lucky, June," Xani said jealously. For the first time since I'd known her, Xani looked at me with admiration rather than the normal dislike. It was a shocking—but nice—change.

"If there's any chance I can introduce you to him, I will," I promised suddenly, not quite sure of where that offer had come from.

"I think I would die. Really. I would just say 'Hi' and it would all be over," she said happily.

"It looks like Mr. Carroll is about to start class. We should probably stop talking," Joseph said stiffly, keeping his eyes locked on the stage where Mr. Carroll had just entered.

"Even your Lukas Leighton aversion can't annoy me today, Joseph. But nice try," I said happily, leaning over and kissing him on the cheek. Talking to Xani had made me infinitely more excited about the whole experience yesterday. It was nice to have someone who was actually excited for me and understood the monumental importance of kissing Lukas Leighton.

Joseph didn't reply to my sudden outburst of giddiness; he just swallowed hard and tried not to let his eyes look like big, round, dinner plates.

After school—and about two hundred retellings of my day of filming—Joseph dropped me off at my house with the promise that he'd be by in a few hours to watch a movie. Gran, who was less than enthusiastic about my love for Lukas Leighton, was waiting in the kitchen with an open bottle of beer. I stopped suddenly in the doorway, looking at the contraband sitting on our kitchen counter.

"Gran, have you been drinking?" I asked, shock filling my voice.

"Yes, June, you've driven me to drink," she said sarcastically. "No Bliss, this is for you."

I simply stood and stared at her for a long while, wondering why the obvious hadn't set into her mind yet.

"Uh, Gran . . . you know I don't drink, right? Never have.

Never will. Because if this is some sort of test to see if I have been, I can assure you—"

"I know you haven't been drinking," she replied, waving away my words with her hand. "It's not for *you.* It's for your hair." She stated this as though it were the most obvious thing in the world.

"I don't think I follow," I answered, still confused by what she was saying.

"We're going to mix beer, egg whites, and mayonnaise and put it in your hair. It'll make it shiny."

I brought my palm up to my forehead and closed my eyes patiently, trying not to look too piqued. "Gran, how many of these crazy food things actually work? Because I'm starting to feel like a human buffet with all of these bizarre remedies."

"Well, you got a part on *Forensic Faculty*, didn't you? That has to count for something," she said.

"True," I answered slowly. I looked over at the open bottle, which was already filling the kitchen with a sickly smell. I honestly didn't understand how anyone could drink something that smelled like that, but if I had to suffer for my art and put the reeking liquid in my hair, I guessed it was the price of fame. "Do you have any nose plugs?" I asked finally.

....

Joseph came over at eight o'clock with two orange sodas and a movie in tow. I placed a bowl of freshly popped microwave popcorn on the coffee table in the living room and plopped down on the couch, gratefully accepting the icy soda he handed me.

"So, what's on the agenda for tonight?" I asked, trying to catch a glimpse of the small stack of movies he had with him.

"I brought a few options. I have a Lillian Gish movie, in case you wanted to tap into your favorite silent film star for inspiration. Or I brought a few newer movies. Whatever you're in the mood for is fine with me. I like all of them," he said with a shrug.

"I choose Lillian, of course," I replied.

"Lillian it is."

Joseph popped the movie into the DVD player and took his place beside me on the couch. I scooted close to him so that I could rest against his side like I always did, and he looked over at me quizzically, sniffing as he did so.

"What?" I asked, suddenly self-conscious.

"June . . . why do you smell like alcohol?" he asked, a look of puzzled surprise on his face.

"Oh. Right. Gran made me put it in my hair . . . apparently it'll make it shinier. Of course, that also means I'll be smelling like alcohol for the rest of my life."

Joseph turned back to the TV to process this information for a moment. "Does any of that stuff actually work?" he asked finally, a hint of amusement in his voice.

"I don't think so. But it definitely makes Gran happy, so I'm fine with it," I responded with a laugh.

We were silent for a moment, watching the black-and-white film with its dramatic music and vaudeville-style acting. I happily snuggled closer to Joseph and rested my head on his shoulder as we watched.

"So I think I'll buy Homecoming tickets on Thursday while you're filming. I just figured we should buy them now so that we don't have to worry about it later," Joseph said.

"Yeah, I think that's a good idea. I'll pay you back soon, I promise," I told him with a smile. Even though neither of us really liked to dance, I figured it would still be fun to get dressed up and go somewhere together.

"Don't bother. I've been working for my dad doing some filing for his business, so I've got a bit of money saved up."

"But you shouldn't have to use the money you've saved on me. Besides, I've got a job now too, remember?" I said matter-of-factly.

"Good point. But I still want to do this properly, where I buy your ticket and pick you up and everything," he answered seriously, making it sound much more like a date than it was supposed to be.

I didn't say anything at first, wondering how I could best

respond. Normally I would say something like, "You make it sound like we're going on a date," but something told me that I shouldn't joke around so much about that kind of thing. Joseph had recently become much more touchy about that topic, and I wondered if it was because he was going on a mission in a few years and didn't want people to think he didn't have his priorities straight. So instead of making a joke or asking why he'd been so serious lately, I just said, "That's really sweet of you," and left it at that.

CHAPTER 14

Seven o'clock on Thursday morning seemed so far off when I left the set on Monday, but as I stood in front of the makeup trailer, ready to start my next day of filming, I found that it had come quickly. Right when I entered Candice's station, Ryan and Benjamin exclaimed, "New Girl!" enthusiastically from the couch. Both were flipping through magazines and drinking coffee from cardboard cups, while Candice sat smashed between them on the small sofa.

"We got you a hot chocolate, New Girl," Benjamin said as he nodded at the only cardboard cup remaining in the cup holder.

"Thanks guys," I answered appreciatively, picking up the cup and letting it warm my hands. I took a seat in the makeup chair but swiveled around so I was facing my three friends. "So, anything exciting happen while I was gone?" I asked, trying to make conversation, since Candice didn't seem too motivated to start on my hair and makeup.

"The costumes were a lot less fun to scrutinize," Candice said dryly.

"True," Ryan agreed.

They were all silent for a moment, indicating that there hadn't been a whole lot happening in the past two days.

"Candice put a plant in the trailer," Benjamin offered

lamely. I looked over at the small green potted plant, unsure of what it was.

"We call it 'The Little Steamer,'" Ryan informed me.

"I see," I said slowly, thinking of what else I should say. "And why do you call it that?"

"It's a thyme plant," Benjamin said simply, while I continued to stare at him.

"Thyme reminded them of time," Candice began, talking as if they were children and she was trying to convey to an adult that we should act impressed by their line of thought. "And time reminded them of a pocket watch, which reminded them of steampunk, which made them call it The Little Steamer. I'm sure they thought they were being clever," she finished sarcastically.

"Candice hasn't had enough coffee yet," Ryan said with a tentative glance in her direction.

"There's not enough coffee in the world to help me put up with you two," she shot back, finally getting up off the sofa to start on my hair and makeup. She pulled out her black binder, which held the shooting schedule and told her what makeup I'd need for each scene.

"I'm doing all precinct scenes today, right?" I asked, trying to remember what scene came first but finding that they were all getting jumbled together in my mind.

"Yeah, so first we'll need you in your stage costume. It'll be the scene right after Edward's murder," she answered, never looking up from her black binder but letting her dark red lips curl up into a smile, showing her amusement at the costume I'd have to put on again.

"Hey, that means you get to act with us today, New Girl," Benjamin said happily, setting his magazine down on his lap. He exchanged a sly glance with Ryan, who smirked back at him. I watched them suspiciously.

"Whatever you guys are thinking right now, stop. You've got these shifty little glances going back and forth and I don't trust them at all," I warned.

"I have no idea what you're talking about," Ryan said in

mock innocence.

"I think maybe New Girl needs to start drinking coffee as well," Benjamin chimed in.

"You guys are impossible," I said with a sigh. They continued to grin at me, making me feel even more wary about doing a scene with them. "I don't see what you could do to mess me up. I don't even have lines with you."

"Ouch," Ryan said in reply.

"Thanks a lot, New Girl," Benjamin added in a hurt tone.

"They added a few lines to the script yesterday," Candice explained, handing me a blue script and returning to pining up my hair in the same style it had been on Monday.

"Oops," I said innocently, looking over at Ryan and Benjamin, who were pretending to pout. Glancing over the script quickly, I saw where the new lines had been added. I now had a small interaction with Ryan and Benjamin while sitting in the precinct waiting to be questioned by Charles and Cutter.

"You're going to wish you had been nicer to us once we start filming, New Girl," Benjamin threatened while Ryan nodded gravely.

"Candice, can't you do something about the two of them?" I joked.

"Don't you think that if I had any control over them, they wouldn't be hanging out in the makeup trailer *all day*?" she asked in exasperation.

"We're a force to be reckoned with," Ryan exclaimed proudly.

"An oncoming storm," Benjamin agreed.

"Great," I sighed.

Soon after I grabbed a quick bite to eat at craft services and got into costume, I met the rest of the cast at the set of the precinct. It was an odd experience to see this well-known set in person. It looked almost exactly like it did on TV except that the ceiling and a few of the walls were missing. Other than that, I really felt like I was at the police station. The thing that amazed me the most about the set was all of the little details that made it feel real, but probably went unnoticed by the viewers. There were half-empty coffee cups, coats on chairs, and even stacks of papers on desks that I took the liberty of rifling through when no one was looking. They were all filled out as if they were police work that needed to be filed. It was simply incredible.

"Excuse me ma'am, but you aren't authorized to view those files," I heard Benjamin say right behind me, making me jump about a foot in the air.

"You scared me to death," I said breathlessly.

"What are you even doing?" Ryan asked, never far behind Benjamin.

"I wanted to see if there was writing on all of the papers," I admitted sheepishly. "You know, instead of just writing on the first few and the rest left blank."

"Why?" Benjamin inquired.

"That's a good question," I said. "To which I have no answer. I was just curious."

"Works for me," he said, shrugging and walking over to a table filled with food and water bottles.

"I see you're in *the* costume again," Ryan pointed out sympathetically.

"Yeah, I can't seem to avoid *the* costume," I agreed heavily, sitting in a chair at one of the prop desks. Ryan perched on the desk and folded his arms.

"It's really not that bad," he said. "I think the fact that you come off as being so innocent kind of makes it less sexy and a bit more costume-y, like you're only wearing it because it looks vaudeville."

I looked down at the costume with its lace and feathers and felt, for the first time since I had put it on, that maybe he was right and I didn't need to be so embarrassed. It was funny how different he was when he and Benjamin weren't bouncing jokes off of each other. He was still goofy and lighthearted, but he also seemed more focused on putting me at ease than making jokes when he was on his own.

"So, I've been wondering something since I met you at the

table read, but I don't want to come off as . . . I can't even think of the word. Nosey, I guess would be the best way to put it," Ryan said, spinning the watch on his wrist around and around as he spoke.

"That's a scary way to start a question," I joked. "But go ahead."

"Are you a Mormon?" he asked, whispering the word "Mormon" as if it were taboo.

I paused for a moment and assessed my current situation. Ryan seemed like a nice guy, so I couldn't imagine him making fun of me or being disrespectful about my religion. At the same time, though, I'd had tons of friends who I thought were really down-to-earth and friendly who ended up getting weird when I told them about my religion. As if there was really something so odd about being LDS.

"Yeah, I am. How could you tell?" I asked, wondering what had given me away.

"Well, first there are the obvious ones: not drinking coffee and being so uncomfortable in revealing clothing."

"But those could easily be attributes of a non-Mormon as well," I pointed out.

"That's true. But I had a Mormon friend growing up. You can just tell. I realize that makes me sounds really weird and creepy, but it's the truth. You actually remind me of him a lot," Ryan said warmly. "That's a good thing," he added quickly, seeing that I was trying to work out the intent of that statement.

"So you're okay with it, then?" I asked cautiously. "I mean, you're not going to go off on a political rant or tell me all of the reasons it would be easier to not be Mormon?"

"From what I can tell, you haven't tried to push your beliefs down anyone's throat here, so why should we do that to you?" he said logically, instantly scoring major brownie points in my book. "I don't have a problem with most lifestyles as long as they aren't looking down on me for not joining in."

I smiled up at Ryan for a long while, glad to be met with

so much respect and maturity from someone I hadn't known for that long. His way of thinking perfectly matched mine on this point, and I couldn't help but wonder why more people didn't feel the same way.

"I'm glad to hear you say that," I admitted truthfully. "Honestly, for some reason a lot of people get kind of . . . hostile, when they find out. Like I've told them I'm against breathing or something."

"Yeah, I've seen that. I think those people have either had a bad experience with an overbearing Mormon, or they believe everything they read about them."

"Which normally comes from anti-Mormon websites . . . so that's a good source of information," I remarked sarcastically.

"It's not fair, but that's why I admire you for being a caring, decent human. I think that speaks volumes about your religion," he said with a smile.

"Thanks Ryan. I really appreciate that," I replied sincerely. He grinned at me for a moment longer before clearing his throat and changing the subject.

"So, do you have your new lines memorized yet? Or line, I guess I should say," he asked. "Because Benjamin and I will be testing you thoroughly."

"Testing me on the actual line, or just testing my patience as usual?" I countered with a smirk.

"Ah, probably a little bit of both," he laughed.

"Yeah, I could have guessed."

"Ryan," said the angelic voice of Lukas Leighton at such close proximity that I started. I hadn't even seen him walk up behind Ryan and then there he was, his voice friendly enough, but hinting at something commanding and dark. "I think it would be best if you went over your blocking with Benjamin again. He seems to be confused."

Ryan kept his eyes trained on me the whole time Lukas spoke, his expression never changing from one of neutral attention.

"Okay," was his only response. He didn't say it in a rude

or sarcastic way. He didn't even sound annoyed, really, but there was something about the way he had given his short answer and left without saying goodbye to me or making eye contact with Lukas that made me wonder if he was as fond of him as he had once appeared.

"Sorry about him. He likes to talk a lot—forgets what he's actually supposed to be doing sometimes," Lukas said apologetically. I hadn't been annoyed by Ryan's presence, but this comment made me wonder if sitting around talking with him had made me look unprofessional.

"That's okay. I probably wasn't doing much to get him back on track, really," I said guiltily, trying to convey that Ryan hadn't been unprofessional all on his own.

"Well that dress didn't help matters, I'm sure," Lukas joked, giving me a winning smile, which instantly melted my heart. I couldn't think of any response, or at least I couldn't get my mouth to work one out, so I just smiled stupidly up at him. "I've missed having you around the set these last few days," Lukas said, leaning against the desk where Ryan had been just seconds before.

"Really?" was my brilliant response.

"Yeah. I actually wanted to text you, but then I realized I don't have your number, which doesn't make any sense," he went on as he pulled a phone out of his pocket.

"No sense at all," I babbled, grinning like an idiot. Was Lukas Leighton really asking me for my phone number? Me? A nobody he'd only known for a few days?

"Number?" he asked, raising his eyebrows at me in a beautifully quizzical way as he passed me his phone. Even those facial expressions that would make other people seem goofy looked like perfection on him. I typed my number into his extensive contacts list, trying not to concentrate too much on the fact that he was watching me with a faultless grin.

"There you go," I said shakily, passing his phone back and feeling giddy at the way our hands touched when he took it from me.

"I'll text you later with my number," he said, answering

my unsaid question just as the director called for everyone to take their places. He walked away from me, but looked back just once to bless me with his perfect smile and a sly wink.

....

The first scene had gone smoothly all through my questioning with Charles and Cutter. Will Trofeos was a terrifying person to be in the room with when he was in his Charles Bagely mode. Lukas seemed to be the same person as his character Cutter, so that wasn't as jarring as having Will trying to scare me into a false confession. The scene was a bit exhausting, but by the time we finished I felt really good about the performance I had given.

As confusing as it was, we then moved on to shoot the scene right before I was brought into the interrogation room. In this scene I was supposed to be sitting down on a bench, waiting for Charles and Cutter to come collect me after filling out some paper work. Before they would show up, however, Ryan and Benjamin (AKA Rich and John) would come up to rattle me a bit and say a few clever lines as per usual. This was a scene I was nervous about. I wasn't worried because I had just been given the lines that morning; it really wasn't a particularly difficult scene, seeing as how I only had one line. I was mostly nervous that Ryan and Benjamin would follow through on their unspoken threat and do something to mess up my performance. By the time everyone was in place and we were ready to begin shooting, I was a nervous wreck. Bates, the director, was quite impressed by my condition, mistaking it for a good bit of acting.

"Just keep that tension up June. You're doing great," he shouted from behind the glaring lights.

"Okay," I responded meekly, not sure what I was doing that he wanted me to keep up.

"And, action!"

I sat on the bench, looking around at the precinct with wide, worried eyes, half acting as Imogen Gentry, and half being genuinely scared for the inevitable "oncoming storm" that was Ryan and Benjamin.

The two boys sauntered up to where I sat, looking suspicious and mildly amused at the same time. I definitely didn't like the looks of this. They both wore dark slacks and white, button-up, collared shirts with their badges hanging around their necks. Benjamin looked me up and down, and then spoke.

"Well, if it isn't the femme fatale herself," he remarked coolly.

"I guess it's true—vaudeville is dead, isn't it?" Ryan added, matching Benjamin's tone. I watched them warily for a moment, trying not to notice how much like their characters they really were. They sat down on either side of me on the bench, much like they had the first day I met them at the table read.

"So, why'd you kill him?" Benjamin asked, leaning in close and making me feel very uncomfortable.

"Wasn't enough 'quiet on the set' for you?" Ryan put in, leaning in just as close as Benjamin. The only way I could avoid looking at either of them was to stiffen my back and look straight ahead, and even then they were dominating my peripheral vision.

"I didn't kill him," I answered quietly, letting my voice quaver a bit as if I might cry. I furrowed my brow and bit my bottom lip, still keeping my gaze trained firmly straight ahead.

"I'm sure you didn't mean to kill him. Maybe you just got tired of being sawed in half every night," Benjamin suggested.

"Tired of being dropped in the water tank or put in the disappearing box," Ryan provided.

"So you filled the disappearing box with gas to make *him* disappear . . . permanently," Benjamin said in a low, threatening voice.

"Guess he should have asked for a volunteer from the audience," Ryan remarked darkly as he rested his chin on his hand. Both of their faces were only inches away now. I had never thought of myself as a claustrophobic person, but being crammed between those two while already being a huge ball of nerves was definitely steering me in that direction.

"Now they have to call in the Vaudeville Vice," Ryan concluded, just inches from me. Had I not been so paranoid about what they might do to mess my scene up, I might have actually enjoyed the hilarity of the whole thing. Ryan and Benjamin were masters of comedy. The way they said these ridiculous lines in such a straight way made them infinitely funnier, but I could hardly concentrate on that when I was keeping watch for any sign of trouble from them.

"Knock it off, you two," Will Trofeos said in his thick accent as he and Lukas walked into the scene, their presence seeming to fill the room with authority. Ryan and Benjamin automatically pulled away from me and stood up from the bench. "We need to bring her in for questioning," he added, nodding to me as an indication that I should stand up and follow him. I did, glad that I was able to get out of the scene without Ryan and Benjamin doing something horrible.

By the time we had left the "room," the director had called cut and the entire set was full of people and noise. I walked over to Ryan and Benjamin, looking at them skeptically.

"All right, what are you guys playing at?" I asked. They exchanged innocent glances back and forth. "You know what I'm talking about."

"New Girl, we wouldn't actually try to ruin your take. We were just joking," Benjamin said seriously.

"He speaks the truth," Ryan agreed.

"Yeah, I still don't believe you," I informed them, shooting the pair a piercing look to let them know I was on to their games as we reset to shoot the scene again.

As fate would have it, we shot that same scene a handful of times and not once did Ryan or Benjamin do anything to throw me off. This, of course, threw me off even more. By the end of the scene I was a nervous wreck, which I let Candice know so that she could make sure they were properly punished. Of course, I knew that Candice's idea of punishing them would be to simply ignore all of their funny comments, which she did anyway.

The rest of the day was spent shooting all of the other scenes I had in the precinct, including the very last shot of the episode. In that scene Lukas and I had a long, heartfelt conversation about how nice it was to work together and what a pity it would be to not see each other again. This, of course, would lead into the next week's episode where they'd have another odd theatre case that they'd ask me to consult on.

The last scene didn't take very long to shoot (unfortunately) so by the time I was back home and ready to go to bed, I had obsessively looked at my phone every minute to see if Lukas had texted me. Joseph hadn't been too happy about that fact while we watched the recorded episode of *Forensic Faculty* from that night, but I'd make it up to him later. There was just no way I was going to miss a text from Lukas Leighton if it came.

Just as I was falling asleep with my phone placed on vibrate right by my ear, I felt it buzz. Opening it up, I read my one new message from a number I didn't recognize.

You left quite an impression on me today. Want to grab a drink after work tomorrow?

In the moments before I fell asleep with a blissful smile on my face I somehow managed to reply to him with a simple:

Yes.

CHAPTER 15

I hadn't told Joseph or Gran about the fact that Lukas Leighton had asked for my number on set. The only person I could really think of who would be excited for me would be Xani, but she and I weren't exactly friends. We were more like acquaintances who shared a mutual interest . . . that interest being Joseph, of course.

And so, sitting in the makeup trailer on Friday morning it was no surprise that I couldn't stop smiling or checking my phone for any possible new texts. Candice watched me closely as she flat ironed my hair into big, loose curls, her intelligent eyes scanning my face every few seconds. I was almost positive she could see through me, but knowing Candice, the last thing in the world she'd want to do was talk about boys, so she didn't ask me a thing.

"Yesterday was fun," Benjamin began carefully, as soon as he and Ryan showed up in the trailer. Even without looking at him, I could tell that his eyes were trained on me to gauge my reaction. "Wasn't yesterday fun Ryan?" he prodded.

"Very fun, Benjamin. I quite enjoyed myself," Ryan responded, looking over at my reflection in the mirror with a wicked grin. I pointedly ignored them, taking my lead from Candice, who always did just that.

"I particularly enjoyed watching New Girl wait for us to

drop the axe," Benjamin said in a fond voice, as if he were remembering a beloved memory.

"The way her eyes get big when she's nervous is just adorable, wouldn't you say, Candice?" Ryan asked.

"Don't talk to me. I'm not awake yet," Candice answered. Her tone suggested that she had thought of a way to kill them using every makeup tool she possessed.

"My favorite bit is seeing the way she's still afraid of us," Ryan went on, undeterred.

"Too true, Ryan," Benjamin agreed supportively.

"You guys are *so* funny," I cut in, worried that this little exchange would go on forever if I didn't stop it.

"Well, thank you, New Girl. We do try," Benjamin said, still using his overly cautious voice.

"You guys made me feel like a crazy person yesterday! I swear that I almost asked anyone else if they could tell what you were up to . . . but then I realized that would solidify my appearance of craziness," I confessed.

"That was the whole point," Ryan pointed out. "We didn't even have to do anything. You made most of it up in your head." He grinned cheekily, making me shake my head at him in disapproval.

"Thank you for that," I answered sarcastically.

"Anything for you, June," he replied.

"Hey, I get to put some ash on you today," Candice suddenly said from behind me, showing more enthusiasm than was normal for her this early in the morning. She held her black binder, looking over the page excitedly. "There's going to be an explosion!" She set the binder down and clapped her hands like a child who had just been told they could have cookies for breakfast.

"I forgot about that," I said, suddenly a little nervous for my first "stunt." I actually had two stunts in this episode. I figured they would normally hire someone to perform these, but since they were relatively small and I was, in fact, a nobody, I'd probably just be doing them myself.

"It's about time I get to do some decent makeup. It feels

like I've been doing nothing but glamour and corrective for weeks," she complained, turning her attention to spraying my hair into submission. The big glossy curls that now framed my face were actually quite flattering and I secretly wished I could do my hair that well on my own. It was definitely a change from the springy ringlets I normally sported.

"Will you do anything special on Edward once he's dead?" I asked, not able to remember the name of the actor playing Edward at the moment. In my defense, I hadn't met the guy yet, so it wasn't like I was just turning into one of those people who don't bother to learn names.

"I'll make his face a little redder and put some blisters on his mouth . . . nothing too exciting," she said dryly, obviously mourning the bloody special effects makeup she normally got to do. She smoothed foundation over my skin as if it were the most tedious task she could ever be assigned to do.

"Maybe I'll convince them to axe Ryan's character," she thought aloud, causing Ryan to make an indignant noise from the couch.

"You'd go crazy without me here," he said matter-of-factly.

"Whatever you say," was her charming reply. "June, go do your other boring scenes and then come straight back to me so I can get working on something worth my time."

"Will do, chief," I answered with a mock salute. I waved to Ryan and Benjamin, who sat on the couch lazily typing away on their phones. It made me wonder if they had brought the sofa into the trailer themselves just to have a better reason to hang around there all of the time.

Each of my scenes for the day would be filmed in Edward's apartment. Will Trofeos and Lukas had already been on that set for a while, filming a scene with the two of them snooping around for clues. Once they finished their scene, Will left the set, leaving Lukas and me as the only actors there. We were going to be doing a scene where I, as Imogen Gentry, take it upon myself to look around Edward's apartment for clues when Cutter, frustrated by the case, returns to the apartment to see if he and Charles missed something in their previous inspection.

"June Laurie," Lukas said with a smile as he walked over to me. "It's about time you got here. I was wondering when I'd get to see you again."

I could understand the words that were coming out of Lukas's mouth, but for some reason, none of them made any sense. Why would Lukas Leighton be happy to see *me*? Especially when he was constantly surrounded by famous actresses and supermodels? It just didn't make any sense.

"Here I am," I replied, resting one hand on my stomach to keep myself from throwing up due to pure, unadulterated joy.

"So, are we still on for drinks after work tonight?" he asked, actually looking hopeful, as if I would ever turn him down. Of course, there was his phrasing that I'd have to clear up, because in my mind, when someone says "drinks," they usually aren't talking about orange soda. There had to be a smooth way of stating that I didn't drink—I just couldn't think of it in the face of such beauty.

"Definitely," I replied with a grin. "I may need a ride home though, if that's okay with you?" For a moment I was worried that he'd see how lame I actually was. He would forget that I had just gotten a part on a huge TV show and realize that I was a 16-year-old girl who didn't have her own car and needed her grandma to drive her everywhere.

"Well, I brought my motorcycle, so as long as you're okay with holding on tight for a while, I'd be happy to take you home," he answered in a sincere, concerned way.

"Thank you Lukas, I really appreciate that," I said warmly, hoping that my tone conveyed just how grateful I was that he was willing to be seen in public with me. I had to admit though, that if Lukas really was talking about the kind of "drinks" I thought he was, I'd have to Google how to drive a motorcycle. I wasn't quite sure how I felt about being the designated motorcycle driver.

"I'm actually not being completely selfless," he said with a glint in his eye.

"Oh?" was the only response I could think of with my heart pounding so distractingly in my ears.

"Taking you home does give me more time to get to know you," he admitted with a charming grin.

"I can safely say I'm fine with that," I answered. I bit my lip to keep myself from grinning like an idiot and tried desperately to think of something clever and witty to say. I was saved from my own horrible rendition of what was "clever and witty" when Bates called for us to get to our first positions for the scene.

For the rest of the day, the only thing I seemed to be able to focus on was what was coming after work. I tried to wrap my head around just how amazing it was that I'd actually be hanging out with Lukas Leighton outside of work. He had been nice to me on set, of course, but that was expected. If you're going to be working with someone, you don't want to cause conflicts, so you'll treat them well. Asking me to spend time with him after work, though? That was something he definitely wasn't obligated to do, which got my hopes up way more than it should have.

I went through the rest of our filming day with a brainless grin plastered to my face. I missed half of what Ryan, Candice, and Benjamin were saying to me in the makeup trailer while Candice painted little lines of "fresh scab" across my face. Hours later, when I came back at the end of the day to have my makeup taken off, I still looked a little dumbfounded that Lukas had asked me out.

"Now, this fresh scab shouldn't be too hard to get off, but it may leave a small trace of red on your skin for a while," Candice was saying as she used an oily liquid to remove my injury makeup. "But I've got some foundation that you can use to cover that up once I remove it, if you want."

I didn't answer her offer, partly because I hadn't really heard what she was saying, and partly because my phone had just buzzed with a text from a number I had now memorized.

Just finishing my last scene. I'll meet you outside of the costume trailer.

I stared at the text for a long time, a monumental smile stuck in place and making my cheeks ache. I closed the phone slowly and let my eyes roam over the makeup trailer, which suddenly seemed very cozy and friendly. The Little Steamer stood near the corner of the mirror, the little round green leaves all angling toward the door where the last slivers of light were streaming in.

"Would you wipe that stupid smirk off of your face? It's ridiculous," Candice remarked in a dull monotone.

"I can't help it," I replied, still beaming from ear to ear.

"This better not be about that handle Lukas Leighton. He's so awful," she said disdainfully.

"Oh, come on Candice, he's really not that bad. He's always been nice to me," I answered, coming to Lukas's defense. After all, he had been extremely sweet to me ever since we started filming. I couldn't help but wonder if maybe Candice and everyone else just thought he was a jerk because they hadn't taken the time to get to know him. They expected him to be a jerk, so no matter what, that's how they were going to perceive him.

"He doesn't kill puppies or anything, but he's so . . . empty. It's like he doesn't really think about anything, he's just kind of there." She said all of this with a perplexed look on her face, as if Lukas Leighton really were some strange creature that she just couldn't understand.

"Have you tried to get to know him?" I asked, already knowing the answer to that question.

"I haven't had a chance," she stated dryly, not really looking like she wanted the chance to get to know him. Candice had finished taking my makeup off at this point and sat down on the couch, rolling her head from side to side to relieve some pain in her neck—possibly the pain that Lukas Leighton apparently provided daily. I grabbed a bottle of foundation and began re-doing my makeup in the hopes that I could somehow look like I belonged with Lukas when we were out.

"If you haven't even tried to get to know him, how can

you make a fair judgment?" I asked, feeling like I had stumped her.

"He won't let me do his makeup, remember? That's why I haven't gotten to know him. Because he's too good for me to work on him. So there you go. Fair judgment made."

I hated to admit it, but she did have a point there. It was odd to me that someone as down-to-earth as Lukas would do something so brusque. I looked back down at my phone, trying to reconcile the two different opinions I was seeing of Lukas. He was either rude or he was as sweet as he had been to me. Unless, of course, there was more to the story that I just didn't know—a side where maybe Candice hadn't been as nice to Lukas as she let on, which I didn't find too hard to believe just judging by how she acted toward everyone. I knew that being dry and sarcastic was part of Candice's personality, but if someone like Lukas came up against that, I could understand why he'd be rude right back to her.

"You don't have to look so put out. Go out with the guy if you want. I don't really care," she said rather unconvincingly. "I was just trying to look out for you."

"Which I'm grateful for," I said with a smile. "It's nice to have a friend who's a girl. All of my friends always seem to be boys."

"I didn't say we're friends," she replied as she opened up a magazine and held it up so that it covered most of her face. The small smile lines that had formed around her barely visible eyes told me everything I needed to know. I had officially made a friend.

"Don't worry, I won't tell anyone," I said as I grabbed my coat and left the makeup trailer. "See you tomorrow, buddy," I added sarcastically.

"I'm not your buddy," she called through the open door at my retreating form.

CHAPTER 16

Straddling Lukas Leighton's motorcycle and holding onto him for dear life was definitely not something I had ever imagined myself doing. But if I'm being honest, it wasn't such a bad way to be terrified of the trees rushing by my head at sixty miles per hour. In fact, I'd go as far as to say it was the best way I could ever imagine having a near-death experience.

All right. Maybe "near-death experience" is being a little dramatic. After all, I was wearing a helmet and Lukas was a surprisingly careful driver. I imagine it had something to do with the fact that if he got into an accident and ruined his face, his career would be over. But I liked to think it had something to do with the precious cargo he was carrying. The precious cargo was me, in case you were wondering.

"So, is there somewhere you'd like to go or should I pick?" Lukas called back while we were stopped at a red light. It was difficult to hear him over the rumbling of his motorcycle and the extensive padding of the helmet I wore.

"I'm sixteen," I answered a bit more loudly than I meant to. Lukas glanced at me over his shoulder, a small smile playing on his lips. I suddenly felt that I should explain this random statement. "I can't go to a bar," I clarified. Really, I should have just said I didn't drink rather than copping out and blaming my age, but for some reason I didn't want Lukas to see me as some boring conservative teenager. And so, against my better judgment, I was attempting to act more grown-up and daring than I actually was (in contrast to my giddy text to Gran letting her know I was going out with Lukas). Getting onto the motorcycle in the first place had been my first step in showing my inner daredevil.

"I didn't really picture you as a bar-hopping type of girl anyway," Lukas said loudly as the light turned green and we took off again. "I was thinking maybe we could get some coffee instead."

Crap.

There was no way out of this one, was there? I couldn't very well blame my age. But maybe I could use the whole not-drinking-coffee thing to make me look unique and freethinking, because everyone drinks coffee, don't they? So how unique would that make me if I were one of the few people who didn't? Of course, I could just be honest and say I didn't drink coffee because of my beliefs . . . but that would require a degree of level-headedness and confidence that I seemed to lack around someone as impressive as Lukas Leighton.

"Sounds good," was my delayed reply. Even though I now had another dilemma to deal with, at least I could throw the "designated driver" scenario out the window.

Now, before you shake your head at how much of a sell-out I was being, you should know I agreed to go to the coffee shop with the intention of ordering a hot chocolate.

And don't give me that skeptical look, oh ye of little faith.

At my response, Lukas picked up the pace a bit, weaving between cars as if, with an actual destination in mind, he had suddenly become more daring. This, of course, made me cling tighter to him. I didn't mind that one little bit, although I could have done without the fearing for my life part.

Pulling into the parking lot of a small, rundown coffee shop, Lukas hopped gracefully off his motorcycle. I tried to do the same but it proved difficult in my heels. I wrestled the helmet off my head and gave Candice a silent thank you for using her extra hold hair spray when she curled my hair. It looked surprisingly good for having been confined to the tight helmet just moments ago.

“I love this place,” Lukas said, lacing his fingers through mine as we walked through the parking lot. I tried not to look stunned at the fact that he was suddenly holding my hand and tried desperately to remind myself that Lukas wasn’t sixteen. Holding hands probably wasn’t that big of a deal to him. It probably wasn’t that big of a deal for most sixteen-year-olds either, but for someone who has only had stage kisses, it was shocking and wonderful all at the same time.

“Is this the coffee shop?” I asked. It didn’t look like the coffee shops I was used to. It was an old, dimly lit brick building with a small, barely noticeable entrance and no windows. A wooden sign on the door read “The Ritalin Rival.”

“It’s a well-kept secret,” he said knowingly. His unsaid "for people like me" hung in the air.

Inside, the shop was the complete opposite of the outside. I expected grimy, unwashed, and dark. Instead I got bright, white, and modern. The springy light wood floors were spotless and white lights seemed to be placed on every available spot on the ceiling. All of the chairs were bold reds, blues, and yellows, with sharp, geometric backs and arms. The bar where a few famous-looking people sat sipping lattes was plastic and see-through, and the stools on which these "beautiful people" sat looked like gumballs that someone had taken a bite out of. There were a few bamboo shoots along the walls springing up out of the ground where the wood floors gave way to dirt, and a constant rhythmic beat played in the background.

“Wow,” I said breathlessly. It was definitely a scene I wasn’t used to.

“I know, right? Isn’t it great?” he asked, his eyes crinkled with excitement.

I wasn’t about to tell him it was very "not me," so instead I smiled brightly and said, “It is something, that’s for sure.” I thought I saw a few A-listers sitting blithely by a tall bamboo plant, talking quietly and exchanging pretty smiles. Even though the setting was so out of place for me, I had to admit that it was like I had entered into a world few normal people got to see. I was beyond flattered that Lukas had wanted to invite me into this part of his life.

A server wearing all black walked up to us and asked for our orders, which I thought was a bit odd, considering you'd usually go up to a cash register and order. But on the list of odd things I'd seen that evening, this was pretty low. Lukas ordered some sort of fancy coffee that probably cost more than Joseph's car, and then the server turned to me. I hesitated for a moment, trying to think of a more sophisticated way of saying "hot chocolate."

"Um . . . do you have anything . . ." I was totally blanking, right in front of Lukas. What was a fancy way of saying hot chocolate? Was there really a fancy way to put it? Not coming up with anything, I gave up trying to look cool. It was only a matter of time before Lukas figured out how different from him I was anyway; I might as well get it over with. "I actually don't drink coffee. Do you have any hot chocolate?" I finished lamely, waiting for all of the celebrities to turn to me with disgust, realize that I was not one of them, and throw me out.

"Sure thing," the server said, giving me a wan smile and retreating to the plastic bar to fill our orders.

"Should we sit over there?" Lukas asked, motioning to a quiet (but not dark, since there were no dark corners in this room) part of the coffee shop. He didn't say anything about the hot chocolate comment, which surprised me. He didn't even ask me about not drinking coffee. Maybe I had made a big deal out of nothing. After all, who cared if I didn't drink coffee? It wasn't really *that* weird. It wasn't like I had said, "Oh actually I like to club baby seals, but thanks for offering me coffee." Now that would be something you could legitimately worry about.

"So I heard Bates talking about your future on the show

today," Lukas said conspiratorially as he settled into a cobalt blue armchair. I took the candy apple red chair adjacent to his and tried to sit as gracefully as I could with my knees almost hitting my chest. Why were these chairs so low to the ground?

"Is this good news or bad news?" I asked, trying to imitate the perfect smile I had seen Joann Hoozer give him so many times on the show.

"They like you," he began, obviously withholding information from me on purpose. He studied my face for a moment, a glint in his eyes. "It sounds like they may keep you on the show for longer than four episodes," he finally confessed. My eyes grew wide at this news. Was it possible that the nobody known as June Laurie could have won over the heart of a big-time Hollywood director?

"I can't even imagine being a regular on the show," I admitted. "It seems too good to be true."

"I'm not saying anything for sure. Just what I've overheard," he said with a sly, beautiful grin.

The waiter arrived once more, placing our drinks on the see-through plastic table between us. The table reminded me of a squat golf tee and I had to resist the urge to say "Fore" as the oversized mugs were placed there, realizing that this would be a June Laurie joke, not a Lukas Leighton joke. Our waiter looked over at Lukas, obviously realizing that I wasn't famous and was therefore not worth his time, and asked if we wanted anything else.

"We're fine, Raul," Lukas answered distractedly. I couldn't help but think that someone named Raul was by default more interesting than someone named June, even if he was a waiter and I was an actress on a show as huge as *Forensic Faculty*. That put me in my place pretty quickly.

Lukas and I sipped at our drinks for a moment, looking around the room at all of the people who undoubtedly led interesting lives. I wondered for a moment if Lukas had an ulterior motive for bringing me to this place. If he really was as bad as Candice and Benjamin seemed to imply, I could see him thinking this would be a good way to show me I didn't belong in the glittery world of celebrities. But then I remembered that Lukas was a human being and not some caricature.

I wouldn't ever describe myself as a brave person. Joseph would willingly attest to that fact. But being surrounded by beautiful people and wondering to myself if I should trust Lukas or not, I found some undiscovered reserve of courage.

"Why did you ask me to have a drink with you tonight?" I asked, meeting Lukas's perfect blue eyes with my average brown ones. He kept his eyes locked on mine, which I thought was a good sign. After all, what dishonest person would look so intently into an innocent and vulnerable girl's eyes if he was about to lie to her?

"I think you're interesting and different from the other girls I meet in this industry," he said with such brutal honesty that any doubts I had about his intentions were swept away. "And you're beautiful," he added as a welcome afterthought.

I blushed, turning what I'm sure was a deep shade of scarlet and letting my eyes fall to the plastic table between us. I hadn't really managed to hold onto my courage for long, apparently.

"You think I'm beautiful?" I asked, like the self-conscious sixteen-year-old girl I was.

"I know you're beautiful," he said smoothly, putting his drink down and leaning over the awkward table so he could hold my free hand.

My head was spinning and the constant rhythmic beat in the background of the coffee shop suddenly seemed to match the pounding of my own heart in my ears. Lukas Leighton said I was beautiful—and not because some clever writer had scripted that for him. He said it because he actually thought that I, June Laurie, was beautiful. I didn't know how I should reply to a statement so unexpected and fantastically unreal. If I said "Thank you," it would seem conceited, but if I tried to play it off like I didn't agree I'd look like I was fishing for compliments. So instead, I just smiled at him. A big, happy, clumsy smile that spread easily over my face.

"This might be the best night ever," I said honestly, wondering why I sometimes let words escape my mouth before consulting my brain first. Lukas laughed his deep, perfect laugh and sat back in his chair, taking in his surroundings with mild interest but keeping me on his radar enough to send chills through my entire body.

....

I can't remember exactly what we talked about for the rest of the time we sat in those squishy armchairs. I did remember learning that Lukas didn't like any soda that wasn't clear because he thought it looked dirty, but that he'd drink coffee like a chain smoker goes through cigarettes. Personally I thought coffee looked way dirtier than Coke, but I definitely wasn't going to disagree with him. He told me about how he liked to sleep with his face buried in his pillow, but how it always gave him dreams that he was breathing underwater. I, naturally, thought this was adorable.

I told him about living with Gran and how it was a constant adventure. I told him how I loved coming home and finding weird concoctions in the kitchen, not for eating, but for slathering on my face. I told him about Joseph and how he was like the brother I never had. And then we talked about nothing in particular.

It was much easier to talk to someone as perfect as Lukas than I would have thought. He was so socially adept that there was never an awkward silence or a moment when we both tried to talk at the same time. It was like he made up for my lack of conversational timing and put me at ease. It was no surprise, then, that as we turned onto Pullman Avenue at ten o'clock that night, I was feeling fully in-tune with him. After talking with him for a few hours, it was obvious to me that he wasn't any of the things Candice and Benjamin said. They had obviously gotten a bad impression of him, because he was the epitome of a sweet, charming prince.

Lukas's motorcycle pulled noisily up my driveway before

he turned it off suddenly, drenching our surroundings in silence. I stepped off the bike and returned his helmet to him, feeling a little lightheaded at how perfectly everything was going. Lukas got off of his bike and stood close to me, looking down into my eyes with confident determination. I didn't want to get my hopes up or anything, but if I didn't know any better, I'd say he was revving up to kiss me goodnight.

I didn't want to ruin this perfect moment by saying something stupid, so I kept my mouth firmly shut and just smiled up into his face in the chilly night air. He leaned toward me just a bit and I let my eyes close slightly as I tilted my head up to meet his. I prepared myself for this perfect moment in this new perfect world with an intense anticipation.

But of course, we don't live in a perfect world now do we? We live in a world where good things happen to June Laurie, but great things are snatched away at the last second, which is exactly what happened when a very familiar male voice said, "You must be Lukas Leighton. It's *so* good to finally meet you. June's told me so much about you!"

Lukas and I backed away from each other quickly, as if we had been caught in some guilty act. It was funny to see that as suave and experienced as Lukas was, he still had that gut instinct to pull away when he thought he had been caught in a sneaky situation.

I was confused, at first, about what had happened, until I realized I was looking at Joseph standing right beside us, grinning up at Lukas like a star struck girl. Only he didn't look like he was actually pleased to meet him. He actually looked a bit odd. The vein on the side of his forehead that always showed up when Xani talked to him was standing out like a huge flashing Vegas sign at the moment, which didn't match his friendly tone and smile at all. It was an odd combination, to say the least.

I wasn't sure how I had missed his forest green VW Bug outside of my house when we had pulled up, until I remembered that I had pulled up with my arms wrapped around Lukas Leighton. I couldn't be expected to notice little details like Joseph's car when I was focused on something else so completely perfect.

"What are you doing here?" I asked through gritted teeth. It wasn't really fair of me to be mad at Joseph for having such horrible timing, but I couldn't help it. Would it have killed him to stay in his car for another minute? He wasn't socially inept, after all. I'm sure he could tell when two people were about to kiss.

Lukas looked over at me, mild confusion lining his beautiful face before a light bulb seemed to click.

"You must be Joseph," he said, looking my friend up and down. Joseph's fake smile faltered for a moment and he actually looked a bit startled and pleased that Lukas had known his name. But only for a moment. Seconds later, he was back to wearing his strained smile and trying to keep his vein from pulsing out of his head.

"I am," he answered without moving his mouth. Both boys continued to stare at each other in silence for a moment, exchanging some unspoken words between them. Joseph had to look up just slightly to meet Lukas's eyes since he was a bit shorter than him. "I just came to bring June her homework assignments," Joseph finally said, catching me off-guard since this was a total lie. My studio teacher had given me my homework assignments on set.

"That's nice of you," Lukas replied shortly, keeping his eyes locked on Joseph like a lion looking at a baby zebra. There was quiet again for a moment and I wondered if I had missed something. I could swear the two boys were holding an entire telepathic conversation that I hadn't been invited to join.

"Well, it was nice to meet you. I hope we'll see you again soon," Joseph said, breaking the awkward silence that had fallen. From my experience that night I had learned how artfully Lukas sidestepped any awkward silence, so the fact that the three of us were caught in one right now suggested something more was going on than I was aware of.

"Right," Lukas answered, flashing Joseph a winning smile before turning back to me. "I'll see you tomorrow June," he said with a softer smile. He leaned over and kissed my cheek, lingering there a moment longer than was normal for a cheek kiss. My face was instantly engulfed in the happy fire that seemed to accompany any closeness I shared with Lukas, and I grinned after him as he took off down the street on his motorcycle. Once he was out of sight and the giddiness had worn off, I turned to Joseph with a look of annoyance.

"What was that all about?" I asked with a frown.

"What? Suddenly I'm not allowed to stop by anymore just because you've started hanging out with *him*?" Joseph asked, the hurt obvious in his voice. This softened my rage.

"Of course you're still allowed to stop by," I said warmly, letting the sad sight of Joseph's hurt fill me with goodwill. "You just surprised me." I didn't mention the fact that he had definitely interrupted what would have been the most perfect kiss of my life. It didn't seem like something that would help him out of his sour mood.

Joseph looked down at the ground, almost guiltily, then back up at me. "Sorry I kind of ruined your moment," he said, sounding sincere despite how much he seemed to dislike Lukas. I shrugged my shoulders as if a kiss from Lukas wouldn't have completed my life, and as if he had simply interrupted some mundane activity.

"There probably wouldn't have been much of a moment anyway," I lied. To him and to me.

"Yeah," Joseph said, playing along.

"So what *are* you doing here so late?" I asked, curious as to why Joseph would show up at my house at ten o'clock at night when that was usually when I was getting ready for bed.

"It's Friday and I was bored. I thought maybe you'd be up for a late night movie since we don't have to get up early for school tomorrow," he offered, sounding more like his old self than he had in a while. "Plus, I had to inform you that Xani will be playing Juliet in the school play, and my life has officially become very awkward."

"Oh, I bet that's been fun," I said sarcastically, already imagining Xani showing up to Joseph's house at midnight saying they needed to practice their kissing scenes.

"Yeah, it's been a blast," he answered with a big, fake smile. "So that's why I need you to distract me tonight. No more worrying about Xani popping out of the bushes to attack me."

"It's just . . . I'm filming a really intense scene tomorrow and I still need to be on set at seven," I said, biting my bottom lip and letting my remorse show on my face. "I'm really sorry Joseph. But maybe we can hang out after that?"

His warm Joseph smile faltered for a moment, and he adopted the look of a child who just turned around to find that their parent wasn't standing next to them in the mall.

"That would be great," he said, though I could hear the disappointment in his voice. I knew it bothered Joseph that I didn't have as much time for him anymore, but he knew what a big opportunity this show was for me, so he'd be understanding, even if he didn't want to be. Besides, maybe having a little time apart would be good practice for when he disappeared on his mission for two years.

"Well, you probably need to get some rest, so I'll go," he said awkwardly, turning and heading back to his car by the curb.

"Hey Joseph," I called after him, causing him to stop and face me. I ran up and threw my arms around his neck, pulling him in for a tight hug. "Thank you for being so understanding about all of this," I said into his neck as I continued to hug him. His arms encircled my waist and he hugged me back, holding onto me like he'd never let go. "You're such a good friend."

I pulled away from him and looked into his warm, chocolate brown eyes, which held just a touch of sadness at the moment.

"I always will be."

CHAPTER 17

Having my hair and makeup done on Saturday morning was an unusual experience. For the first time since I'd joined the show, we weren't shooting at the studio. Instead, all of the cast and crew were inside a small old theatre downtown, trying to find places to squeeze equipment, the craft service table, and the makeup and wardrobe setup. Candice had been shoved into one of the theatre's smaller dressing rooms backstage; her makeup bags all sat overflowing onto the floor.

I sat patiently in the swiveling vanity chair and listened to Candice mumble about lack of respect and doing makeup in a sardine can. Miraculously, Ryan and Benjamin had somehow managed to find small, uncluttered spots on the floor to sit amidst the chaos of makeup brushes and bottled makeup sealer.

"Would you guys really rather be sitting on the floor in a crowded makeup room, when you could be in a nice, spacious, makeshift cafeteria meant specifically to cater to your every need?" I asked the pair as Candice was attempting to glue huge fake eyelashes onto my lids.

"Why would we want to be there when we could be here listening to the melodic and compassionate voice of Candice?" Benjamin asked seriously.

"Bite me," was Candice's automatic response.

"She loves me secretly," Benjamin remarked, turning his attention back to his phone.

"Do you guys even have a scene at the theatre?" I asked, not recalling ever seeing their characters at this location in the script.

"Just a short one. You know, gathering evidence and all that," Ryan answered. He had been staring at a box of injury pallets silently until this point, looking distracted.

"Hey, New Girl, how long can you hold your breath?" Benjamin suddenly asked, amusement playing in his eyes.

"Don't even start," Candice said instantly, her monotone voice full of menace.

"I was just asking," Benjamin replied, making his eyes wide and unassuming.

"The water tank doesn't actually lock, does it?" I asked, referring to the rather frightening scene I'd have to do today. It involved being dangled above a large water tank Edward and I used in our act, and then being dropped into it by our killer, who quickly shuts the lid, locking me inside and forcing Charles and Cutter to decide if they'll save me or go after him.

"These things do happen," he said mysteriously.

"Seriously Benjamin. I'm going to kick you out of the makeup room in two seconds if you don't shut it," Candice threatened. I knew Candice was my friend (though she'd never admit it) but I couldn't understand why she felt like standing up for me so much today. I wasn't complaining, but it was very out of character.

"Candice doesn't like water shoots," Ryan said by way of explanation. "They creep her out."

"Why?" I asked, my curiosity getting the better of me.

"Think about how much goes wrong during a shoot. Someone forgets to bring a battery for something. The gel over the light melts. The boom goes out. They forgot if they got coverage of some stupid little insert shot. I'm not trusting those people to get a water stunt right," she said with a tone of utter authority, giving a theatrical little shudder for effect.

While I had to admit she did have a good point, I could definitely have done without this lovely little thought being planted into my head right before I'd be plunging to my icy death.

"New Girl, you're looking a little pale . . . er," Benjamin said from his spot on the floor, actually sounding a bit serious.

"It's because you guys scared her about the stunt. Now she's going to freak out and forget how to open the box," Ryan said accusingly, not helping my nerves at all.

"You said the box doesn't lock," I almost shouted, looking at Candice with slight hysteria in my eyes, one eyelash dangling off of my lid like a madwoman.

"It doesn't. There's no way you could get stuck in there," she reassured me. "And even if you did, they're not filling it up all the way. The top of the tank is covered by metal and that part will be all air. So no matter what, you'll be able to breathe . . . for a reasonable amount of time"

I thought this over for a moment, trying to decide whether this was adequate consolation or not.

"If I drown today, I'm coming back to haunt all three of you," I threatened darkly.

....

I stood alone on the stage, waiting for everyone to get organized. Of course, when I say "alone," I mean as alone as you can be on a film set. I knew there was a mic on or around me somewhere, and if I spoke, the sound people would be able to hear my every word. That was one of the first lessons Gran taught me when I started acting—never say anything bad about someone you work with while you're on set, because someone is always listening. This thought made me reflect back on my conversations with Candice and the boys in the makeup trailer where we had analyzed Lukas's goodness (or lack thereof) for extensive periods of time. But I was almost positive no one had heard that—or if they had, they certainly weren't showing any signs.

I couldn't see much as I stared off into the audience, since the lights shining on me made it almost impossible to see anything. I sighed deeply and looked down at my costume. I was, again, in my ridiculous stage costume. My chest was cinched in so tightly that I thought I'd faint, and my fake eyelashes were so long that I looked like a porcelain doll. I had to admit that the skirt made of iridescent green feathers was pretty amazing, no matter how uncomfortable the rest of the costume made me feel. I brought my hand up to my wild, curly hair, feeling that it was snuggly pinned into submission and piled on top of my head. I had never acted in a period piece, but I was beginning to feel that this is what it must be like: all curls and corsets.

I closed my eyes for a moment in the heat of the lights and imagined how perfect Lukas and I would be in an Austen-esque film. Lukas would have those beautiful, manly sideburns and tight breeches the men always wore, and I'd wear some empire waist, flowing gown that would make me look like a princess. And of course we'd both have British accents, which would automatically make us infinitely more attractive.

I let myself get lost in this wonderful land of accents and lovely clothes until an actual British accent (or at least something that sounded pretty similar to one) brought me out of my reverie.

"Are you Imogen?" I heard the voice ask, directly in front of me. I opened my eyes and blinked a few times, wondering if maybe I had willed this man into life.

"Me?" I asked, though it was pretty obvious he was talking to me. There wasn't anyone else on the stage. He demonstrated this by looking around the stage once to verify that my question really was as stupid as it sounded.

"Yeah," he said simply, bringing his hand up to his mouth and beginning to bite his nail.

"Imogen?" I asked dimly, until I finally realized what he was talking about. I was pretty embarrassed by how long it took me. "Oh yeah, I play Imogen on the show. My name's

June," I said, extending my hand. He took it with his free, non-nail biting hand, and gave me a quick smile.

The boy continued to stand there, nibbling on his thumb and carefully observing the commotion happening offstage until I finally cleared my throat as an indication that he hadn't told me who he was.

"Rafe," he said, leaving me to wonder if he had just said his name, or somehow insulted me in some unknown English slang. Realizing that this boy would be no help in identifying exactly who he was, I tried to figure it out for myself. I was guessing, using my extensive knowledge of the script (or just my common sense) that he was playing Edward. We were, after all, the only two people in this scene if you didn't count the audience, and somehow, people never did.

Rafe was a tall, lanky boy—well over six feet, which put him several inches taller than Joseph, Lukas, and Ryan. He reminded me of a lit match. He was pale and towered over me, with copper colored hair that seemed to be untamable, even though I could smell the product Candice had used in it. He was wearing eyeliner, which I supposed was part of his character, and an old, tight-fitting, ratty gray suit that looked like it had seen better days. His eyes were a sort of amber color and never rested in one spot. It felt like he was a big ball of nervous energy, between his nail biting and shifting eyes.

"So, Rafe, are you playing Edward?" I asked out of politeness, even though I was pretty sure I already knew the answer. He looked over at me as if he didn't know I had been standing there the whole time.

"Yeah, I'll be the one dying here pretty soon," he said, slight amusement in his voice despite his anxiety-inducing habits.

"Have you been on a show like this before?" I pressed, feeling like there were a lot of awkward silences growing between us.

"I've been on *this* show before," he said in his thick (was it British?) accent.

"Wait . . . as Edward?"

"No. As various people. You'd be surprised how well they can get away with using the same actors for smaller roles. I've been on the show three times now, just wearing wigs or being mangled beyond recognition. That sort of thing," he said, dropping his hand away from his mouth as though tired of biting those nails. Instead, he began to tap out a drumbeat on his legs while he stood talking to me. This guy couldn't stop moving.

"Wow. I had no idea they did that on shows," I said, genuinely shocked.

"Not all shows, just ones who know they can get away with it and have the budget to hold onto an actor they like by changing up their look a bit. Of course, I can't be in big roles more than once or people would notice."

I pondered this new information for a moment, wondering if Bates had been talking about keeping me on the show as someone else. That would definitely be a pity. I liked playing Imogen Gentry. Leaving these thoughts for another time, I tried to continue making small talk with Rafe, though it was difficult since he, unlike Lukas Leighton, didn't bother trying to fill awkward silences.

"So, are you from England?" I asked, wondering why his accent didn't sound quite right. It was almost as if he were speaking with an English/Scottish accent, but one where he rolled his Rs excessively. Even that wasn't a good description. It sounded more like rolling your Rs, but only once. Either way, I had no idea where he was from.

He looked at me for a moment, one coppery eyebrow raising into the mess that was his shaggy hair. "England?" he asked, as if I were crazy.

"Well, it's just . . . you have a British accent," I offered, trying to recover from however I had insulted him.

"I'm from South Wales," he said making me feel like this had been more obvious than the fact that the sky is blue. "And people don't have British accents. They have Welsh accents . . . or English, or Scottish, or whatever you'd like.

'British' is a bit of an all-encompassing word."

"Oh, yeah . . . of course," I said, attempting to recover from this awkward situation. I wasn't a stupid person, but I definitely put myself into situations where I often looked pretty dumb—right now being the perfect example. I decided not to mention the fact that I had absolutely no idea where Wales was and had only heard of it because of Princess Diana.

"So, you landed yourself a pretty comfortable gig on this show, eh?" Rafe asked, ending his pant leg drum solo and starting to run his fingers absently through his hair. I could now see why, despite the product Candice had used, his hair was standing on end. I got the feeling this guy would make Woody Allen and Jim Carrey seem calm and relaxed.

"Yeah, I hope so. I'm really loving it so far," I answered, looking at the disappearing box behind us that would soon become Rafe's coffin.

"Rafe, you look perfect," I heard Bates call out from some unseen spot in the audience. Frankly, if I tried to look past the blinding lights, all I saw were spots in my burned eyes.

Rafe gave a little two-fingered salute to our unseen director and walked to the edge of the stage, presumably for further instruction. Not knowing what else to do, I followed suit. He knelt down (a pretty impressive sight to behold when all six-foot something of him bent in half) and muttered something under his breath that I didn't quite catch. I decided to keep playing the politely interested co-star and pretended not to notice.

"So, Rafe, we'll have you do this how we originally discussed. Forget about what we said this morning," Bates said, stealing a quick glance in my direction that caught me off guard. Had they talked about *me* this morning? Was that a bad thing?

"June, you don't need to say anything. Just be very showy and help Rafe into the box. Once he's in, give a few beats before you try to open it again, and then act like it's stuck. He needs to be in there almost a minute," Bates instructed.

"We'll shoot him actually falling out of the box later today after he's gotten his makeup done, but we'll just have you keep going so it doesn't look too jumpy."

I was pretty sure I understood what he was trying to say, so I nodded silently, assuming that if I did it wrong they'd just stop me and have me re-shoot anyway. I was becoming much more relaxed on set, which was a nice change for my stomach's sake. Rafe and I stood up and walked back over to the disappearing man box in silence.

"Also, it's carbon monoxide poisoning now, not arsenic," Bates called out, somewhere behind the lights. "At least, I think that's what they said."

Rafe gave a little full body shake, presumably to help him get ready to start filming, then turned and gave me the biggest, toothiest smile I'd ever seen. "Showtime," he said. Apparently he was very excited about filming.

Bates called out a few instructions to other crewmembers and then set the shot up, instructing us to get to our first positions. I stood beside Rafe, slightly left of center stage, and fluffed the feathers on my skirt up a bit. We waited a moment as Bates got caught up in some conversation with the director of photography, and I turned to Rafe, suddenly confused by what appeared to be an empty audience.

"Where are the audience members?" I asked, worried that I was the only one who had noticed this huge missing piece of the puzzle.

"They'll probably shoot the audience scenes later, if they show them at all," Rafe said in a muffled voice, having gone back to biting his nails again. Apparently waiting a few seconds for Bates to call action was enough for Rafe to slip back into his easily awakened boredom.

"You two ready?" Bates finally called out. We both nodded, not mentioning that we had been ready for a while. "Camera?"

"Speeding."

"Sound?"

"Speeding."

"Action."

Rafe walked grandly to the middle of the stage, his presence now anything but small. He grinned out at the empty audience and bright lights before giving a majestic sweep of his hand, indicating toward the disappearing man trick. I followed quickly behind him, trying to look like I had any idea what I was doing. I definitely thought we would spend more time blocking this scene out, or that Bates would at least tell me what he wanted me to do.

"Ladies and gentlemen," Rafe began—rather stereotypically, I thought. "Tonight you have seen many a strange wonder. You've experienced the excitement of my lovely, levitating lady," he exclaimed in his thick accent, bowing slightly in my direction. Apparently I was the levitating lady. I looked out at the "audience" and put my hands up in a "ta-da" gesture.

"You've felt the suspense of sawing this sweet supporter clean in half." He once again gave me a little bow. It was starting to sound like Imogen Gentry really got beaten up during this show. No wonder Cutter and Charles suspected her.

"But now, prepare yourselves to dive into the dramatic denouement of the disappearing man!" he exclaimed. I hadn't read any of these lines in the script and I wondered if it was Edward or Rafe who was taken to speaking in alliterations.

Attempting to keep a straight face after Rafe's ridiculous rant (apparently now I was thinking in alliterations), I followed him to the large painted box at center stage. He spun the box around to show that there was no way he'd be able to escape through the back and then stepped in, giving a hearty wink in the general direction of the camera before I closed the door on him.

And there I was—standing alone in the middle of the stage with a camera and millions of lights pointed at me. I had absolutely no direction to go on except, "make a few gestures and give him about a minute in the box."

Trying to interpret those directions as best I could, I

looked back out at the audience with a mysterious smile on my face . . . or at least, what I hoped looked like a mysterious smile. I presented the box, looking something like Vanna White, and tried to do a little spin in front of it so that I could get to the other side and hold my arms out like an idiot. Unfortunately, that didn't happen. Instead, my toe caught on the uneven wooden floor halfway through my spin and I came tumbling into a heap on the floor right in front of the box. And of course the best part was that it was all caught on tape. Lucky me.

"Cut," I heard Bates yell from behind the camera. There were a few scattered snickers, but I couldn't make out where they were coming from. Then Rafe opened the disappearing man trick and poked his head out.

"What happened?" he asked Bates, not even seeing me on the floor. It didn't take long though, and he soon emitted a loud, rumbling laugh.

"Thank you," I said sarcastically, my cheeks feeling like they were on fire. At least Lukas hadn't been here to see that. He probably would have been polite enough to not laugh (unlike Rafe), but I still wouldn't have wanted to trip like a clumsy oaf in his presence.

"Are you okay, June?" Bates asked from his mysterious position behind the lights. At least he sounded like he was trying to be sympathetic, even though I could hear the smile in his voice.

"I'm fine. Sorry. The floor is uneven," I mumbled, trying to pretend like nothing had happened. I quickly got to my feet (with no help from Rafe, I'd like to point out) and dusted off my skirt, relieved that I hadn't ruined the feathers.

We reset and shot the scene a few more times after finally receiving some direction from our director. You'd think, given his title, he would have told me what he wanted me to do in the first place, but no such luck, I guess. I messed up a few more times, much to Rafe's amusement, but we finally got the scene captured. Bates was as happy as a kid at Christmas by the end of it.

I was anxious to get back into the cramped confines of the makeshift makeup room so I could tell Candice how embarrassing the whole ordeal had been. I quickly checked in with the assistant director to make sure I knew what my next scene was and then scampered away to see Candice.

The dusty and hot makeup room was piled, floor to ceiling, with Candice's makeup cases and men. More men than usual, that is. Benjamin and Ryan sat on the floor texting like fiends, while Rafe, who had somehow managed to slip past me unnoticed, was sitting in the makeup chair with Candice fawning over him in a disconcerting manner.

"Don't give Candice flowers and candy to woo her," Benjamin began saying to no one in particular, "Give her fake blood and liquid latex. Apparently I've been playing this all wrong." He looked up at me, indicating that I was the one he'd been talking to all along.

"Looks like you'll have to rethink your strategy," I said knowingly as I picked my way through the piles of makeup to sit next to Ryan. I stumbled slightly over a powder brush and Ryan instantly sprang to his feet, surprising me by his gentlemanly behavior.

"Careful, June, the floor is a little uneven," he said with a smirk, making me forget my mental impression that he was a gentleman.

"It *was* uneven," I muttered under my breath, taking a seat beside him.

"So, how was your date with Mr. Wonderful?" Ryan asked casually. Benjamin gave him an odd look that I couldn't quite decipher, but he ignored Benjamin, so I did too, focusing on the more worrisome fact that they somehow knew about my date with Lukas.

"What do you mean?" I asked cautiously, wondering if there was any point in pretending like I didn't know what he was talking about.

"June, this is a film set. You can't keep a secret here for long. It's just too many people, too close together," he explained.

"For *way* too long," Candice added, sounding pretty happy despite her sour comment. I figured it had something to do with the blisters she was now applying to Rafe's face.

"It was fine. We just went out for coffee," I said, purposefully picking up a discarded magazine on the floor and holding it up over my face.

"You don't drink coffee," Benjamin pointed out, never taking his eyes off of his phone.

"I had hot chocolate," I answered, keeping all of my responses short so that I wouldn't be implicating myself in any way.

"And what happened after that?" Rafe asked with sarcastic enthusiasm, obviously not happy that they were all so interested in my love life when there were other topics to be discussed, like nail biting and anxious twitches.

"I went home," I said.

"Did you invite him up to your place so you could 'slip into something a little more comfortable'?" Ryan asked, his voice lighthearted.

"Yeah. I introduced him to my grandma who I live with because I'm sixteen years old and in high school, slipped into something more comfortable, and then told him to hurry up and have his way with me because I had to be in bed by curfew. It was a pretty steamy night," I said dryly.

"I see your point," Ryan said, breaking the awkward silence that followed my little story.

"That sounds like a good night to me," Rafe exclaimed, giving his two cents in a thick accent.

"I don't know why you went out with him in the first place," Candice remarked in her familiar monotone.

"New Girl is obviously too blinded by his charms to see his true evil, Candice. We can't fault her for that," Benjamin said with a sad, slow shake of his head. "Maybe a dunk in the tank will do her some good."

I groaned audibly at the reminder. I had been doing a pretty good job of letting myself forget about my little "stunt" throughout the morning, but there was no avoiding it now. I only had a few more scenes to shoot that day before I took the plunge, and I prayed with all my might that the tank didn't somehow lock once I was in there. I told myself over and over in my head that there was no way this stunt could go wrong, but somehow I wasn't very convincing.

CHAPTER 18

The thick, itchy rope wrapped around my wrists did little to keep me dangling high above the water tank. In fact, I was pretty sure it didn't do anything at all. Hidden strategically behind my hair and beneath my sparkly costume was a body harness that reminded me of a very revealing bathing suit made of thick straps. While the harness did distribute my weight pretty evenly, it was still amazingly uncomfortable. I had no doubt in my mind that if I weren't a "nobody," they'd have a stunt double do this scene for me. But as it was, there I stayed, dangling above a tank full of icy cold water and slowly losing feeling in my legs (which I was pretty sure wasn't supposed to be happening).

They had lifted me up above the water tank at the very last second when they were ready to film so that I wouldn't be dangling there long, but after a few takes this painful position was beginning to lose its appeal. I closed my eyes against the headache that had been slowly forming and silently cursed the itch on my cheek that I couldn't scratch with my hands suspended above my head.

"Are you doing all right up there, June?" Bates called from somewhere below.

"Fine," I mumbled around the damp cloth acting as my "gag," trying to sound like a good sport when I was actually quite unhappy with my current predicament. If I'm being honest, though, the dangling above a water tank thing wasn't the worst part of it. The worst part was that after we captured this scene, I'd be dropped into the tank below, have the lid shut over my head, and pray that something didn't go wrong with the stunt.

The stunt coordinator told me before they tied me up that if need be, they could empty the tank in less than ten seconds through the grate in the bottom. While this did comfort me a little, it gave rise to new and more complex worries. What if I panicked in the tank when there wasn't anything wrong, and they emptied it in response? Then I'd have to get dried off and do the scene all over, subsequently costing the show hundreds of dollars in time spent because I'd freaked out over nothing.

I hadn't ever realized how stressful acting was. You didn't just have to worry about lines. You had to worry about how much you were costing the studio every time you made a mistake, especially with a water scene. I always loved watching bloopers on DVDs with Joseph, but at that moment, dangling above a tank of freezing cold water that they had sworn was room temperature, the concern about creating my own bloopers made me feel slightly nauseous.

"Okay, I think we have the scene where we want it up to the drop, so this next shot we're actually letting you go June," Bates called up to me.

"Sounds good," I lied around the gag cloth.

"Now just remember, when you hit the water, don't panic," he said slowly, making me wonder if my worries were that evident on my face. At least acting scared wouldn't be too difficult. "The lid will shut and you hit the glass and pretend to push up on the lid until Lukas runs over and gets you out."

The way he said everything made it seem much easier than I was imagining it. If I could just see it as a list in my head, I might actually be able to pull it off.

"The most important thing is what we see when you first

drop in the tank. We can shoot your underwater shots all day long, but the first scene where you go from being dry to wet we want to get just once, if we can."

Oh great. No pressure.

Bates called action and Lukas, Will, and Jim Little (who was playing the theatre owner in love with me) all sprang into action, shouting at each other and making threats while waving guns like crazy people. I tuned them out for the most part, getting into the zone while allowing myself to look distraught and helpless, like a damsel in distress.

I was vaguely aware of Jim's cue line about me making a lovely corpse when I felt the click behind my back. The mechanism holding me suspended in midair released and there was a moment where nothing happened and I wondered if the stunt had broken. I felt everyone's eyes turn to me, cast and crew, before the sickening feeling of falling finally hit me and air rushed past my head. I let out a little involuntary scream which was muffled by the gag in my mouth, and then hit the water as Will and Jim ran out of the shot for the chase scene that would be spliced with my rescue scene.

At first everything was silent (and freezing, might I add) when I hit the water. All of the shouted lines turned into nothing more than thick, heavy words muffled by the water. Then I felt a thousand little bubbles rush up my body, making a mad dash for the surface in the icy silence.

And then I heard it.

The dull thud of the heavy metal lid closing above my head.

My eyes shot open wide, and I became terrified that I would drown right then and there. The world outside of the tank looked glassy and blurry all at the same time ,and I could see a dark shape rushing toward me. I assumed it was Lukas, but if the stunt coordinator had decided to come rescue me early, I wouldn't have minded that either.

Remembering that I had to do some actual acting, I slammed my bound hands repeatedly against the glass wall in front of me. I looked around hysterically, beginning to actually believe that I was Imogen Gentry, trapped in a water tank and about to die. Some of the long feathers of my skirt floated up around my face, making me feel even more claustrophobic, while the tiny fishing weights holding the rest of my skirt down made me feel like I would be pulled down to the bottom of the tank, preventing me from swimming to the surface at the end of the scene.

In reality, the tank was only about seven feet tall, so I'd only have to push off the bottom, not "swim" to the top. But this was a fact that was lost on me in the moment.

I could feel my air running out as Lukas pretended to throw all of his weight into opening the heavy lid. I knew he was eventually supposed to grab an axe and cut the lock holding the lid on, but surely they didn't want me to stay in here until he finally did that, right? As it was, I had already been in the tank for about thirty seconds, which I realize doesn't sound like a lot of time, but when your hands are tied, your mouth is gagged, and you're being dragged down by tiny little weights, it feels *a lot* longer.

I saw Lukas run to the side of the stage, presumably to get the axe, but I didn't think I'd be able to wait for him to open the tank. I could feel my body involuntarily swallowing, trying to force me to take a breath against my will as I continued to hit the glass walls around me. Small pinpricks began to make their way up my arms and legs, but I couldn't tell if that was the feeling returning to my limbs or the first signs that I was about to be part of a freak on-set accident.

Finally psyching myself out enough, I pushed my feet off the grated floor, my arms above my head and ready to open the lid. At first when they made contact with the metal ceiling of the tank, nothing happened, and the dread took all of one second to spread through me. I saw a large bubble escape my mouth as I opened it in shock, but only a moment later the lid lifted seemingly by itself, letting the welcoming sight of studio lights stream in. A strong hand reached into the tank and grabbed the rope around my wrists, pulling me to the surface of the tank.

Water sprayed everywhere as I tried to breath out of my mouth, still covered by the cloth gag. I began to cough from the unexpected barrier and quickly tore the annoyance away from my face so that it dangled limply around my neck. Continuing to sputter in an unattractive manner, I felt a warm hand touch my ice-cold cheek.

"Are you okay, June?" Lukas asked, his voice full of concern and his face the perfect picture of a prince charming who'd just rescued his princess. Okay. Maybe that was a bit much, but that's still what it felt like right at that moment. Lukas had been the one to pull me out of the tank. "I would have opened the lid sooner, but you held your breath a lot longer than they expected you to, so they told me to go grab the axe instead just in case we could get that shot in. I'm sorry I didn't just open it," he said, making me want to kiss him right then and there. Of course—everything he did made me want to kiss him, so that wasn't saying much.

"It's all right. I'm fine," I sputtered, shaking from the cold water and complete terror I had experienced moments before. "I'm just glad you opened the lid. I couldn't get it open for some reason."

"Yeah, it's pretty heavy," he explained, though I wasn't sure if this made me feel better that there was nothing wrong with the lid or worse that even when it wasn't broken, I couldn't get out of it myself. Lukas allowed his hand to continue cupping my cheek as he gazed at me with a perfect smile.

"Can you please not touch her? I have to fix her makeup," Candice said, suddenly beside us, though neither of us had seen her approach. Her tone was dry and flat as usual, but I could sense an uncommon menace in it. Lukas sighed, looking unabashedly annoyed with Candice before rolling his eyes and walking over to Will Trofeos and Jim Little, who had just reappeared on the stage.

"Tool," Candice muttered under her breath at Lukas's retreating form.

"He pulled me out of the water tank," I said in a shaky voice, still unsteady from my little scare.

"Yeah, and he got in the way of a dozen other people who were rushing to get you out of the tank too," she countered in a hushed voice. "It's not like he rescued a baby from a burning building. He opened a lid." Candice looked over her shoulder at Lukas, who was watching her closely even though he appeared to be talking to Will.

"He's still a nice guy," I attempted as Candice removed the black makeup that had migrated from my eyes down my cheeks. I could only imagine how scary I looked, freezing with makeup melting all over my face and my lips trembling from how cold I was.

"Haven't you ever heard that sociopaths are some of the most charming people?"

"I hardly think he's a sociopath," I answered defensively.

"Oh, I don't know. Manipulative, promiscuous, superficial charm, inflated sense of self. Sounds about right to me," she responded, her mouth twitching in the corner, almost like she was smiling.

"Fine, if you find me murdered and hidden in a crawl space, you can name him as the number one suspect," I said sarcastically. "But until that happens, you should at least try to be nice to him."

"Yeah, that'll happen," she said with a scoff as she finished touching up my makeup. "Don't drown," she remarked as she walked away, shooting a dirty look in Lukas's direction. He walked back over to me the second she had left the stage to perch behind the cameras once more.

"What's with her?" he asked, looking more amused than angry by Candice's obviously cold feelings toward him.

"She's having a bad day," I lied. I didn't want any conflict between them, but I also didn't want Candice to lose her job just because she didn't know how to keep her emotions at bay.

"Apparently," he said with an eyebrow raise. He shook his head, presumably shaking off whatever bad feeling he was having toward Candice, and then turned to me with a winning smile and said, "Ready for another go?"

....

Lukas and I walked through the silent, dark parking lot of the theatre after work that day. I was surprised that there weren't any paparazzi surrounding the building, although Bates had told everyone to keep quiet about the location of the shoot. Apparently whenever *Forensic Faculty* shot outside of the studio, they had a bit of a crowd control issue. But at that moment, walking alone with Lukas, I was glad for the absence of any spectators, including Gran, who was apparently late picking me up.

Lukas and I stopped at his motorcycle. He leaned against it, looking like an angel, and I tried not to let my giddiness show on my face. Here I was, standing alone with Lukas Leighton after having spent an entire day with him fussing over me and making sure I felt safe in the water tank. It didn't get much better than that.

Lukas pushed a few stray curls behind my ear. My dark curly hair had finally dried after much persuasion from Candice and the blow dryer. That girl could somehow work wonders with my hair. She had managed to coax it back into the big glossy curls she had created before, much to my amazement.

"You were really brave today," Lukas said softly, letting his hand rest on my jawbone. I was pretty sure being this close to Lukas was exactly what being hypnotized would feel like. My head grew fuzzy and all I could do was smile stupidly at him. It was like being given laughing gas at the dentist. Everything just felt perfect and happy. A bus could mow me down right then and there, and I would simply giggle about it.

"All I had to do was hold my breath," I said, trying to sound modest even though I was pretty proud of myself for making it through that horrible stunt.

"You can sound humble all you want, but I know it was a scary thing to do," Lukas whispered, the softness of his voice making the situation seem much more intimate. I shivered slightly at the lines his thumb was tracing on my cheek, and he stood up to his full height, taking a step toward me. "Are you cold?" he asked.

"A bit," I replied, wondering what exactly he was going to do to warm me up. All he really needed to do was look at me and I'd burst into flames, but the fact that he was getting closer and closer to me definitely worked too.

Lukas pressed his body against mine, his strong form feeling warm and unfamiliar. He wrapped his arms around me and pulled me into him so that my head rested on his chest. I could hear his heart beating in a slow and steady rhythm. Strong and self-assured, just like him. My heart, on the other hand, was doing its best to imitate a hummingbird's as it pounded embarrassingly fast against my chest.

I closed my eyes and took a deep breath, trying to memorize every perfect detail of this moment. I felt Lukas inhale, as if he was preparing to say something, but his words caught in his throat and he pulled away from me, looking over my shoulder. I could see his face illuminated suddenly by the familiar (and unwelcome) sight of headlights.

"Gran," I breathed, disappointment lining my features.

"Actually, I think it's your friend," Lukas said, his voiced filled with something that I'll call disappointment. At least, I'm hoping that's what it was.

"My friend?" I asked, a bit slow on the uptake, having just had my brain scrambled by Lukas's unfathomable perfection.

"Joe. Right?"

"Joseph," I corrected automatically, more out of habit than an actual desire for Lukas to get his name right.

Turning reluctantly away from Lukas, I could see the well-known sight of Joseph's green VW Bug. He seemed to have developed a bad habit of showing up at the most inconvenient times lately.

"Hey June," Joseph said as he walked briskly toward Lukas and me. "Annette had something come up, so I said I'd pick you up from the shoot. Sorry I'm late."

"That's fine," I said with a sigh, unable to completely hide my exasperation over another interrupted moment with Lukas. I turned back to him with an apologetic look on my face. "Thanks for walking me out." Lukas smiled warmly at me, glancing over my shoulder at Joseph for a moment as he did so. It wasn't an uncomfortable, "why is this guy watching us so closely?" kind of look, but more of a "yes, I see you standing there and I really don't care" glance.

"I won't see you for more than a week if we wait until the next episode starts shooting," he said with a hint of sorrow in his voice. "So let's make sure we don't wait that long." He added the last part so quietly that I wondered if Joseph had heard it at all.

"Okay," I managed to whisper, a grin spreading across my face.

"See you later Joe," Lukas said.

"Joseph," both Joseph and I said in unison, though Joseph sounded annoyed while I just sounded dazed.

Lukas pulled me into a warm hug and gave me a lingering kiss on the cheek, nestling my ear with his nose and causing my body to break out in goosebumps from head to toe.

"Goodnight June," he said before turning away and making his grand exit on his motorcycle. I stared after him for a minute, in a complete happiness-induced fog.

"Anyway," Joseph said loudly, obviously trying to snap me out of my haze, "Are you tired from working all day, or are you up for a little adventure?"

I could hear the falseness in his voice. He wasn't using his normal, comfortable Joseph voice, but the one he used when he was acting comfortable in an uncomfortable situation. This, of course, made me feel horrible. Joseph and I had been attached at the hip since birth, and now he was using his acting voice with me. I didn't think things had gotten *that* weird between us, but I knew I had to fix it quickly. I walked over to him and linked my arm with his.

"Allons-y!" I said in my best French accent (which was pretty horrible) as we walked toward his car.

CHAPTER 19

I adjusted the full skirt of my knee length navy blue lace dress around my legs as Joseph drove on the freeway toward Simi Valley. He had been silent most of the drive, but I could see him mentally talking himself out of his bad mood. That was the benefit of having known each other for so long—I could read Joseph like a book. Right now the title of his book was, "I'm mad at June because she has a new friend she's spending more time with than me, but I shouldn't really be mad at her because this is a great opportunity for her, so I'm going to be rational and start talking to her again: The Joseph Cleveland story."

"So, where is this big adventure going to take us tonight?" I asked, deciding to help out a bit with breaking the ice. After all, I could see where Joseph was coming from. If he got a part on a big show and decided to suddenly start spending all of his time with Joann Hoozer (who I wasn't very fond of), I'd be pretty mad too. In fact, I think I'd be a lot less friendly than Joseph was, so he earned brownie points for trying so hard.

"If I told you, it wouldn't be much of an adventure, now would it?" he asked cryptically, his old self shining through his cautious exterior. I almost had to wonder if he was thinking *I* was going to be weird around him and he was just bracing himself for new, high-maintenance June.

We had gotten off the freeway and were driving through surface streets in an area I wasn't familiar with. A lot of the streetlights were out, casting the sidewalks in an ominous darkness.

"Have you brought me here to kill me?" I joked.

"Not quite," he replied, pulling into a dirt lot full of cars, litter, and children running around with balloons tied to their wrists. We had arrived at a large (normally empty) park that was currently filled with carnival rides, tents, and booths. The sugary smell of cotton candy hit my nose, mixing with the buttery aroma of freshly popped popcorn.

"A carnival!" I exclaimed, my face lighting up. Joseph knew me so well. "I didn't even know there was a carnival going on right now."

"That's what makes it such a surprise," Joseph replied with a knowing grin. He seemed to be pretty much back to his old self, much to my relief.

Walking through the carnival was a surreal experience after having spent so much time dressed up in old-fashioned vaudeville clothing. The plum and cranberry colored striped tents surrounding us were all bursting with such an array of noises and smells that my senses were going crazy. Orange paper lanterns were strung between the tall oak trees above us, casting jittery shadows on the grass underfoot. All around there were bubble machines, making the air thick with shiny, soapy bubbles looking like glass orbs drifting on the wind.

"This is perfect," I said happily.

"I'm glad you like it," Joseph replied, his face glowing with pride at his discovery.

We didn't talk about the whole "Lukas" issue once as we went on the Ferris wheel, ran through the fun house, and did everything you were supposed to do at a proper carnival. I picked at a large globe of pink cotton candy as we walked through the rows of booths selling garlands for your hair and other things you'd think were a good idea at a carnival but would get home and never wear again.

"Do you hear that?" Joseph asked as we neared the end of the booths and came to a darker area in the park, thick with oak trees. I strained my ears for a moment.

"The music?" I asked. I could hear the distinct sound of organ music traveling on the wind. It had been faint at first, but now that I recognized what it was, it somehow seemed more obvious.

"I think it's getting louder," Joseph remarked, his eyes focused on nothing in particular in front of him, as if he could sense where the music was coming from without seeing the source. "Must be an organ grinder walking around," he concluded, coming out of his daze to look at me. We were leaning against a massive oak tree, separate from the rest of the chaos of the carnival, but still watching it like an old favorite movie.

"Thanks for bringing me here," I said. "Today was kind of hectic and scary . . . it's nice to do something normal with a friend and not worry about if I'm messing it up or costing the studio a bunch of money or anything like that."

"I'm glad you still want to do this kind of stuff with me," he answered, sliding down the tree trunk so that he was sitting on the soft grass. I joined him on the ground, letting our shoulders touch as we leaned against each other. "School has been horrible without you. I think Xani's becoming more aggressive without you to scare her off."

I covered my mouth with the huge ball of cotton candy to hide my laugh. "I'm so sorry," I said with a giggle. "How many times has she made you rehearse your kissing scenes?"

Joseph shuddered next to me at the question. "Oh my gosh, June, you have no idea. It's been like running across the 405 during rush hour and trying not to get hit! She follows me everywhere," he exclaimed, his eyes wide and his smile bright. This was the Joseph I loved so much—the fun Joseph who could talk to me about anything and turn it into a joke.

I grabbed his face and turned it toward me, making his lips pucker out like a fish as I squeezed his cheeks. "Hmmm, your lips *are* looking a bit chapped," I joked, releasing his face and turning back to watch a pair of clowns walk past us toward their cast trailer.

"It's my burden to bear," he said with mock sadness, shaking his head slowly. "I have such a hard time keeping women from falling in love with me."

"Well, if it gets to be too much to handle, I'll come rough her up for you."

"Yeah, because I could see you 'roughing' someone up. What are you going to do? Lillian Gish her to death?" he asked with a laugh.

"Something like that," I replied, hitting him lightly on the head with my cotton candy.

"Well, if that's how you intend to fight, you'll need all the blessings you can get. Let's get you home so you don't sleep through church tomorrow."

"Yes sir," I said with a mock salute. "And Joseph just think—in three weeks, the play will be over and Xani won't have a good excuse to attack you anymore . . . though I'm not sure that'll stop her."

"Thank you for those comforting words, June," Joseph replied, helping me to my feet so that he could take me home.

CHAPTER 20

It was an entire week before I finally saw Lukas again, but that didn't stop me from thinking about him and all of his perfection twenty-four/seven. The rest of the cast continued to film scenes throughout the week, but I had finished up my last scene for that episode on Saturday, and therefore had more than a week until I started working on the next episode.

I was slightly shocked when he actually texted me a week before, asking if I would spend the next Saturday with him. It took me all of two seconds to reply with an adamant yes. Now, as I clung to his strong form while he drove his motorcycle through the city, I replayed my week's worth of Lukas Leighton fantasies.

Since Lukas had picked me up at noon, we had already eaten lunch, done some shopping, and strolled through the park. I wasn't sure what else he would want to do, or how long it would be before he got bored with me, but he seemed perfectly content to continue driving me around the city just to walk around and talk. I did my best to remember all of the bad things Joseph, Candice and Benjamin had said about Lukas, but no matter how rational I tried to be, that image of Lukas didn't match up with how he'd treated me. He didn't stand to gain much from being nice or spending so much time with me, and yet he went out of his way to do both. It didn't seem like the actions of a person who was really a scumbag.

Lukas pulled up to a little sidewalk café and helped me off his motorcycle, not letting go of my hand as we took a seat at a small table. I was vaguely aware of the fact that everyone was watching us (or Lukas, at least) but I was so caught up in his bright blue eyes that I hardly noticed the stares.

"So, when do you start filming the next episode? I've hated not having you on set this week," Lukas said, holding my hand over the small round table. I rested my free hand on my chin and kept my eyes locked on his, attempting to not be so obviously infatuated. (And failing miserably, I might add.)

"I think I shoot my first scene on Monday," I answered, glad that I'd get to see Lukas soon no matter what. Who said dating people you work with is a bad idea? It just meant that even when Lukas and I were too busy with work to make plans outside of shoots, we'd still be able to see each other.

"That's good. At least now I won't have to make excuses to see you," he said with a winning smile, still holding my hand and turning me into a puddle with every word he said. The sun was setting now, and I was surprised by how late it had gotten. I could have sworn Lukas had just picked me up a few hours ago.

As the waiter came to our table and took our order, I could feel my phone buzzing in my purse. I glanced down at it but didn't pick it up to see who was calling, not wanting Lukas to think I was being rude.

"So June, what do you think you'll do after you're done on the show? Are you going to keep auditioning for TV, or do you think you'll try to move toward movies?" he asked, sounding almost like a reporter for a newspaper.

My phone buzzed twice, indicating that I had a new voicemail.

"I don't know. Honestly, I think I'll audition for any part I can get. I'm not too picky. Although I'd love to be in a movie," I answered dreamily. I didn't know for sure (obviously, since I'd never been in a movie) but it seemed like movie sets were much more glamorous than TV sets. But then again, what did I know? Until I'd been on *Forensic Faculty*, I hadn't known they had stand-ins just to test the lighting. "What about you? Do you have any big movie plans coming up?"

Lukas's face broke into an easy smile at my question, the light from the candle on our table casting an orange glow over his skin. The sun had now completely set, leaving us surrounded by the blue night, broken up only by the orange globe of light cast by our candle. I felt my phone buzz again—another call coming through—and I considered checking to see who it was. That is, until Lukas squeezed my hand and reminded me exactly why I was there.

"I've only done a few films, but I'm trying to move away from TV," he said with a shrug, as if this would be the easiest thing in the world. I guess when you're Lukas Leighton, life just works itself out for you.

"Do you have any auditions lined up?" I asked, genuinely interested in what his plans were for the future. A small part of my mind was trying to work out who would be calling me so many times in a row. I could feel a small nagging at the back of my mind, as if I had forgotten something obvious and important, but I couldn't quite place what it was. Something told me it had to do with my phone, which was now buzzing again.

"I've got one for an epic action movie that should be fun," he said offhandedly. "*They* asked *me* to audition, so I'm not too worried about it."

"Uh-huh," I answered, now completely distracted by the fourth phone call I was receiving.

"Are you okay?" Lukas asked, obviously taking note of my lack of interest in his story.

"What? Yeah, sorry it's just . . . I'm really sorry. I don't mean to be rude, but I just need to check my phone really fast," I said.

"That's fine," Lukas said, though I could see that he was slightly annoyed that I wasn't enraptured by his story.

As I slid my phone open, the screen read *four missed calls.* All four of my calls were from Joseph, which gave me a sick feeling in my stomach. I had definitely forgotten something important, but it just wasn't coming to me for some reason. Joseph had also left me two voicemails and four text messages. Not wanting to be completely rude to Lukas, I opted for reading the texts rather than listening to the voicemails. As I read my four missed messages, a feeling of horrible guilt engulfed me.

8:04 PM: *June, I'm at your house all dressed up and ready to go. You'd better not be getting your hair done or something ridiculous like that.*

8:07 PM: *Would it be cheesy if I bought you a corsage for Homecoming? Not that I did. Because I'm not cheesy at all . . . I swear.*

8:10 PM: *Annette just said she thought you were out with Lukas. You're not still out with him are you?*

8:20 PM: *June, did you forget about me?*

Reading Joseph's last message to me, I could feel the blood draining from my face.

I had forgotten about him.

I hadn't just forgotten about him—I had completely stood him up. He had made such a big deal about buying my Homecoming ticket and making sure everything would be perfect, and I hadn't even had the decency to show up.

"Are you okay?" Lukas asked, pulling me from my mental crisis. "You don't look so good."

"I need to get home. As fast as you can possibly get me there," I said urgently, throwing my phone into my bag and jumping up from the table.

"So, no dinner, then?" Lukas asked, following quickly behind me as I tore through the café toward his motorcycle.

....

It felt like it took hours to get back to Simi Valley from Los Angeles, and I was helpless to make the trip go faster. I tried to think of something to tell Joseph when I got there, but there wasn't anything I could say. I had completely forgotten about him and there was no way around it. I was a horrible friend to the boy who'd been my best friend since before I could crawl. My phone buzzed a few more times as Lukas drove not nearly fast enough on the freeway toward my house, and I could only imagine what these new texts from Joseph said.

When we finally pulled onto Pullman Avenue, I couldn't decide if I was relieved or terrified by the fact that Joseph's green VW Bug was still parked outside of my house. The whole ride home had convinced me how little I could say to Joseph to apologize for what I'd done, and I'd half hoped that I could take the coward's way out and not have to face him just yet. But as Lukas pulled into the driveway, I could see Joseph sitting in the front seat of his car. I couldn't see his face clearly enough to read his expression, but it didn't take a genius to figure out what it probably looked like.

"I really have to go talk to him. Thanks for today though," I said absent-mindedly to Lukas over my shoulder. Lukas said something in return that I didn't quite catch and rode off down the street in mere seconds.

I had walked quickly to Joseph's car, wanting to get to him as fast as possible to explain myself, but as I reached him, I stopped outside, not opening the door or making any move to enter the passenger seat. If I was being honest, I was scared out of my mind. If I had been in the right and could explain myself to Joseph, I wouldn't have hesitated letting him know exactly what had happened. But as it was, my only excuse was, "I forgot about you."

Joseph looked at me through his dirty windshield for a moment, his face holding only resignation and not the anger I expected to see there. He slowly opened his door and got out of the car, walking over to where I stood on the sidewalk. He was dressed up in an old-fashioned brown suit and tie with his wild hair tamed and gelled into place. He held a see-through plastic box with a white flower in it.

"Did you forget?"

He didn't say anything else. He didn't have to. Those three words caused the heat to rise up in my cheeks and tears to threaten in the corners of my eyes.

"I didn't mean to. I just . . . didn't think about it," I said slowly. Joseph brought his gaze up to mine, his eyes sad and serious.

"I think that might hurt more than if you had just decided you didn't want to go with me," he muttered. "I wasn't even worth remembering."

"Joseph, I didn't say that," I began, but he brought his hand up to silence me.

"June, you know I love you. You know I always have. You can lie to yourself and say we're just friends and we just like spending time together, but deep down you know it's always been more than that for me. And I'm really happy for you that you're so happy, but I can't keep beating my head against a wall. It hurts too much to constantly think maybe you're starting to love me too, only to find out that I'm still just a convenience for you," he said. Every word made me feel smaller and smaller.

I could say that I was shocked to hear him say he loved me, but he was right—somewhere inside of me, I knew that he loved me and that all of our time spent together only intensified those feelings. I tried to speak, but I couldn't find the words I wanted to say. I wasn't even sure there was anything I wanted to say, or if there were just feelings that I couldn't translate into words.

"Even if you don't love me back . . . " he began, his eyes beginning to water even though he quickly looked away to try to hide it, "I don't see how you could have forgotten about me. I don't understand how I could be so insignificant to you after all of this time."

"Joseph," I said in a choked voice. He turned away from me, tossing the white flower onto the sidewalk and jumping into his car. He started the engine and glanced at me with a look on his face that I would never forget, before driving away down the street, his tires squealing against the asphalt.

I stood alone on the sidewalk, tears streaming down my cheeks and a sick feeling in my stomach. I tried to justify what I had done, but couldn't seem to find any scenario where I wasn't a horrible person. As I listened to the sound of Joseph's car fade into the night, I pulled out my phone and read his last text message.

8:45 PM: *I guess he wins, huh?*

CHAPTER 21

I didn't see Joseph at church on Sunday, and he didn't pick me up for seminary on Monday or Tuesday. I couldn't try to corner him at school because we'd started filming the next episode already, so I was on set all day. I called his phone during every filming break we had and tried texting him repeatedly, but it was like talking to a ghost. I didn't hear even a hint of a reply to any of my attempts. I was even starting to wonder if his phone had died just to make myself feel better.

Gran had lectured me the night of Homecoming about having my priorities straight and making sure I wasn't falling into the trap of forgetting what was important in life. I appreciated her efforts, but honestly, she didn't need to lecture me. I already knew that I had messed up. I think she realized how bad I felt, because after her little talk with me, she didn't bring it up again and didn't ask any questions when she noticed Joseph hadn't come to get me for seminary.

I didn't go around announcing my status as an awful friend on set, but I think Candice, Benjamin, and Ryan could tell something was wrong. I was pretty good at pretending like I was listening to their random conversations and laughing at their witty jokes; I mean, I was an actress, after all. It wasn't something that I found difficult to do. But even trying my hardest to act interested in what was going on around the set, I think they knew.

On Tuesday night as Lukas drove me to my house, I started to wonder if everything Joseph had said about him was right. That night after work, Lukas had taken me out to dinner at a nice restaurant. He had said all the right things and acted interested in anything I said, but now that I was starting to see what a good little actress I could be in everyday situations, I couldn't help but notice the way Lukas *always* said the right thing. I was starting to find it hard to believe that he really agreed with each word I spoke.

When we left the restaurant to get into Lukas's car, (he had opted to drive his sports car today rather than his motorcycle) he lingered in front of the paparazzi, letting them snap pictures of us and holding me close. For some reason, it was all starting to feel less and less like a dream come true and more like a scene in the show. But that just had to be my crazy guilt over Joseph talking. This was everything I had always wanted, wasn't it?

We drove to my house in silence. I couldn't really think of anything I wanted to say, and it bothered me that Lukas never asked what had happened with Joseph that night. In my normal star struck state, I would say that Lukas was being a gentleman and wanted to protect my feelings. But now I was beginning to think he really didn't care what had happened between Joseph and me because it didn't serve whatever purpose he was trying to achieve with this relationship. Then again, maybe I was being too hard on poor Lukas. Just because I had turned out to be a horrible person didn't mean everyone else in the world was too.

When we reached my street, Lukas parked his car at the sidewalk in front of my house rather than in the driveway. He kept the car running with its mellow music playing quietly in the background as he turned to me. I could see in his eyes that he was about to tell me something serious, and for just a moment I forgot all of my worrying about how awful I had been to Joseph. Maybe Lukas was about to tell me just how much he needed me in his life and how he couldn't believe he'd lived in a world without me in it. No. Wait . . . that was a line from one of his movies. So scratch that. I didn't want him to repeat his scripted lines to me. But maybe he was going to tell me something to that same effect?

"June, you're a beautiful girl," he said finally, when I felt like I couldn't take the suspense any longer. Even in my stressed state I could appreciate the incredible-ness of what he, Lukas Leighton, huge Hollywood star, had just said to me. "There's no point in denying it. I like you. And I think you like me too."

I was going to try to respond in the affirmative to his statement, but my voice seemed to be rebelling against me so I nodded mutely.

Lukas opened his mouth like he was about to utter some other magical statement, but then he stopped, as if thinking better of it. Instead, he leaned toward me and slowly brought his lips to mine. To say that I almost had a heart attack would be a huge understatement. Lukas Leighton was kissing *me*—June Laurie: unimpressive high school student. The kiss was deep and experienced, if not a little awkward due to the armrest between us. I tried to twist in my seat so that I was at least sort of facing him and not just straining my neck in an attempt to kiss the most beautiful, famous guy there was.

Even though it was crazy, for some odd reason I couldn't get my mixed-up mind to stop comparing this kiss to the one I had shared with Joseph while we rehearsed our skit together. Even though Lukas's kiss was like kissing someone who had gotten a doctorate in making out, it wasn't as . . . what is the word I'm looking for? It wasn't as . . . meaningful. It didn't quite feel as heartfelt and utterly special as it did when I kissed Joseph. I couldn't believe that I was even thinking this, but at that moment, I would almost rather be kissing my best friend who I had always claimed I didn't have feelings for, than Lukas Leighton (who every girl wished they could kiss).

Even with this confusing revelation passing through my

mind, I couldn't deny that kissing Lukas was like fulfilling a guilty pleasure. I was kissing the most eligible bachelor in Hollywood, even though I was starting to suspect that the rumors about him being a huge jerk were less like rumors and more like well-tested truths. As Lukas kissed me, he brought his hand to my waist (which I'm not quite sure how he managed in our awkward position). His kiss was getting hungrier and more intense, making me feel like we were definitely not on the same page right at that moment.

And then it happened: confirmation that Ryan, and Candice, and Benjamin, and Joseph had been spot-on.

Lukas was slowly trailing his hand from my waist upward to a place he definitely wasn't allowed to be. I grabbed his hand before he could claim his grand title of, "creepy older guy trying to get to second base with an inexperienced and naive younger girl." I instantly pulled away from him and gave him a puzzled look, hoping that maybe, just maybe, I had misunderstood his intentions.

"What are you doing?" I asked, my eyes full of unspoken accusation.

"Are you serious?" he asked in return, giving a short laugh and looking at me like I had just said something very funny. "Is it because we're in front of your house? We can go back to my place if you want. Actually, that would probably be better. More comfortable," he said, pulling away from me to put his car into gear.

"Wait," I exclaimed, stopping him before he pulled away from the house. "I don't think you're understanding what I'm saying. That's *not* okay." I tried to sound tough and resolute, but my voice just sounded shaky and weird. I could feel my hands trembling, partly because I was shocked that Lukas had turned into a creeper in my eyes, partly because I was genuinely nervous that I was telling him something no one had probably ever told him before, and mostly because everyone had been right. I had been the naïve one all along. It was a hard realization to come to; I won't deny it.

"What do you mean it's not okay?" he asked. I had to

hand it to him—he still sounded honestly confused, as if he couldn't grasp the fact that someone wouldn't want him to feel them up in his car. Very classy, Lukas.

"What, haven't you ever heard of someone having standards?" I asked, my voice sounding a bit stronger now that I was beginning to realize that losing Lukas Leighton's affections might not be the worst thing to ever happen to me.

"Are you kidding? What are you, five years old? It's just sex. It's not that big of a deal!" he exclaimed, sounding angry now that he fully understood what I was saying.

My mouth dropped open in shock. Here I had thought he was just kind of a dirtbag, but now that I knew what he *really* wanted to do, I was fully convinced of his off-the-scale dirtbag level.

"You were seriously going to try to sleep with me in your car? In front of my grandma's house?" I asked, my voice much louder than I had intended. "That's the most disgusting thing I've ever heard." My whole "old fashioned" obsession had been based on a love of class, and this scenario was probably the least classy thing I could have imagined. Apparently Lukas wasn't big on romance—he was big on making a girl feel like he was romantic and caring so that they would sleep with him in his stupid expensive car while listening to cheesy pseudo-alternative music. Gross.

"You do realize who you're turning down, right?" he said after a moment of thought.

That was the straw that broke the camel's back. How had he changed so quickly?

"You're disgusting, and conceited, and kind of an idiot. I wouldn't sleep with you if you were the last person on earth," I said slowly and seriously as I unbuckled my seatbelt and climbed out of the car. "Thanks for a great night," I said cheerfully, my voice dripping with sarcasm as I slammed the door and stormed up to the house.

I felt like every nerve in my body was standing on high alert as Lukas tore off down the street. I was so completely indignant that he really thought I was that cheap. Did I give off the vibe that I would actually do something like that? The worst part about it was that everyone else had so clearly seen what I had been trying to deny the entire time: Lukas was a huge jerk.

I felt one hot tear slide down my cheek, though I wasn't really sad. At all. I was mostly brimming with adrenaline and kicking myself for not saying the millions of witty comebacks that were now traveling through my brain at light speed. At least I had managed to sort of put him in his place and let him know he couldn't have everything he wanted.

As I stomped up the stairs to my bedroom, I heard Gran asking me what was wrong from the kitchen.

"Lukas Leighton is the biggest creeper alive," I shouted down to her.

"I could have told you that, Bliss," she called back up. "In fact, I think I did . . . several times."

"Yeah, I know," I said huffily, plopping myself down on my bed and instinctively pulling out my phone to call Joseph. As my thumb went to dial his number, I stopped, remembering why I had been so upset these past few days. I wondered if it would help if I told Joseph what a jerk Lukas was, but the more I thought about that idea, the more it felt like he would think I was running back to him because I couldn't have Lukas. That wasn't the case at all, but I wondered if that's how it would appear.

Was it really my fault that I was a bit slow on the uptake? Should I really be punished because I didn't recognize my feelings for Joseph right away, and because it took a little longer for me to come around? Well, maybe . . . but still. Joseph knew how thick-headed I was going into this whole friendship. He should at least try to be more understanding. But it didn't really matter, because now I was determined to make things right. I would get Joseph to see how sorry I was, or I would bother him to death trying.

I could feel my mind working overtime on the perfect way to get him to listen to me, though after what I had done to him, it might take a bit of a miracle. Before I went to bed that night, though, I figured I could at least let him know I wasn't completely clueless anymore. Picking up my phone, I sent him one single, solitary text, even though I knew he wouldn't respond.

You were right.

CHAPTER 22

Nothing big had changed by the next morning. Joseph still didn't pick me up for seminary, I still felt horrible, and Gran still had to drive me to set to face the now-undesirable Lukas Leighton. The only thing that had changed was my resolve to prove to Joseph that I was sorry and I really did love him back. It was an odd revelation to me, but after I had admitted it to myself, it made so much sense.

Of course I loved Joseph. How could I not? He knew me better than anyone else and he loved me even though I was irrational, paranoid, and a complete stress case on the best of days. He loved me for who I was and I loved him back, even if it did take me slightly longer than him to realize it.

I knew I could possibly get Joseph to respond to my texts and voicemails if I told him I loved him, but it hardly seemed romantic to tell someone that over the phone. That was something Lukas Leighton would do . . . and he wouldn't mean it. He would just say it so that he could sleep with you.

Jerk.

I was shaking the entire time I waited for Lukas to come to set, but when he finally did show up, his behavior threw me off more than I had imagined it would. He wasn't cold toward me, but he also wasn't his usual suave, flirty self. Instead, he acted like we were strangers meeting for the first time. He was congenial and only spoke to me when he needed to. Even though he was the world's biggest scumbag, I had to admit that he was a good actor.

Sitting in the makeup trailer right before lunch, I stared at myself in the mirror. I looked about the same as I always had (maybe a bit more tired and stressed) but somehow I felt more grown up. It was as if realizing how poorly I'd treated Joseph all these years, while also turning down Hollywood's biggest heartthrob (ha!) had forced me to mature and take matters into my own hands.

Candice was busy pulling peacock feathers out of my hair from the scene I had just shot, while Benjamin texted away madly on his phone, occasionally asking Candice to marry him. Ryan, however, kept his gaze fixed on me. It felt almost as if he were trying to figure out what I was thinking just by staring long enough.

"New Girl, did you sleep with Leighton?" Benjamin blurted from the couch in the makeup trailer. Candice stopped pulling feathers from my hair and watched my reflection in the mirror while Ryan straightened up, suddenly tense.

"Why do you ask?" I responded, keeping my voice neutral. Even though I didn't really want to relive that nightmare, I was pretty excited to tell them how I had shut Lukas down.

"Today on set he treated you like he treats all of his 'morning after' companions," Benjamin said bluntly. "There's only one reason for that."

"Oh my gosh, June, if you seriously slept with that tool, I'll go jump off a cliff right now," Candice threatened, putting one hand on her hip and giving me her best four-foot-nothing-in-heels stare down.

"There's actually not only *one* reason Lukas might treat me that way," I said knowingly, trying to hide my grin but failing miserably.

"I think I'm going to be sick," Ryan said, looking like he meant it.

"Oh, come on you guys. Do you really think I would sleep

with him?" I asked, slightly indignant that they really thought me capable of that.

"Stranger things have happened when young star struck girls come into the presence of the great Lukas Leighton," Benjamin said with disgust. Candice made a gagging sound behind me, her crimson lips forming a large "O."

"Actually, what happened between us last night was much better than that," I confessed, happy to have the perfect audience for my "turning down Lukas" story.

"I don't think I want to hear this," Ryan exclaimed, pretending to cover his ears.

"So, last night, Lukas brought me home in his car," I began.

"Car," Candice and Benjamin said together.

"That's the first sign," Ryan added.

"He pulled over and played some soft music," I went on, trying to drag this wonderful story out as long as I could. "We kissed for a while and I was thinking life was pretty good."

"Please stop," Candice said.

"And then Lukas decided he was going to be a little hands-y," I continued.

"No seriously. Stop," Ryan pleaded.

"And so I told him that he was disgusting, and an idiot, and that I wouldn't sleep with him if he was the last person on earth . . . It was pretty romantic," I finished grandly, still wearing my look of faux bliss.

"Wait, back up. You told him what?" Benjamin asked, his face the perfect mask of confusion.

"Oh, and I slammed the door in his face," I added, proud that I had found the three (out of four) people who hated Lukas most in this world to share this experience with.

"That's the most fantastic thing I've ever heard," Ryan admitted in admiration.

"Okay. I will officially let you call me your friend now," Candice said. "Oh, I would pay such big money to see the look on his face when you told him no!"

"I think I underestimated you, New Girl," Benjamin said with a nod. "Ryan, it's like our little baby is all grown up."

"And off ridding the world of guys who give us all a bad name," Ryan added, pretending to dab at fake tears in his eyes.

"I'm not going to lie . . . it felt pretty good," I confessed.

"It probably felt like the most epic thing ever because it was," Candice said happily clapping her hands, having taken the last of the peacock feathers from my hair.

"Ryan, go get the girl a cookie or something. She deserves it," Benjamin ordered. Ryan instantly jumped to his feet to oblige.

"Here, I'll come with you actually," I said following him out of the trailer. "I need to get up and walk around. I feel so energetic right now."

"The bold new June," Ryan remarked as we walked past sound stages toward the lunchroom. "Any other new developments I should know about?"

"Well . . . there is one thing," I began, wondering if I could use Ryan as my sounding board for the whole Joseph fiasco.

"Shoot," he said, indicating that I should continue.

"Do you remember me talking about Joseph?"

"He's the one you've known since before you were born, pretty much, right?" Ryan asked as we passed a bunch of nuns (or at least actors dressed up as nuns) in Tiffany blue habits.

"Yeah, that's him. Well . . . I accidentally blew him off for Lukas a few days ago on a pretty big day and he sort of got really mad at me and told me that he loves me but never wants to speak to me again because he's loved me for so long and I don't love him back and it's just getting too hard for him to deal with it anymore," I said all in one breath.

"Wow," Ryan answered with wide eyes. "That sounds . . . complicated."

"It is," I mumbled miserably.

"So, what are you going to do about it? Do you still just

want to be friends with him, or . . . " he trailed off, letting his question hang unfinished in the air.

"That's the thing. I think I've never wanted to admit that I really like Joseph because we've been good friends for so long and I didn't want to ruin that. But after hearing him say he loves me it made me . . . less scared. Does that make sense?"

"Yeah, it does. I think it's easier to know how you feel about someone once you know how they feel about you. It's not as risky," Ryan said wisely.

"I think you're right," I conceded. "I think I always felt something for him, but assuming that he just thought of me as a friend made me want to put up my defenses against my feelings so I wouldn't get hurt."

"So, are you going to go for it, then?" Ryan asked, stopping in his tracks and facing me, his blue eyes gazing at me intently.

"If I can get him to listen to me, I will," I said, sighing deeply at just how complicated everything had become recently.

"Well, he sounds like a good guy, so I hope it all works out."

"Thanks Ryan," I said sincerely, glad to have him to talk to after feeling so alone the past few days.

"I have to admit, I was kind of hoping that with Lukas finally showing you his true colors you'd be . . . I don't know . . . available," Ryan said, looking at me meaningfully. "You're just so wholesome and kind. That's sort of hard to find in this industry sometimes. Or in this city, for that matter."

I swear, there had to be something in the water because a few months ago, a boy had never so much as glanced twice at me (except for Joseph) and now they were coming at me from all angles. It was flattering, but making my life very weird at the same time.

Hearing Ryan say he'd hoped we'd have a shot together was an unexpected surprise. Of all of the crazy things that had been happening lately, Ryan was definitely the most mature and stable guy I had known through all of this, and he seemed to be sweet like Joseph, though a little old for me at the moment. Funny how big an age gap can seem when you're both younger. If I had been twenty-one and he was twenty-five, it wouldn't seem like a deal. But as it was, sixteen and twenty just didn't work out too well.

"You're an incredibly nice guy," I remarked honestly. "And if you told me you wanted to be with me in a few years, I'd marry you on the spot," I said with a giggle, pulling him into a hug. He hugged me back tightly for a moment before pulling away.

"I guess I'll have to either get the time machine from studio D or get your number and track you down in a few years, then," he said with a good-natured laugh.

"Deal," I agreed happily as we resumed our walk to the lunchroom, arm in arm.

....

The next day we only had a half-day of shooting due to a small cast "party" where we'd watch the episode we had just made. It wasn't much of a party. It was more like a small table of food in a tiny theatre where we'd be watching the final cut of the episode with a small handful of the cast. We were allowed to bring someone along if we wanted, but I didn't have anyone to bring so I just showed up and sat next to Candice, Benjamin, and Ryan.

"So, what's this I hear about you completely shooting Ryan down when he tried to confess his love for you?" Benjamin asked, never one to be subtle or tactful.

"I did *not* say that," Ryan cut in defensively.

"The way I heard it, you took his engagement ring and threw it back in his face," Candice said, in a rare moment of joining in with the joking.

"June, I swear, all I said was I may have mentioned thinking you were a nice person and we decided I was too old for you," Ryan said evenly, his cheeks turning an adorable shade of red.

"It's okay, Ryan, you can tell them what really happened,"

I said, causing Benjamin and Candice to look at me with sudden interest.

"What really happened?" Benjamin asked, obviously feeling that he had been left out of some juicy bit of gossip.

"Ryan and I went to Vegas after work yesterday and eloped, but then my grandma found out and got mad. So we got an annulment," I said matter-of-factly.

"She got the kids and I got the summer home," Ryan added, giving me a secretive wink.

"I hate you guys," Candice said affectionately.

"No, I think that's just residual hate you're feeling from what just walked in," Benjamin stated with a look of disdain on his face. We followed his gaze to the door and saw Lukas standing there smugly with a girl on his arm. She had bleached blonde hair, something that would almost pass for a dress if it had a bit more material, and a few spare parts that were definitely not God-given.

"Words can't describe how much I hate that guy," Candice muttered darkly.

"That's okay. I can use the words if you won't," Benjamin said helpfully.

Lukas looked over at me for a moment and raised an eyebrow quizzically. I couldn't quite understand what that facial expression was supposed to mean, so I just gave him a polite smile in return and turned back to my friends.

"He's such a tool," Ryan growled angrily, catching the less-than-kind look Lukas had just given me.

"Wow, the claws are really coming out, aren't they, Ryan?" Benjamin joked, impressed by his friend's anger on my behalf.

"I just don't understand how he can be such a jerk," Ryan said, his brow furrowed in frustration.

"That's because you're nice, so you can't think like him," I answered, nudging Ryan with my shoulder and trying not to look over at Lukas and his ostentatious new toy.

"Why are we still talking about him?" Candice asked, her voice threatening to fall back into its normal dry monotone.

"We're not. Benjamin and I were just about to ask if you girls wanted something to drink," Ryan said, having cooled down.

"Is this what we've been reduced to, Ryan? Getting drinks for extras and *the vanities*?" Benjamin said, shooting a look at Candice.

"If you call my department 'the vanities' one more time, I swear I'll kill you and make it look like an accident," Candice said in an off-puttingly sweet voice, winking at Benjamin as she did so.

"Soda it is," he answered, grabbing Ryan by the elbow and pulling him away as quickly as possible.

"Okay, now that they're gone, I wanted to talk to you," Candice said, suddenly becoming serious and turning toward me with interest. "Ryan told me about the whole Joseph thing."

I wasn't quite sure what was happening, but it almost seemed like Candice wanted to talk about boys with me. I tried to search my mind for a scenario where this made sense and didn't completely throw me off, but I couldn't seem to find one.

"Really?" was all I could manage to say in my shocked state.

"Of course he's not listening to you, June. You hurt his ego," she said matter-of-factly. "It's not like you just told him 'no, I don't like you back'. You made it seem like you completely forgot about him. That's got to hurt the poor boy if he's really liked you as long as he claims he has."

"Are you really talking about relationship stuff with me?" I asked slowly, just to make sure I was actually hearing the words coming out of her mouth.

"Keep that up and the offer will be revoked," Candice said, suddenly monotone once more.

"No, no . . . keep talking. I need all the help I can get," I said.

"You need to do something big. Don't just call him or text him or show up at his house. Do something big and extreme and maybe even slightly embarrassing. It's the least you could do, really, considering how embarrassing it had to be for him to be forgotten."

"I don't really know that embarrassing myself is going to make this any better," I said warily.

"No, June, you're not getting it," she answered in frustration. "You're not embarrassing yourself just for the sake of doing it. You're putting yourself out there as much as he did by telling you that he loves you. You're taking a risk to match his and showing him you're on the same page."

"But he won't listen to me. It doesn't matter how much I try to tell him—it's like he's wearing ear plugs," I said miserably.

"Then get him in a situation where he *has* to listen. One where he can't get away without hearing what you have to say first," she answered, looking surprisingly adamant and involved in this whole situation. I never would have thought I'd be getting relationship advice from Candice, but it sounded pretty good to me, so who was I to turn down a good suggestion when I had none? "You need to do something big, June. You're an actress, aren't you? You're dramatic."

"Something big," I repeated slowly. "I think I can manage that."

CHAPTER 23

By Saturday night, my brilliant idea for something "big" still hadn't hit me. I think Gran was starting to worry about my constant moping around the house, because not once did she try to put some weird fruit blend on my face to make it "glow." She walked past my bedroom door way more often than she needed to, claiming she had to put laundry away, or get something from the cupboard, or make sure the smoke alarm had batteries in it (even though there was no smoke alarm there). With every trip past my door, she'd linger for a moment, looking at me as I lay on my back and stared at my ceiling.

At a quarter to six, she finally came into my room, looking a bit dressed up for an evening in, and sat on the edge of my bed.

"Bliss, I know you're upset about everything that's happened with Joseph, but you've both been friends for a long time. It'll blow over. These things always do," she said warmly, placing her hand on my cheek and smiling at me.

"I don't think this is the type of thing that blows over Gran," I said sadly. "But thanks for trying to make me feel better."

She sighed deeply, standing up from the bed and walking back toward the door.

"I take it you aren't going to the play tonight, then?" she asked.

"No," I said miserably. "I'm going to stay here and figure out how on earth to set this right."

"All right, Bliss. I'll let him know you wanted to come," she promised, giving me a little wave as she left.

I waited until I heard the garage door open and close again before I let out a shuddering sigh. A few tears rolled sideways down my cheeks and pooled in my ears. I had definitely messed up big time. The numerous texts and calls I'd sent to Joseph throughout the day were as silent and unanswered as ever. I had even plucked up the courage to go over to his house, but his mom had told me he was at a final rehearsal for the play tonight. If it hadn't been such a believable alibi, I would have wondered if Joseph were standing behind the front door whispering what she should say to me.

I paced my room for a while, thinking that maybe walking around would help me find a solution. I was wrong, of course, but it was always worth a try. About twenty minutes later, my phone buzzed, catching me by surprise. My heart jumped in my chest for a moment, and I wondered if it could be Joseph texting to ask why he didn't see me in the audience.

I didn't recognize the number when I picked up the phone, but I read the text anyway:

Have you done it yet? –C

At least I had Candice to cheer me on from the metaphorical sidelines and make sure I didn't chicken out. I was pretty sure she'd eat me alive if I came back to set on Monday without any good news to tell her.

I'm trying. I answered, hoping that would placate her. I resumed my pacing, now moving down the stairs to pace the kitchen, in case a change in scenery could help. My phone buzzed once more, and I tried to stop thinking it could be Joseph.

Not hard enough.

I looked at my phone incredulously for a moment, as if it would tell me what on earth Candice wanted me to do. It wasn't like opportunities to make someone listen to you just fell into your lap. They had to be well planned out and opportune. This wasn't an everyday occurrence.

And then I almost kicked myself for being so dense.

It might not be an everyday occurrence, but it was definitely a *today* occurrence. Glancing at the clock on the microwave, I sprang into action, trying to do a million things at once. I grabbed the closest pair of shoes I could find—which happened to be a pair of uncomfortable heels—and bolted out the door, heading for the end of the cul-de-sac that shared a brick wall with the school's football field. I might not have had a car, but I had legs and a house that was thankfully close to the high school.

I scaled the brick wall (which was difficult to do in heels) and ran across the dark football field (also hard to do in heels). It felt scandalous to be running through the school at night when I wasn't supposed to be there, but the excitement added to my adrenaline. I considered the emotions a good thing, since I was pretty sure I'd back out if I weren't completely wired and ready to charge.

I slowed to a quick walk once I reached the auditorium, where I could hear the sounds of the play going on. I didn't stop at the doors where the audience, entered but instead followed the familiar path backstage where my fellow classmates scurried around trying to change costumes, remember lines, and not trip over the black-clad stage crew. From the sounds of the lines being spoken, I guessed they were almost to the very end of the play.

I saw Xani standing near the stage, looking anxious, and then I knew what I had to do. It was a long shot on so many levels. I took off my heels so I wouldn't make any noise and slowly crept up behind Xani, grabbing her by the arm and pulling her further away from the entrance to the stage so I could talk to her. She looked shocked to see me, though probably not as shocked as I was to see her normally blonde curly hair covered in a brown wig that looked almost identical to my hair.

"June, what on earth are you doin' here?" she asked in her thick Southern accent that I silently hoped she wasn't using while playing Juliet.

"Xani, I know you don't like me all that much, and this is probably the craziest thing I could ask you to do, but can I please borrow your costume?" I asked desperately, realizing how short we were on time and how unlikely it was that she would agree to this. This would be her big chance to kiss Joseph on stage, after all (even if it would be while playing dead).

"Excuse me?" was all she managed to say, which honestly was a better reaction than I was expecting to my outlandish request.

"I know this sounds crazy, but Joseph hates me right now and he won't listen to anything I say. I know you like him. I know that. And I know that means you probably don't want to help me win him over. But I also know that you're a good person and you realize how important this is to me," I pleaded quietly.

Xani didn't say anything for a moment. She actually looked pretty mad at me for even asking her to do something so extreme. I wondered if I had underestimated the craziness of my plan. She stared at me a moment longer, first looking angry, and then looking resigned as she kicked her shoes off.

"If you're going to take away my big moment, you might as well help me unzip the dress," she said in a tone that sounded like it was trying to be upset but was mostly just accepting of the current situation.

"Seriously?" I asked, not sure if I should trust that she'd really given in that easily.

"If I thought I had even a small chance with that boy, you wouldn't be able to pry this costume from my cold dead fingers," she said as I helped her out of the dress. "But he's been miserable for the past two weeks. It's like he's not himself anymore, and I like him too much to let him keep feeling so awful," she finished with a shrug. "I don't know what you did to him, but you'd better set it right."

I felt myself tear up a little, but I didn't let my emotions get the better of me (for the first time ever). I had a job to do, and people were already moving around backstage to get ready for the next scene. My new scene.

I quickly pulled my clothes off, very aware that I didn't have a flesh-colored bodysuit under my clothes like Xani did. I tried to ignore the fact that I was living out the popular nightmare of being in your high school surrounded by your peers in nothing more than your underwear, and quickly pulled the dress over my head.

"Oh June, the stupid wig is stuck to my head. I've got like, a billion bobby pins in here," Xani whispered urgently, trying to pull at the fake hair as the stage went dark so that the next scene could be set.

"Don't worry about it. I think it's close enough to my hair that they won't be able to tell," I said, slipping on Xani's shoes. I said about a thousand silent thank-yous that Xani and I were about the same size, though the dress was a bit loose on me. It didn't really matter though, since I'd be lying dead on the tomb.

"Okay, you need to run out while it's dark and lay on that box . . . I mean, tomb, in the middle of the stage. You've read it right? Don't wake up until he kills himself," Xani instructed in a hushed but panicked voice. I would almost think she was more nervous than I was about this.

"Xani, I honestly can't tell you how much this means to me," I said, pulling her into a quick hug.

"Yeah, yeah. Go get him!" she said, giving me a thumbs-up and pushing me out onto the darkened stage.

This was it.

I half walked and half ran to the "tomb" in the middle of the stage, and then climbed up onto it. I lay down so that my hair covered my face for the most part, hoping no one would notice that Juliet was suddenly a different person—at least, not until it was absolutely unavoidable.

Through my closed eyelids, I could see the lights turn up on the stage and hear the familiar sound of someone's microphone being turned on from the tech booth behind the audience. A pair of footsteps echoed on the stage and I wondered why there were two people walking on. Maybe someone had seen me trade places with Xani and they were coming to drag me off the stage, thinking I was some spotlight-obsessed teenager.

As the two figures spoke, I realized it was supposed to be Paris and his servant, coming to pay their respects to Juliet. I had completely forgotten how long this last scene actually was. I would have to wait for Paris and the servant to hide, then for Romeo (Joseph) and Balthasar to enter. Then Balthasar would leave and Romeo would kill Paris. I'd just have to hope that I could contain my nerves for that long, because the more I thought about it, the more I realized how painfully long this wait was going to be when all I wanted to do was tell Joseph how I felt right then and there.

I tried not to listen to the lines being spoken and focused on exactly what I would say. I couldn't ruin the play for everyone just because I had been an idiot, but I needed to be able to get my point across as well. It would be tricky, and I'm sure my words wouldn't be Shakespearean, but the audience would forgive me. Most of them probably wouldn't even know the difference.

I lay there silently, trying to ignore the deafening beating of my own heart as Romeo killed Paris and brought him to lie near my tomb. I could hear myself breathing loudly but tried desperately to tune it out and just concentrate on what I would say—which I still had absolutely no ideas for, by the way.

I felt Joseph sit on the box next to me and heard him recite his lines loud and clear. It was almost odd to have him so close to me now, after not having seen him in a while. My arm tingled where his hand rested on it, and suddenly I knew exactly how Joseph had felt being around me all this time. I was a little giddy to have finally realized how I felt about him. Now that I knew I loved him, it made the stakes that much higher. If I didn't get this right, I could completely ruin my only chance of getting him back.

Joseph shifted his weight next to me and I could only guess what that meant. He was turning to kiss me.

"Eyes, look your last. Arms, take your last embrace. And, lips, O you the doors of breath, seal with a righteous kiss. A dateless bargain to engrossing death," he recited, his hand moving the hair from my face.

I have to admit, at that moment I would have given anything to open my eyes and see the look on Joseph's face. I could feel his whole body tense up, his hand freezing on my cheek and his breath catching in his throat. It took all of my willpower to not smile or laugh. Even though I knew the situation was extremely delicate, the circumstance itself was pretty amusing. Even in my panicked state, the humor was not lost on me.

After an uncomfortable moment of complete and utter silence, I began to worry that he wouldn't kiss me. Maybe he'd just storm off the stage and my only chance to talk to him would have failed. I heard someone in the audience cough, probably just assuming that Joseph was nervous to kiss a girl onstage.

Finally, after what seemed like hours of waiting for him to decide if he was going to play along or bolt, I felt him lean down toward me. I thought he might whisper some angry remark, but then I remembered he had a microphone taped to his cheek. He pressed his lips against mine very briefly before pulling away. It definitely didn't feel like the time we had kissed while rehearsing our scene together. This was a forced kiss.

My throat tightened at the fact that the first half of my grand gesture apparently hadn't been well received, but I was hardly counting on him to forgive me just because I crashed his play. The second half of my plan was the real bid for his affection.

"Come, bitter conduct, come, unsavory guide. Thou desperate pilot, now at once run on the dashing rocks thy sea-sick weary bark. Here's to my love," he said, jumping right back into character after his little moment of shock.

"O true apothecary! Thy drugs are quick. Thus with a kiss I die."

I felt his body lurch forward violently before falling sideways so that he was laying right next to me, blocking my view of the audience.

I opened one eye cautiously only to find Joseph facing me, both of his eyes wide open and looking like I'd better have a good explanation for my presence. I stared at him silently for a moment, hoping I could somehow convey in a single look how sorry I was. We lay there for a moment, staring at each other until Joseph motioned upwards with his eyes. I gave him a puzzled look and mouthed a silent "What?"

"Get up and finish the play," he whispered between gritted teeth.

"Oh, right!" I said. I wasn't sure how they had rehearsed this whole scene, but I wasn't exactly going by the book (or play, I guess) anyway, so I sat up on the tomb and looked down at Joseph. I could hear a wave of whispers sweep through the room. Apparently I didn't look as much like Xani as I had hoped.

I could see my friend Jared standing off to the side of the stage, frozen mid-stride. Apparently I had also forgotten that the friar was supposed to come in and talk for forever. He looked at me in shock and then slowly backed off the stage, causing the audience to laugh. I'd have to remember to apologize for stepping on his scene. Well . . . if I was really thinking about it, I'd have to apologize to a lot of people for a lot of things after this was all said and done. But that would have to wait until I had gotten the most important apology off of my chest.

Trying to channel my inner Shakespeare (which was definitely not easy), I looked down at Joseph and placed my hand on his cheek, turning his face so that it was pointed up at me.

"Oh Romeo," I began, wishing I had read more Shakespeare so I'd at least have some idea of how I should word this. Gran may have thought I had all of Shakespeare's works memorized, but trying to translate your own muddled thoughts into a work of art was a whole new ballgame. "How tangled our lives have become. We confess our love with our lips and with our hearts, yet neither is heard nor appreciated until it is too late." Saying these pseudo-Shakespearian lines felt like the cheesiest thing I had ever done. But Candice was right—Joseph had put himself out there for me, so if I had to look like an idiot to show him how sorry I was, I would do it.

"You brought your love to me and I brought you to a tomb. I reflect and wish I had admitted to myself and to you, that my affections matched yours from the very first moment. But I was naïve and . . . " What was a Shakespearian word for "an idiot"? Gosh, this was a lot harder than I had thought it would be. There was a long silence while I tried to think of a good way to put what I really wanted to say in the context of the play. I wanted to tell him how sorry I was, how I hadn't meant to be a jerk, how I wished I had gone to Homecoming with him rather than being with Lukas.

Unable to think of any possible way to fit all of that into the storyline of *Romeo and Juliet*, I looked down at Joseph. His eyes were closed but his face was bright red. I couldn't tell if he was embarrassed for me, angry, or just burning up under these stage lights. Leaning down toward him slightly, I smiled. It may have not been the most eloquent apology, but he had definitely heard it.

"I'm sorry," I said finally, my words echoing around the auditorium. My hair covered our faces as I leaned over him and brought my lips to his. Now, I may not be a Shakespeare expert, but I was pretty sure dead Romeo was *not* supposed to kiss Juliet back. Joseph grabbed my hand, hidden behind him and kissed me back with full force. His kiss was like falling into a pile of laundry fresh out of the dryer. It was warm and comfortable and made me feel like I was home.

I had to physically pull myself away from Joseph to finish the play off, though I did see the way he was smirking with his eyes closed, his shaggy dark brown hair falling across his forehead, as I turned to face the audience once more.

I couldn't remember exactly what Juliet was supposed to say next . . . something about a happy dagger, which seemed a little odd. So I improvised.

"Well . . . I have checked my Romeo's lips thoroughly for poison and can attest that none remains," I said with a shrug. I could hear a few giggles throughout the audience at this statement. "So now with a dagger, I'll loose these mortal chains." All right, all right, I know that's not what she says. But I figured maybe Mr. Carroll wouldn't kill me after this was all done if I at least made it rhyme.

Pulling the prop dagger from Joseph's belt, I raised it high in the air and plunged it deep into the folds of my dress. I made a pained face for a moment and then let myself die, laying my head on Joseph's chest and entwining my fingers with his. The audience actually applauded, which I found a bit surprising A) because I had just killed myself over a boy, and B) because I had just completely butchered one of the most famous plays in history. But beggars can't be choosers, and it looked like I had accomplished my goal, so I smiled against Joseph's chest and listened to his heart beat for the rest of the scene. It felt like the dénouement took forever, since all I wanted to do was talk to Joseph.

When the lights dimmed on stage, Joseph and I ran off to the wings while everyone else went on to take their bows. The crowd's applause echoed all through the auditorium. I did notice in my frazzled state that Xani had changed back into one of her previous costumes and was now heading out to take her bow. Joseph stood in front of me, his face flushed.

"You need to get out there and bow," I said urgently.

"Did you mean what you said?" he asked, ignoring me.

"I did. Every word . . . well, more than every word actually, because I wasn't clever enough to fit everything I wanted to say into the story . . . sorry," I said sheepishly.

"I can't believe you hijacked our play just to talk to me," he laughed, admiration showing on his face. Candice was right—sacrificing my pride for him really had showed him how much I cared.

"It was the only way to get you to listen," I answered with a shrug.

"Well, I heard you. Loud and clear."

"Not quite. I didn't get to tell you that I love you. Completely and unconditionally and really quite stupidly. I've tried to ignore it all this time, but that doesn't make it any less true. I love you, Joseph Cleveland," I said earnestly, feeling all of my stress lift from me with that simple admission. "I love you like those idiots in romantic comedies who make all sorts of bad choices because they're so blinded by their love. I love you more than any silent film I've ever seen, or any piece of old-fashioned clothing. I love you more than acting. And I certainly love you more than I could ever love some immature, disgusting, snobby A-lister."

I beamed at Joseph and my eyes actually teared up, which was embarrassing. "It almost hurts how much I love you."

Joseph gave me the happiest smile I think I had ever seen on his face. He opened his mouth a few times to say something, but couldn't quite seem to ever get the words out. So instead of trying to match my ridiculously ineloquent ramblings about how much I loved him, he brought me close to him and gave me a proper, unrestrained and completely amazing kiss. He held me tightly, one hand on my waist and the other tangled in my hair as he kissed me deeply. He only pulled away once in the darkened wings of the applause-filled backstage to whisper his response.

"I love you too, June Laurie."

Don't miss the next novel in the June series:

Chasing June

Turn the page for a sneak peek at the first chapter!

CHAPTER 1

A rusty old Volkswagen Bus can mean a lot of different things to a lot of different people. Okay . . . so maybe that's not true, and saying so might just a bit overly dramatic. To most people, a VW Bus probably means, "hey, that person can't afford a car with more paint on it than rust." But to me, standing on the front lawn of the house I grew up in, it meant freedom. Or at least, it meant I was starting a new and scary chapter in my life.

It had been more than two years since I had first landed that life-changing role on *Forensic Faculty* and launched myself into the world of some of the sleaziest Hollywood people and some of the most wonderful Hollywood people. I had been kept on the show for more than my original four episodes. Apparently the focus group liked the dynamic that Imogen Gentry brought to the show, so I had stayed on throughout my junior and senior years of high school. That meant I became known to everyone in my school as, "That one girl on *Forensic Faculty*."

It wasn't bad, though. Joseph helped to get me through the wrath of the online *Forensic Faculty* fandom, which was full of girls who hated me simply because my character was Lukas Leighton's love interest. I hadn't realized, going into the show, just how crazy people would get about a fictional character. What Imogen had done on each episode the night before would greatly impact how people at school treated me the next day, which meant Joseph and I kept our group of friends limited. At school it was me, Joseph, and Xani, (who, even though she could admit I belonged with Joseph, wouldn't stop herself from shamelessly flirting with him every chance she got). Outside of school, I turned to Ryan, Benjamin, and Candice.

Putting aside the reflection for the moment, I looked around my front lawn at my small but perfect group of friends and family. They had come to see me and Joseph off for our big departure to college in Utah, and I couldn't help but smile at what I saw. Ryan, Benjamin, and Candice stood in a small circle looking at Benjamin's phone and laughing about something. Joseph and my Dad, who had come home from his constant work-related traveling for this farewell, struggled to shove one of my bags into the back of the VW Bus. Gran stood and talked with Joseph's parents, looking misty-eyed and sentimental. I wondered if Gran would start taking acting jobs again now that she didn't have my budding career to focus on.

After a few episodes of *Forensic Faculty* aired, I had started getting offers for other parts. Most of them were smaller TV roles, although a few were small parts in big movies. As much as I had wanted to break even further into the acting world, (Gran was practically salivating over the roles I was being offered) there were always reasons I couldn't do it. It seemed like every role I was offered had something questionable in it. I hadn't realized that having such high moral standards was going to hurt my acting career so much. Each time, I gracefully turned down the parts I was offered, beginning to feel like the only roles that would be free of "questionable content"' would be kids movies where I did a voice-over for a talking animal.

All right. That's a bit extreme.

But I was honestly kind of grateful I couldn't find any clean roles in Hollywood, because it made the decision to go to college *much* easier. When Joseph and I got our acceptance letters to Brigham Young University in Provo, Utah, there wasn't a question in my mind that I was doing the right thing. Besides, maybe once I had graduated, I wouldn't keep getting offered parts in dirty teen comedies and could instead act in dramas or romantic comedies. At least, that was what I told myself to make me feel better about leaving Hollywood right as my career was starting to take off.

Gran swore I'd probably never be able to get my foot back in the door if I left for school, but I told her I'd be okay with that, since the only door open at the moment was the kind you'd find behind the red curtain at video rental stores.

"New Girl, come here," Benjamin said, pulling me from my reverie and still using my old nickname even though we'd been friends for more than two years now. I smiled at the three of them and walked over to see some video of a cat holding onto a ceiling fan . . . at least, that's what it looked like from where I stood.

"Thank you for that," I said sarcastically, shaking my head at them.

"You're lucky you're leaving. That's the third time today he's made me watch that stupid video," Candice stated dryly.

"I'll miss you too," I said with a big cheesy smile, pulling her into a tight hug, which she didn't reciprocate at all. It was like hugging a two-by-four, although the plank of wood might have been more affectionate.

"Personal space bubble," was all she said, making me hug her tighter for a moment before releasing her.

Candice was really my only girl friend. Xani didn't count as a girl friend because she only hung around to get to Joseph. Candice, on the other hand, was an actual friend. We rarely hung out without Joseph, Ryan, and Benjamin, but it was nice to feel like even though I was going away to school and leaving the show, I'd still be their friend. It made leaving less difficult when I knew I had something worthwhile to come back to. And of course, Joseph felt blessed to be able to hang out with Ryan and Benjamin, who played his favorite characters on *Forensic Faculty*.

"If you get bored with the whole school thing, make sure you come back. We'll get Bates to bring you back on the show," Ryan said, his deep blue eyes crinkling at the edges as he smiled. He was sporting a bit of a five o'clock shadow these days, making him look much more "leading man" than the "witty sidekick" his clean-shaven baby face had made him. Even though he was still on the show, he had been picking up more and more roles lately, finally getting the recognition he deserved.

"You'll be the first to know," I promised, pulling him into a hug. He held me tightly for a moment longer than I thought he would, and kissed me on the cheek as we pulled apart.

"He'd better not be the first to know," I heard Gran say behind me. I turned to face my eccentric, flame-haired grandmother, who smiled, obviously resisting the urge to cry. "If anyone is hearing about your return to the great city of Hollywood, it'll be me," she said, shooting Ryan a mock threatening look. He held up his hands in defeat.

"You win, Annette," he said. "I can live with second in line."

"Everything's all packed up and ready to go, Button," my dad said next to me. I hadn't even realized he and Joseph had managed to stuff everything into the cobalt blue and white (and rust) VW Bus.

I turned and faced my dad, trying to memorize everything about him. I already barely saw him on a regular basis because he lived in different states (and sometimes countries) most days out of the year. But now that I was going away to college, I'd see even less of him. His dark hair had gotten grayer over the years and he wore glasses now, but his brown eyes were the same as mine and our smiles were identical. I didn't think any amount of time apart would ever erase our similarities.

Joseph, who had just finished saying his goodbyes to his parents and herd of siblings, walked over to join the group.

"I love you, Dad," I said as my dad gathered me into a warm hug.

"I love you too, Button," he replied, kissing the top of my head and making me feel like I was far too young to be setting out on my own.

"Keep in touch," Candice said as I hopped into the passenger seat and rolled my window down. She realized, then, that she had said something vaguely friendly and instantly corrected herself. "Ryan will probably jump off a cliff or something if you don't."

Ryan rolled his eyes at Candice.

"He didn't deny it," Benjamin pointed out.

"I'll miss you guys. But I'll be back for Christmas, so keep Ryan away from any high places until then," I said seriously.

"Will do, chief," Benjamin said with a salute.

Joseph and I waved our final goodbyes as his new (to him) car pulled out of the neighborhood and on to everything that lay before us.

ABOUT THE AUTHOR

Shannen Crane Camp was born and raised in Southern California, where she developed a love of reading, writing, and anything having to do with film. After high school, she moved to Utah to attend Brigham Young University, where she received a degree in Media Arts and found herself a husband in fellow California native Josh Camp. The two now call Utah home permanently (although they can't be kept away from the California beaches for long). Shannen loves to hear from readers, so feel free to contact her at Shannencbooks@hotmail.com or visit her website for more information: http://shannencbooks.blogspot.com

Made in the USA
Charleston, SC
15 December 2012